Dear Mrs. Lindbergh

W. W. NORTON & COMPANY

New York   London

Dear Mrs. Lindbergh

A
N O V E L

KATHLEEN HUGHES

For information about permission to reproduce selections from this
book, write to Permissions, W. W. Norton & Company,
Inc., 500 Fifth Avenue, New York, NY 10110

Manufacturing by Quebecor World, Fairfield
Book design by JAM Design
Production manager: Anna Oler

Library of Congress Cataloging-in-Publication Data
Hughes, Kathleen, 1972–
Dear Mrs. Lindbergh : a novel / Kathleen Hughes.— 1st ed.
p. cm.
ISBN 0-393-05785-2
1. Parent and adult child—Fiction. 2. Lindbergh, Anne Morrow,
1906– —Correspondence—Fiction. 3. Missing persons—Fiction.
4. Air pilots—Fiction. 5. Iowa—Fiction. I. Title: Dear
Mistress Lindbergh. II. Title.
PS3608.U558D43 2003
813'.6—dc21

2003013972

ISBN 0-393-32622-5 pbk.

W. W. Norton & Company, Inc.
500 Fifth Avenue, New York, N.Y. 10110
www.wwnorton.com

W. W. Norton & Company Ltd.
Castle House, 75/76 Wells Street, London W1T 3QT

1 2 3 4 5 6 7 8 9 0

For my parents

James Edward Hughes 1937–2001

and Sheila Priester Hughes

Flying again. The things I had forgotten. Things going under that still suspended wheel. How slow the cars, the pattern of houses doubled with their shadows, box like houses. How still the water! A boat cutting the water like shears—the heavy satin, rippling back, falling away on either side, frozen water-falls, woven cloth fields . . . and over the earth, a clear, calm light, quiet. One could sit still and look at life—that was it. The glaze on life again, that glaze that art puts on life. Is that the fascination of flying?

—*Anne Morrow Lindbergh, March 30, 1933*

PROLOGUE

*I*N HER MIND'S EYE, Mother is on the back porch of the
small house in Cedar Bluff, looking west at the evening, at
the cornfield spreading like a hand from the backyard, at
Dad's landing strip which traverses the field as a tendon from
wrist to middle finger. She has finished the dinner dishes and
her body is completely still but for her hands. Her face is
placid; her lips are calm; she stands without leaning or shifting. She is drying her hands on her apron but she is also
wringing the soft, worn, yellow-flowered fabric. Margaret is
not afraid to go wrap her arms around Mother's legs or to slip
under those hands, yet still she watches instead of going there.
The sun is setting. Yellow light pours over the top of the cornstalks, pooling in the front yard and streaming through the
white latticework beneath the porch. It is summer, always
summer in this image, and the crickets have started but the
combines and tractors and Dad's plane are at rest. The radio
is on somewhere inside the house; Dad and John are listening
to the baseball game.

Alternately, Margaret thinks of bedtime and being tucked
in. She says, "Tell me something while I close my eyes," and

Mother, with her smooth, soap-smelling hands, pushes the hair off the child's forehead. She begins, "Once upon a time airplane wings were completely flat." And when it's so cold outside that they crawl under the covers together for a few minutes, Mother talks about the Jenny. "She rattled and shook like a tin shed in a hurricane and she could fall from the sky with the leaves in November. But there are still people like your father and myself who will always love the Jenny most of all because it was the first and the simplest."

They had their own Jenny, or a Curtiss JN4D. She sat in the shadows behind the garage and by the time Margaret was ten, she had wild wheat growing up through her fabric belly and moss spreading over her wires. Dad gave up flying her after he nose-planted the poor girl landing during a storm before Margaret was born. Of her parents' generation of flying people, the Jenny was the Model T. She was their first love. Life began there.

ONE

After crashing into a cornfield, an Air Mail
pilot asked the surprised farmer, "Where's Cleveland?"
The farmer replied, "Cleveland's dead!"

—*Col. Carroll V. Glines*

THEY LOOKED AT the stringy, high cirrus clouds in the western sky. Henry rested his hands on Ruth's hips, standing behind her, and he leaned in to smell her hair, fresh from the air and musky from work and sleep and love. He could smell the bread she'd baked for supper, her pillow. He turned her toward him and then slipped his hand in between their bodies, onto her not-yet-rounded belly. Ruth's hands went to his arms, across his shoulder blades, down his spine. She closed her eyes for a moment.

"I'm sorry you aren't coming with me," he said. "I'll be lonely up there."

"You must be able to fly to Chicago blind by now," she said. "I'm not sure what I'll do with myself."

"You can start knitting booties," he said.

Ruth grinned and looked away. She said, "I don't like to knit." A breeze raised goose pimples on her arm. She shivered and Henry pulled her in, wrapped his arms around her. It was unusually warm for November but she should've worn more than a sweater. On either side of the narrow landing strip, the cornstalks were matted down and moldy with the rain and frosts they'd had; everywhere, the soil was a concerning mixture of freeze and mud. Ruth shut her mind's eye against the picture of a hunk of mud or rock flying into the propeller and breaking or jamming it, even though they'd walked the length of field already, together, to check for such things.

The Jenny stood ready behind them. Her tan wings and body stood out against the cool blue fall horizon, the spurts of brashly colored maples and oaks and chestnuts, and the white farmhouse and red barn and silvery grain silo down at Ruth's parents'. The ground would go white with snow and ice, then melt to a black sticky mess before tendrils of crop would start anew on the farm, but Ruth's belly would begin its rounding long before that, with their first, who would be called John Henry.

"Safe flight," Ruth said into his neck.

"Safe week," he replied.

She nodded and pulled away from him and wrapped her arms around herself, chilled as much by the air as by the fact that she would not be getting in the plane with her husband.

"Take care of the little one," Henry said as he tugged his helmet and goggles out of his flight suit pocket. He kissed her once more and then turned, walked to the Jenny, and hoisted himself into the front cockpit. She watched him get settled in, then walked to the front of the plane and reached up to the top of the propeller. "Contact?" she said.

"Contact."

And Ruth heaved her weight down and the propeller stuttered, caught, and whirled to life. She stepped back, back, sixty feet back, and she shaded her eyes as the plane turned to face south and Henry raised the throttle. In another minute, he started bumping down the field, finally lifting off and turning to head due east. By the time Ruth turned to cross the field to home, he was a large fly on her horizon.

As she fell away behind him, vanishing into the wide-open, empty field, Henry settled into his flight back to Checkerboard Field, Chicago. He looked at his compass and peeked over the side of the plane to be sure he had the railroad in sight. He would arrive just after sundown, the familiar beacon swinging out to greet him and bear him down from the star-spangled, wind-blown heights of an autumn midwestern night, 1928.

~

THREE YEARS EARLIER, Ruth's father had told her she was crazy to marry him. He'd questioned her at the dinner table: "You gonna be my full partner in the farm, all eighteen-odd years and a hundred pounds of you? You gonna sleep well at night without him next to you? What if there's trouble?" Next he shook his head and scowled: "Marrying a man who's gone five days a week, and flying around in an aeroplane every one of those five days—idiocy, Ruthie, craziness! You read in the papers about these Air Mail men dying by the dozen." He stopped to take a bite of food, swallowed slowly, and continued: "A man flying is the craziest thing I ever heard of. If God meant us to fly, he would have given us wings."

"If God meant us not to fly, he wouldn't have given us the brain to invent the airplane," Ruth said before she could stop herself. "And besides, we've seen the barnstormers at the county fair together—remember Ruth Law?—and you said, I remember, 'Now, that's something, Ruthie. Isn't that something?' I *remember*. Now, suddenly, you're so shifty. You simply want me to marry one of these awful boys from town."

As she reached for her water glass, her hands were shaking, and she caught her mother's eyes flashing toward her, urging, *Don't talk to your father like that*.

Ruth sighed. "He won't always be gone so much, Daddy." She got up, retrieved the pot of coffee from the stove, and set it on the table in front of him. "Pretty soon there'll be enough business that he'll come to Iowa City every night." She poured coffee into his cup and continued. "Besides, flying is not that crazy. You should let Henry take you up sometime. You would love it, Daddy. I know you would. You can see for miles and miles. You can see to the Mississippi from up there—almost all the way down to Davenport!"

"How would you know?" he said, his faint Irish brogue more distinct whenever he was agitated—"*How d'ya know, eh?*"—setting his coffee cup back down after he'd started to lift it.

Ruth smiled.

"Ruthie?"

SHE WAS AN only child of the first order to her father—and a girl. With seven miscarriages before her, Elizabeth had almost died delivering Ruth and was not able to have any more children, which meant no boys. Paul Sheehan never expressed disappointment in this, and maybe he didn't allow himself to feel it, but he was, accordingly, devastated by his son-in-law's disinterest in farming. He didn't oppose the marriage, however, because Henry was basically a good man and Ruth loved him.

Paul loved chess and in the spring when it was bet-hedging time as to when to plant, he always wanted to play. "Ruthie," he'd call into the house. "Ruthie, chess." He'd pull the wooden board out from next to the icebox—hand-painted red and blue with leftover paint from the wagon he'd made for her fourth birthday.

As he made a show of dusting off the porch table where they played, he said, always, "It's the most important decision a farmer can make each year. Can't yield more than you plant. You can't."

Paul Sheehan played chess because there wasn't much else for him to do and if he was unoccupied he was likely to end up in the kitchen, trying to do something but incapable of most everything there except puzzling over the speed of his wife Elizabeth's hands with a knife. She hated being watched, and besides, the kitchen wasn't so big—he would bump her for sure, eventually, and then one of them would get hurt or mad or both.

They drank lemonade out of blue Mason jars whose lids had gone off, and until Ruth was nine or ten, he explained his every move. "This puts me within two moves of check-mate," he said. "Unless you sacrifice your queen. See it?" He wanted her to see two moves ahead of each turn. "There's always a most certain move," he said. "The key is to find it out and then to answer it."

At the end of three games—they never played more than three, it was some facet of his Irish superstition—Paul would lean back, extend his legs, crossing them at the ankles, and dig his finger at the wet pile of sugar in the bottom of the jar. He would scoop up as much as he could in his first knuckle, then raise it to his mouth. He chewed the lemon slice, too, and watched his curly-haired daughter across from him on the porch swing, her feet planted on a leg of the table, gently rocking herself back and forth like the almost-waves of a river. Even the horses, a few dozen yards to the left, turned their attention to him.

"It's all a careful dance, Ruthie," he told her. "Chess, farming, life. It's all a dance and there's always something leading you. Always."

Her father repeated this adage to her whenever she was "being headstrong," and by the time she was thirteen, she could mouth the words along with him. And she thought about how he lived. She couldn't see that her father was always following something or someone else. No, it seemed to her that aside from waiting to plant, trying to anticipate nature's next move, and then trying to get out of check when a too-heavy rain or a drought or an insect visitation ruined the crop, Ruth could not see that her father was a follower in the dance he lived. Not when, some thirty years before, he had picked up his mother, his two younger brothers, and all their belongings and moved them to Cedar Bluff from Mason City, where his grandfather and grandmother had settled after moving from Ireland in 1833. Two consecutive grasshopper plagues and then a major flood ruined that land three years running around 1880. Paul's father, who was known to be a little mad anyway, took to believing there was a curse on the land. He became obsessed with the plagues of locusts and frogs that the Israelites had suffered before Moses led them back to Israel. It was the same thing, he said. God was testing their strength. Finally, he decided he wasn't strong enough and so he propped up his rifle beneath his chin and pulled the trigger with his toe. Fifteen-year-old Paul buried him, then packed up the house and moved the family south, to Johnson County, where the soil was supposed to be richer. Those weren't the actions of a follower, Ruth thought.

The only clue that remained in Paul as a testament to his early life, besides his refusal to attend church—and the only thing close to fear that Ruth knew in him—was his hatred of grasshoppers. The sight of just one would set him cursing; the sole of his boot would flatten the thing with a sick crackle before Ruth could cup her hands around it. As he would then scold her for feeling defensive of the bugs, for going against her own father, she tried to imagine the peaceful eye of a swarm of the large, celery-green insects, with them swirling around her, stilled unto themselves, without their legs or antennae moving, yet moving in thousands, maybe even millions, as a whole.

⌒

HENRY HAD ONE clear visual memory of riding the coal-powered paddle-wheel ferry with his father, Captain John; he remembered standing on the top deck and watching the murky waters of the Mississippi sliding under the boat. He had a clear image of the sharp hills of McGregor as they approached, and the hotel, post office, store, and saloon nestled into the side of one of those hills; and if he turned to look behind him, he would see the flat marshy lands where the Fox River met the Mississippi, wetlands that rose and fell through the year, with rainfall and snow and drought. He remembered the timbre of his father's voice—it seemed chestnut-hued, not too deep but resonant.

Henry would've been on the ferry with his father when lightning struck it if he hadn't been in bed with typhoid. A fire killed Captain John before he could reach shore. Henry lay in bed and watched the lightning make the dark bedroom shades glow, felt the thunder rattle the roof. He knew his father was on the boat and he heard his mother's sighs and the twins' frightened whimpers coming from the kitchen every time a new blast of light and noise came through. Henry kept counting between the lightning and thunder.

He was asleep when Ed and Dorothea Ferrer came in with the bad news, but he awoke, hungry and damp with sweat, when he heard his mother's sobs in the living room.

"You should sell the boat, Anne. Let Ed sell it and why don't you and the children go up to Plain for a while. Spend some time with your folks. Do you some good. You need rest after the typhoid, or you'll come down with it yourself."

"We'll stay right here, thank you, Dorothea. Can't haul Henry a hundred miles right now. Besides," she said, "maybe I'll run the boat myself." She began to sob again, lower, quieter, like she was wearing out, and someone pushed a chair back and went to the stove and put a log on.

Henry stayed in bed until the shades had a certain, constant slant of light on them. Then he slipped out, for the first time in weeks, hoping maybe he'd dreamed it all, found his mother asleep in her rocking chair, and he climbed into her lap as the first true sunlight in days touched her face.

By the time Henry and the twins arrived at their grandparents' dairy farm in Plain, just a touch west of Madison, Anne had died of the typhoid Henry had given her and she was buried next to her husband. Henry was seven years old and, besides his parents, he missed the river, his canoe, the ferry, as if they, too, had been blood relations. Grandmère and Grandpère were quiet, devout French Catholics and they had to let the hired hands go in order to afford three hungry, growing mouths—which meant the hands that went with those mouths had to pitch in. Henry loved herding the cows into the barn at night. Although he was no taller than the smallest calf, the cows would warily watch his stomping approach across the pasture and as he circled around behind them, they would all turn, their eyes wide and fixed with alertness, their ears straight out, only their tails and their nostrils moving. When Henry raised his hands and started running at them, screaming, "Ya, ya," their hooves scrambled and they ran away thirty paces before turning to see him again, still coming, and ran thirty more paces. In this manner, seven-year-old Henry got them all the way back to the barn. He had a dog to help, a little collie that only ran at the cows when Henry did, and then eventually a Shetland pony as uninspired as the dog.

Henry liked the cows and he loved his grandparents, yet he never imagined growing up to be a farmer. When he thought of farming, he thought of Uncle George, his father's brother, who was the reason Henry's parents met. "George didn't want anything to do with the fur or ferries over in Prairie du Chien, so he went up to Plain to farm," Captain John once explained to his son. "And when I went to visit George the first time, I saw your mother in church, and knew I had to marry her. I'd never seen a face like hers—an angel, except"—he laughed, pinching her arm playfully as she passed nearby them— "you couldn't exactly be sure whose ranks she broke with in the big battle. Beezlebub or Michael."

As for George, he was a terrible farmer, although everyone insisted it was just bad luck. Henry learned this part as he grew up in Plain. George's hogs got sick, his cows gave bad milk, and his chickens killed each other. Finally, George just farmed what he needed for himself, cut down and burned his own trees, and locked himself up in the cabin for a good year. People talked, because no one knew what he did in that year and one of the larger cows took up residence on the porch, lying down—she wasn't even sick—and eventually a few of those floorboards gave way. When people went to see him—stepping around this cow and knocking on the front door—he did not answer, even though there was smoke coming from the chimney and footsteps could be heard inside. Then one day he was just gone. It was later believed that he went to St. Louis first and then Texas, where Plain people said folks were crazier and George would fit right in. He was never in touch with his nephews and nieces after his brother John died. But Henry thought a lot about this uncle during his own time in Plain and came to believe George was an oilman, and he believed that his own attempts at farming might end like George's.

Henry's decision to join the Army as soon as he could, just

after the Armistice, had nothing to do with wanting to be any part of a war, but it did have to do with stories of this uncle he'd never met, seeing the world, and, to his mind anyway, the farm having one less mouth to feed. His grandparents were quietly angry at his departure but they still gave him a St. Christopher medal for safe passage.

A captain in Chicago, faced with this Wisconsin farmboy, still too fresh to shave, needing a new hole in the smallest belt they could find, first asked to see his birth certificate three times and then made him a stable keeper at a major Allied air base near Lyon, France. He spent several cheerful if lonely months there, leaving the base and wandering about the city and the French countryside in total silence since he was only starting to learn the language, loving the strangeness of it all, and, of course, the beauty. He met his first real friend, a Frenchman, Philippe, while sitting on a bench outside his quarters, listening to a record by a young George Gershwin on his prized Victrola, and watching an enormous plane— with three tailwings and a wingspan broader than any hangar Henry had ever seen—come in for a landing.

"That's marvelous," Philippe said. "Can I listen with you?"

"Sure," Henry said, and they listened in silence for several minutes, while the bomber came to a stop within their line of sight. "Do you know what that huge airplane is? I've never seen anything like it."

"A Caproni Ca-36," Philippe said. "Italian, a bomber."

Henry nodded and watched the behemoth rumble around the airport. Planes like that—it both strained the credulity of flight and reinforced that credulity. If that thing could fly, then flight was real.

"You are not a pilot," Philippe said, mostly sure.

"No, oh no," Henry said. "I'm not so lucky as that. I tend the horses."

Philippe nodded.

They listened to the entire record twice, and then Philippe said he wanted to buy it.

Henry said it wasn't for sale but then Philippe said, "I'll take you flying." And Henry was sold, as Philippe knew he would be.

The first trip, in a fast, exhilarating Nieuport 28, which still had its Vickers guns attached and the Allied roundel on its wings, was freezing, unnerving, and wonderful. Henry, who finally hit a growth spurt that first year in France, kept sticking his head as far out of the cockpit as he could and looking at France, green and brown and white and gray and jagged, with pools of undulation, then of smooth flat, far below them. His stomach felt inverted, inside out, something, and he thought, once, that he might vomit. But when they finally landed, Henry told Philippe that he could keep the record, and Philippe responded, "Would you like to learn to fly yourself? I can teach you." Henry said he'd give him every record he owned, which was not so many.

Lesson one took place the following afternoon, and Philippe said that Henry was a natural. "Think that the stick is an extension of your arm," he said as they removed the chocks from the wheels. Philippe wore a great white silk scarf when he flew, just like the famous aviators in the newsreels and papers. He guided Henry through takeoffs, landings, great wide sloping turns; fast climbs and gradual descents; one engine fire and several sputtering stalls. They went up in bad weather so that Henry could know what it felt like to fly when you weren't sure of the horizon or your altitude or the direction of the wind or the location of a good field for landing. The rides were frequently so bumpy and jarring that Henry left Philippe's Nieuport with a headache; other times, however, it was as if they floated on one breeze alone. Although Henry's French could barely get a meal ordered or directions asked, he became very proficient at describing the wonders and calamities of flight: *Ça me stupéfie. Elle s'est écrasée au sol. Elle est en perte de vitesse.*

There were all sorts of pilot heroes around Henry on the Allied base, urging his passion forward. They seemed to have done everything—fighting in the war, flying mail to Casablanca and over the Pyrenees, and setting new distance records. They talked about the legends—Pequet, Dal Mistro, Saint-Exupéry—as their friends. They made Henry almost wish he'd cracked up a plane in cotton-ball-thick fog in Tangiers, Casablanca, Nice, anywhere. Just so he would have a good story to share. He couldn't help but dream of running down a German Fokker in a SPAD or a Sopwith Camel. He tried to imagine the rush of air and the smell of gasoline and oil and mortar rounds. He imagined diving down on the German, gathering speed while staying invisible, obscured by the enemy's wing with the hated black and white cross-pattée at each wing end and on the tailwing. Yet Henry never imagined—never wanted to know—the exact moment that so many pilots talked about on the base—the moment when the enemy turned to look at you, when you saw fear wash over his face, a split second before you pulled the trigger back and held it there, when you knew you'd won.

Henry, he was captivated by the diving and the furious, precise cowering in the enemy's blind spot, climbing into the sun so that the enemy was blinded and lost sight of you—all the daredevil flying over the jungles and deserts of Africa, or the mountains, rivers, cities, and farms of France, Germany, Turkey, Russia. It seemed graceful and magical. The violence with which many pilots met their end terrified him—whether they were shot down by the Germans or slammed into the ground by weather or the plane itself. But Henry knew such violence was the price a real pilot had to be willing to pay.

Once, Philippe nearly killed them both by putting the plane down at the edge of an avalanche field near Grenoble. It was better than hitting the side of the mountain, Philippe pointed out, which would certainly have killed them. Instead, on their nearly blind landing in a mountain meadow that was edged by boulders of all sizes, the wingtip caught on one of the rocks and spun the plane around and over, onto its back. They both sat still and quiet for a minute, held in place, upside down, by their seat straps. "*Tu es là?*" Philippe said tentatively.

Henry was terrified but also thrilled and amused. "*Oui,*" he responded in the deepest, most serious voice he could muster. "*Je suis ici.*"

WHEN SHE WAS LITTLE, Ruth didn't play house, and as she grew up, she didn't think much about the boys in town and whether or not they'd be good husbands someday, although some of her friends at school did. It wasn't that there was a principle at stake—she simply wasn't interested. Instead, whenever she could, she went to the pine grove on the south edge of the farm, where the ground was soft and the dense pine needles hushed and mellowed the whole world, making her feel far away, yet safe. There, she pretended she was someone famous—Betsy Ross or Pocahontas; Joan of Arc or Queen Victoria.

There were also the letters. She had written them for nearly as long as she could remember. At some point, yes, early on, it had been a diary, *Dear Ruth*, in a leather-bound book that had been the last present her father's mother, Margaret, had given her. She was six, just learning to write in cursive, and Grandmother had died the previous year. When the book ran out of pages, it was a drought and there was no money for extravagances. It was exceptional that year, even, when her mother bought her some paper and ink and her own pen. But somehow Ruth couldn't write a diary if she didn't have a book for it. Clean white paper was for *letters*, she decided, not a diary, and her mother suggested she write to her cousin Beatrice, the same age, in Minnesota but Ruth couldn't even put a face to that cousin. So she invented a pen pal, Ingrid, who lived in Sweden and rode a bicycle to her school on the sea. After school, she fished for herring and braided her hair and wrote letters back to Ruth.

In the first grade, Ruth's teacher assigned them to write letters to President Wilson and then to an important person of their choice. Ruth first chose Alexander Graham Bell but then changed her mind and wrote to the first lady doctor, Elizabeth Blackwell, and the teacher, charmed that Ruth remembered a lady whom she'd mentioned to Ruth once, did not tell the child that Dr. Blackwell had been dead a few years. In the sixth grade, given the same assignment, Ruth chose a lady barnstormer, Ruth Law, whom she'd seen at the state fair over the summer. It had taken them three days to get to Des Moines in the Model T, as it took a flat tire outside little What Cheer and there was a day lost to fixing it. But they got there in time to see Ruth Law, who went up in an old plane that sounded like a congested four-cylinder, or so Paul Sheehan said, and she outflew her teammate named Bob something. Bob couldn't fly as low as Miss Law, nor could he corkscrew his plane over their heads. Ruth didn't even know why Bob was there, actually, besides to prop the stool next to the plane when Miss Law needed to step out of it.

And Ruth couldn't believe it when, six weeks after she sent her letter, Miss Law sent her a signed picture postcard of herself. After that, Ruth told Ingrid she didn't have time to write anymore. She had new letters to write, new people to meet.

August 1920

Ruth Law
Ruth Law's Flying Circus
c/o: Iowa State Fair
Des Moines

Dear Ruth,

I saw your performance at the State Fair last week and it was splendid! Your loop-the-loop, so big, so close to the other planes, and I almost fainted there at the top of the loop, I was so sure you would simply fall to the earth, but there you stuck, magnetized to the sky I don't know how, and down you swooped like you'd planned all the while, more graceful than a hummingbird, surer than a hawk. You made me feel like I could fly, too, and maybe I'll get a chance to try it someday. We can be the Ruth and Ruth Flying Circus!

I'll be thirteen years old in about a month, and I would very much like to be a nurse or a doctor. I live in Cedar Bluff, which is just about 100 miles east from Des Moines. Maybe you've flown over sometime, as we're not too far north of the railroad tracks and route 6. I wonder where you are from and how you got into a plane for the first time. My father says he'd never let a woman drive an automobile he was riding in, so I don't think he'd like it if I went up in a plane. He jumps barrels on ice skates when the neighbor's pond freezes over, my father does, three at a time once, but he took my skates away after I jumped over just one barrel two winters ago. He said it wasn't ladylike.

My friend Mary Hitchens says she saw you fly at the Muscatine County Fair in just your skivvies. She likes to stretch the truth a bit, Mary does, and I told her I didn't believe her. But she still insists. Wouldn't it be too windy and cold to fly without any clothes on?

I hope to see you when you come through Iowa again.

Sincerely,
Ruth Sheehan
Cedar Bluff, Iowa

She was dazzled by Ruth Law's show and still more so by the postcard the aviatrix sent to her, but it was medicine, nursing, on which Ruth set her real sights. It was reasonable, after all, and increasingly commonplace, that women would learn medicine to take care of people; barnstorming, meanwhile, wasn't really something to be *serious* about doing. Watching, loving, yes; *doing*, no. Besides the Blackwells and Clara Barton and Florence Nightingale, it was wartime—or war posters, anyway—that showed Ruth how important nurses were. And they got to see Europe's real gingerbread houses, the leaning Tower of Pisa, the Eiffel Tower, and maybe even the Sphinx! The distinguished and affable (and, alas, dead, as she eventually discovered) Elizabeth Blackwell gave Ruth her first genuine heroine; the nurses "over there" showed Ruth where she could go.

In the pine grove, Ruth would collect giant sycamore leaves for blankets, corn silks for bandages, and corn kernels and acorns for medicine, and then she cured the kitten she'd brought with her, usually of leprosy or influenza. She pretended to visit people's houses in the middle of the night to save them or their children; she imagined her own office in town with a lock on the door and on the medicine cabinet, and a big rolltop desk, like old Dr. Fischer's. Back inside her house, when her mother or father had a real splinter, Ruth had the softest touch of anyone, and loved the ritual of warming some water, getting the clean tweezers and maybe a needle.

As she advanced through the school's upper grades and continued to focus on the idea of nursing, she thought of going far away from Cedar Bluff, if only temporarily, and then decided she liked this thought. She would go to an orphanage in Chicago, she decided, or a hospital in New York or Boston—or California, even, simply because it was said to be beautiful. The wagon trains used to pass just south of Cedar Bluff and a whole pile of Mormons who decided not to continue on had settled one town over, in West Branch, and some Mennonites had settled Amana and Kalona, twenty

miles to the west. She'd take a train, she decided—the wag-
ons were both tedious and a little dangerous, people dying
under the wheels all the time, and such weather and mountains, eventually, and thieves and marauders. Or, when her
father retired the Model T and bought a new car, maybe she'd
take the old Ford and drive herself, though she'd have to run
away with it in the dead of night. Her father didn't believe
women should be driving. His wife, he said, was too frail.
Ruth, thinking of how much more strength it took to do the
laundry than it did to steer a wheel, always chuckled when
he asserted this, and he always pretended not to notice his
daughter's chuckle.

Or maybe Ruth Law would come back through and young
Ruth could hitch a ride on her way west. That would be
something.

Ultimately, she imagined, after a brief spell away, she'd
work in the hospital in Iowa City, helping with the babies,
maybe—wouldn't that be safe and close to home? She might
take up practice later on with a doctor like Dr. Fischer, or
whoever was coming to relieve the old man, who walked with
a cane but still seemed to know just about everything there
was to know. Even right there in Cedar Bluff—she'd still be
doing what she loved. A lifetime on the farm as a wife and
mother, on the other hand, terrified her. She imagined she'd
expire from boredom. There was a nursing school right in
Iowa City, just ten miles away, and she first wrote to them in
1923, when she turned sixteen and had one more year left
before school in Cedar Bluff was exhausted.

When they wrote back, accepting her but asking for some
money, or some statement of how she planned to pay for

school, Ruth took the letter to her mother. Elizabeth was a quiet, kind woman, not without her own will and temper, and yet she was far more subdued than Ruth, at any age. They were one another's physical doppelgänger, however, the honey-brown hair, slightly curly, and rich, pooling brown eyes. "You should talk to your father about it," Elizabeth Sheehan advised her daughter.

"But he'll say no. Can't you talk to him first?"

Elizabeth said she'd do what she could.

"College is not for girls and most absolutely not for *farm* girls—you're lucky to have as much schooling as you do," her father said a few nights later. "I didn't finish grammar school and I turned out all right, didn't I?"

Ruth didn't move, but her chin trembled, barely, and her stomach shimmied and twisted.

"Where did you think we were going to get the money?" he continued.

Ruth stared at her mother, begging for help, but getting none. "It's a *nurses'* college, and it's full of women," Ruth said. "Maybe I'll just pay for it all myself." She knew his face would be darkening, tightening, and he would be wondering how he had raised such an unruly, ungrateful daughter. Her mother looked at her quickly, once, her eyes saying, *Don't do this, not like this, he's your father, be respectful.* Then the dogs howled and her father stood up to see if there were coyotes near the chickens. Left alone with her daughter, Elizabeth still said nothing, offered no condolence. Ruth reached for a piece of bread and then carefully, slowly, sopped up gravy off her plate, imagining it as blood, which sickened her but felt better than this disappointment, this anger.

July 1923

Dear Ruth Law,

I don't think I want to be married, not like my mother and father anyway, and not to any one of these boys in town. My friend Anna talks about how kind and hard-working George Klemman is, and my friend Mary is sweet on Tom Hitchens because he says he's going to study the law and Mary's father is a lawyer. Those boys are nice enough, but they're about the only nice ones, who don't smell like a farm anyway, and the rest of them can't add two and two if it's not swine or cattle they're counting. Oh, I know my father would be ashamed, and he'd wonder what makes me think I'm so good, but the fact is, I don't know really what's wrong with the boys in Cedar Bluff, just that none of them make me laugh or smile.

I was sweet once on Gus, Mr. Cilek's nephew from Chicago who came out for a few summers when I was terribly small. He told me about the streetcars and a big fire that nearly burned the whole city down, even with so much water right nearby. And he told me about some of the dances and music he hears there, and about the trains right through the city, and the lake—it just sounds so beautiful. My father told me Gus was a troublemaker back home and that he got sent to Cedar Bluff so he wouldn't go to jail, but I wouldn't believe him. My father's afraid of boys that come around me, just like he's afraid of grasshoppers. Mary and Anna, too, were afraid of Gus, they said they'd heard what city boys were like, but I didn't listen to them, either. And Gus was grateful for my faithfulness. He never once held my hand, but he did give me a cricket

at the end of the summer, and told me if I listened carefully I'd hear the song it was cricketing for me. That was
kind, I thought, even though I was only 10 years old and
he was close to 16 and I think he liked me like a little sister. He called me Pip.

The Cileks, unfortunately, are a little strange—even my
mother, who does her best never to judge anyone, says so.
They raised their oldest son Dean as a girl for nearly four
years until Dr. Fischer finally said that if they tried to enter
him in school that way, he'd be forced to tell the teacher.
Dean lost most of his hearing sometime when he was born
and he hated being out in the fields to boot, which made
Mr. Cilek think he'd just be better off as a girl, and why
not try it? They put him in dresses and called him Deanie
and let his hair grow long until it could be braided. My
mother told me she thought it was the cruelest thing she'd
ever seen anyone do and I could tell she'd like to have
nothing at all to do with the Cileks except then Dean
wouldn't have any friends at all. I'm three years or so older
than Dean and we would look after him sometimes when
his parents were in church—they didn't like to take him
out much, like they knew there'd be problems if all of
Cedar Bluff found out. Instead, we were about the only
ones to know, I think, and Sheehans aren't the type to
spread gossip, that's what my father says, anyway,
although I told Anna and Mary and made them promise
not to tell. I don't think they've told to this day, actually.
Now the Cileks have Charlie, too, who's all boy, one hundred percent.

My mother told me once she didn't think Dean would stay
around these parts, and just a few nights ago, he proved
her right, hopping a train out of here, and I don't think
we'll ever see him again. He's only 12, too young to be liv-

ing with hoboes, but maybe he'll make it all the way to California and find a good job and be happy. Mr. and Mrs. Cilek expect him back any day, but I think they're wrong, and so does my mother. My father, who is probably Tom Cilek's best friend, was glad to see Dean leave. Even though he's just 12, and deaf and a little strange to boot, my father thinks he'll be all right. "Tom burned that boy's bridges around here years ago," he says. "He's better off anywhere else."

There's so much to do before I can get married, I can hardly think about it. I'd rather be a nurse than a wife anyway. You get to do more. Or, best of all, I could be a barnstormer, like you!

Sincerely,
Ruth Sheehan

It was a warmish day the following spring, 1924, and thick clouds hovered low all across the sky, as if each one were hung on a string that at any moment might snap, letting the cloud crash down, smack open and flood the earth.

Henry had been threading his plane through these clouds. The ceiling was low, just six hundred feet or so, and sometimes he would be lifted right back into gray blindness. He missed the first pass at Iowa City, circled back, and the second time was enough of a charm. He got water, fuel, and then went back up. But then the engine was funny, too high-pitched, without any burps or hiccups, and there came an abrupt stall. Henry put her into a little dive to see if he couldn't get enough oxygen to start her up again, but she was adamant and there wasn't much diving space, so he leveled out as best he could and lined up with the first field he saw without any cows in it. The de Havilland floated down as if she'd planned it all along. The field was bumpy as any spring-plowed field is apt to be, and she came to a stop several hundred yards from a barn and house. Henry got out and looked around but no one approached. No sign of Paul Sheehan. When the engine was cool enough, he discovered the cracked cylinder, and knew there was no getting on to Chicago just then.

Paul Sheehan started out of the barn toward the house in time to see the pilot, wearing the bulky flight suit and goggles around his neck, walking toward him. He looked up the field, where the airplane was parked. When Henry was within hand-shaking range, Paul extended his, and said, smiling, "I can't say you're welcome anytime—there'll be corn in that field before long. I just seeded a week back."

Henry laughed, expressed his appreciation, and explained the problem, looking up at the darkening sky once or twice.

"I guess my hearing must really be going," Paul said. "Even though I was tending some loud milking cows, I'd think I'd have heard you."

"Not likely," Henry replied, "since my engine was stalled. Nothing to hear." He asked Paul for a phone and as they walked to the house together, Henry answered the man's questions about the plane, starting with how she ran on an eight-cylinder engine just like any other. The farmer seemed incredulous. "So I suppose someone can make my new tractor fly," he joked.

"Depends how big a lady she is," Henry replied. "Although

you'd never believe the size of some of the things I've seen flying. Man-made elephants with wings. Enormous."

On the phone, the field manager in Iowa City said the truck would take a half hour and it would drive the mail to a train first, then come back and help him. Henry was to go meet it on the road, at the end of the farm drive. Paul took Henry to the kitchen and introduced him to Elizabeth, who offered him a glass of water, which Henry accepted. Elizabeth smiled at him politely, but without much interest, said she hoped the water was cold enough.

"It's perfect," he said, handing the empty glass back to her. "You'll have to excuse me now—I've got to go gather the mail and meet my truck." Then he headed out to the end of the driveway.

Ruth came along, walking home from town, deep in her own misery. She wasn't to be a doctor or nurse, she wasn't even to leave Cedar Bluff—the exhaustion of her last resort, of a year's efforts, confirmed by final letters in her pocket from the college in Iowa City and from a girl's college in Minnesota, St. Catherine's, where her teacher Miss Jenkins had attended, saying, there was simply no arrangement available to her without her parents' permission; it just wasn't their policy. She had been shocked when the Minnesota college wouldn't help her—it was *for girls,* after all—but now, with these two closing their doors, there was no one. She wept as she walked, kicking a rock or mud clod when she happened upon one. Why couldn't her parents understand—why were they being so unkind? She was nearly seventeen, but she felt the world was closing in around her.

But what about that lady pilot she'd seen at the state fair,

Ruth Law? Could she help, if Ruth wrote to her and asked, *begged*? No, she supposed not. And as she kicked a few more rocks, she wondered, Why do I want to go so badly, anyway, and can I change enough, can I let this go?

~

A QUARTER MILE ON, nearly home, she smelled Henry before she saw him—the oil and gasoline on him; it wasn't like her father smelled, not even after crawling around a broken-down tractor all day, and what disgusting annoyance, she wondered, would she encounter now? She braced herself for the odd, semi-leering Charlie Cilek, their youngest, or the stinky Billy Luhrman, who helped her father. As she got closer, however, and heard him whistling "Pop Goes the Weasel," she discerned his flight suit and helmet—not Tom or Billy or some other local, but a pilot! Right there before her. Was this a joke or a mirage? Where was his plane? She looked toward the fields but saw nothing—since the barn hid the DH-4. She tried not to stare, in case he was real, and as she got closer, ten feet away, she saw he was not only real, but as handsome as anyone she had ever seen—green eyes and dark brown hair beneath whatever coating of dust and grease and gasoline she smelled, which, coming from the plane, made him all the more attractive. And he seemed a bit awkward himself, or maybe he hadn't seen her, not boldly calling out hello or teasing her like other boys.

Could this be true, or was she still walking along, kicking dirt, imagining things? She feared all of a sudden that her face looked like she'd been weeping, and she quickly tried to dry her eyes with the sleeves of her dress. She knew it wouldn't help enough and thus she hoped that she'd be able to get by him without drawing attention to herself. Anyway, she'd never see him again—some fluke, anomaly, must've brought him there, to miserable Cedar Bluff, and thus what was the point in speaking him today, whyever? She kept her face down as she reached the driveway, nodding hello without looking at him, and turned toward home.

Henry had been looking up and down the road for the truck when pretty young Ruth strode and kicked her way into his vision. He enjoyed watching her from a comfortable distance—she was *mad*—but when she got closer, turned her face out of sight, and walked very fast and surely right past him, without a word, he almost let her go. He felt certain she was barely fifteen and that her father would nearly kill him for talking to her; yet he needn't say anything forward, he told himself. And what if she just *looked* young? *Say something*, his brain commanded. And before he could stop himself, he'd spoken up to her small back not yet too far past him, two arm's lengths, maybe. "I've landed my plane in your father's cornfield up there," he blurted. "She's got a cracked cylinder and I'm waiting for the truck to come fetch the mail and help me fix her. I mean, I'm not just loitering here at the end of your driveway trying to embarrass you. Some day, isn't it? On your way home from school?"

Ruth stopped, although she wanted to keep walking. Still, it felt impolite not to answer. "Sure is," she said, half turned, looking at the sky instead of him. "It keeps wanting to rain." There was a silence long enough then that Ruth thought she'd head on. "Well," she said. "I hope the clouds stay sealed for you. If you're flying again today."

"Sure am," he said quickly, trying to keep her there. "Got to get the de Havilland back to Chicago. I started the morning in Omaha." He showed her his filthy hand as he extended it, showing her he meant to shake, but wouldn't. "I'm Henry Gutterson. From Wisconsin. Prairie du Chien first and then a little town called Plain."

Ruth turned to face him, giving up on her tear-streaked face. "Ruth," she said, pretending to shake his hand in the air. "Ruth Sheehan. I think I've heard you fly overhead sometimes. Seen you, too. Is that possible? Or would it be another pilot?"

He was hopeful. She talked like a young woman, not a girl. "It's likely that it was me," he said, letting himself smile all the way.

She asked more questions about the Air Mail Service, then, and set her books on the fence post and leaned back against it to listen. Might as well talk to this handsome pilot she'd never have the good fortune to see again.

"We're slow and we crash a lot," Henry told her, "and President Harding was always wanting to shut us down. Unless we figured out a way to fly at night." Then came the thirty-six-hour marathon flight, he explained, connecting San Francisco and New York with two planes meeting in Chicago. "In March, for God's sake. Two of the four men starting out crashed—one in the Wyoming Tetons and one in the Alleghenies, Pennsylvania."

As he talked, explaining how a man named Jack Knight single-handedly saved the Air Mail by flying the whole way from North Platte to Chicago even though he was suppposed to trade off in Omaha, Henry wasn't quite sure if she was listening and found it interesting, or if she was just being polite. She was looking at him dead-on, carefully, her brown eyes taking everything in, but still, he didn't feel sure.

Of course, Ruth was utterly captivated—this Jack Knight flying over her in the pitch-black of a snowy February night, farmers below lighting fires to help him trace a path, to pray for him, and where was she? She would've helped, if she'd known. And now here was Henry, a real live pilot, standing before her, about to take off again from her cornfield. She would tell him about seeing Ruth Law and her magnificent stunts, but she didn't want to seem impolite by interrupting him.

"They say some pilots die because they just go crazy and can't help but drive their planes into the nearest mountain-side or even straight into the ground," Henry continued. "One fellow once—not on the cross-country marathon—jumped out without his parachute. The plane crashed a mile away, and they couldn't find anything wrong with it apart from the crunched-up mess of the entire body of the thing." When he finally stopped talking, listened to his last words lingering between them, he was suddenly embarassed that he'd told her this story—it was so dark and awful. A cold breeze blew and it felt like it might, at last, rain. He couldn't think of another thing to say now. He flushed and prayed she'd say something instead.

Ruth turned and looked upfield. "Your plane's behind the barn?"

"Couple hundred yards, yes," Henry replied.

"That's why I can't see it," Ruth noted.

"I can show you," Henry offered.

"You've got the truck coming."

"Right."

Ruth loved that he was awkward; he was sweet. She looked around them. The grass was clumpy and only newly thawed—the usual for early April—and although it was only fifty degrees, it felt balmy after a screaming subzero winter. Snow and ice still clung to the tallest grass along the fence. It started to rain gently—soft, cool, misty bits. "I saw Ruth Law's Flying Circus once at the state fair," she said.

"Oh? When was that? Did you like it?"

Ruth nodded, a broad smile taking over her face. "Yeah. It was beautiful. It was, let me think. I was about twelve, maybe thirteen. About four years back, I guess."

"Right," Henry said, looking at her full-on now, taking in her beauty and the spark in her eyes, her face, as well as the fact that she came up to about his shoulder, and *he* was short. Her mother had been tiny, too, he recalled.

Then Ruth asked a question: "What's it like, flying?"

Henry thought about this. "Maybe a little like diving off something into water, a little like spinning around and around, and a little like being shaken upside down and backwards."

None of these descriptions told her much. She tucked the hair behind her ear that had come loose from its comb in the wind. "I'd go now with you, if you'd take me," Ruth said. "Flying, that is. I would've gone with Ruth Law, if she'd ever come back. We could've been the Two Ruths Flying Circus."

He laughed gently. "Yes, I suppose you could've."

In the last few minutes before the truck from Iowa City arrived, they both enjoyed the warmth of this last gentle laugh. They looked up the road to see if the truck was yet coming, hoping it was not. "Well," Ruth asked, "what other stories can you tell me before you leave? I don't expect I'll ever meet an Air Mail pilot again—"

"I hope that's not true," Henry interjected.

"Well." She looked down, felt her neck warm with color.

"I'll tell you how I learned to fly. How about that?"

"Lovely." Ruth shifted in her lean against the fence.

And Henry began the story of meeting Philippe, the Gershwin records, the crack-up in the Alps. She listened, wishing she could close her eyes to memorize his face, his voice, so that when she lay awake that night in bed, miserable once again with disappointment from the schools, she could remember that this Henry was out there, that men like this were out there, all she had to do was find them, since marriage seemed the only progress her life could next make. She would very likely never see the perfect blue Mediterranean beaches and white sand he described, or the craggy Alps, but with someone like Henry, she could have them *through* him. He could tell her what the farthest horizon looked like, how to recognize it. Could he really fly in clouds? She didn't particularly think he was brave so much as lucky. He seemed different from the men in town, including her father and his friends, because he looked at her the entire time she was talking, waited for her to finish, and then said something else, or asked a question. She liked the smile that always seemed to rest in the corners of his mouth. Even when his mouth was downturned, he seemed on the verge of smiling. He had a heavy watch on his wrist, silver metal with a black face and a couple extra dials on it.

And then, all of a sudden, as they heard the truck rumbling up the road, and as Henry curtailed his story in order to say a brief and proper goodbye, saying indeed he hoped to see her again, she was overwhelmed with anger and resentment for his landing there at all. Damn him for coming and going as he pleased, she thought; damn him for coming at all. He would leave, and she would stay, and why in the world would he ever return to her?

It was a flurry then. He hopped in the truck and went up to the barn for the mail. Then he was at the plane, working on her, getting her set just as night fell, and Ruth was upstairs in her bedroom, feeling sorrier for herself than ever, pulling a pillow over her ears when she heard Henry's voice on the porch, saying farewell and thank you, and her father's voice saying, "Come back anytime. We'll feed you dinner."

As Henry strode toward his plane, he wondered the same thing, except it wasn't *why*, it was *how*. In France, he had lain awake, thinking of a moment somewhat like this—going to his plane, a woman he loved waiting behind him, this woman wanting, willing, to go up there with him, to see the world, the farm, from above, to fly low over his beloved Mississippi. He dreamed of teaching this woman how to fly, if she wanted to learn, as Philippe had taught him, and then their children. This Ruth, she would want something like this, too, he felt sure of it.

Yet he had nearly stayed in France with Philippe, who believed they should fly in Africa for Latécoère. "I can't land a plane on a tennis court," Henry told him one day at a café, not looking up from a news story about a Latécoère pilot landing in Spain only to find the strip was two thousand square feet—roughly the size of a tennis court—instead of two thousand feet long as had been requested.

"Nor I. You will not need to. Conditions are getting better all the time."

"I'm not French. I'm American and I want to go home. My French is terrible, among other things."

"Bah," Philippe said with a dismissive hand flick. "But you are nearly French. You speak better French than most Americans, and in Africa, every place you go has someone who speaks French or English. And," he said, thinking of something new and wagging his finger at Henry, "you speak of flying and airplanes in French, and that's the most important."

"Like I said, I don't speak French," Then he slowly looked around him in the café, at the beautiful lipsticked and perfectly hatted women gazing languidly across tables at men with starched shirts and close haircuts. He looked down the crooked brick street at another café, a bakery, a butcher, and at children squatting, playing jacks on the sidewalk. He looked back at Philippe, who was smoking with his eyes squinted, watching Henry look around.

"You love it here, no?" he said. "What's there for you in America?"

That day in Cedar Bluff, three years after Philippe's question, he thought he might know, at last: Ruth.

T W O

The German Army is at the gates of Paris.
There is nothing for you to do but surrender.

—Message bomb dropped by German airships in 1914

M ONDAY AND TUESDAY, the police found nothing suspicious or helpful at the farm. Wednesday evening, four inches of lake-effect snow fell in Chicago, stacking up on even the finest of tree branches, windowsills, windshield wipers. Giant evergreens just strewn with blinking multicolored lights wore a gentle white frost, and in Lincoln Park, where Margaret and her husband Terry lived, their red brick townhouse stood out against the white sidewalks and plowed blacktop street, even in the dark. There was that hush, too, in which the whole city goes quiet under snow. Up in Wilmette, where John lived, it was notably heavier—they got six inches, prompting schools to close and his grandchildren to toddle out onto his wide lawn and pitch dramatically backward into their first snow angels.

On Thursday, Margaret must've called Lori, her secretary, six times from a deposition out in Naperville—John checked in there, too, since they figured it easier to give the police one point person to call, and it was Margaret—but still, there was nothing.

On Friday, Margaret and John decided it was time to go over to Iowa and have a look around the house. Susan, John's wife, and Terry would stay back. Just the siblings, one shy of his fifty-eighth birthday and the other of her fifty-fourth. They planned to leave first thing Saturday morning. Friday evening Terry, also a lawyer, was home before Margaret was, and he helped her put a new set of styrofoam covers over the rosebushes, weighing them down with bricks, as her mother had suggested. The frost had been visiting her garden for a few weeks now, but she'd gotten by with bedsheets. She was skeptical of the styrofoam, as it seemed like the featherweight, turretlike covers would catch the slightest breath of wind. Yet her parents' farm in Cedar Bluff was a far windier place and if they worked there, then her own tiny rose garden plot just off the patio behind their townhouse should be fine. They moved quickly in the cold early December dark, still in their overcoats and suits, Margaret praying that her already arthritic thumbs and knees wouldn't be set off, and Terry not complaining—couldn't he do this the next morning?— although he might have if circumstances had been different, and afterward they went to the small place around the corner for soup and sandwiches and the Bulls' game.

Margaret set the alarm even though she knew she'd be awake before dawn, listening to traffic increase from about five-thirty on, newspaper and milk and food delivery trucks, and buses, mostly empty but for night shift workers coming home for the dawn, swishing up and down the avenue. At six-thirty, Margaret climbed out of bed and into the shower, her hair covered so she wouldn't have to dry it, while Terry trudged downstairs and made a pot of coffee, set out a thermos. He had offered to go to Cedar Bluff—would've liked to, even, but it made sense that Margaret and John would go alone. At seven, John arrived, alert and chatting about an NPR special on Jefferson Davis that he knew Terry, a Civil War buff, would like. John said he had some muffins, so Margaret finished her juice, took her Premarin, kissed Terry on the cheek, and left.

In the passenger seat of her brother's Mercedes, she turned the radio down just barely, as it was such a lot of noise for a quiet, still morning. John looked bothered for a moment, then relented. Once they were on Lake Shore Drive and not stopping and starting any longer, she opened the thermos and poured them both coffee, to which milk was already added. She asked him about the conference where he'd spoken the previous day about a new sinus surgery, and he said simply, "I'd give it a B-plus, all things considered." She noticed that the hair in his sideburns was shifting from a slate or flinty gray to white silver and she thought of asking his thoughts on retirement, or at least scaling back in a few years. Her sister-in-law had recently complained, before all this with her parents disappearing, that John still worked sixty- or seventy-hour weeks most weeks. Margaret had initially found this shocking, until she added up her own workload and found it to be in the same ballpark. And so she was truly interested in what John would say. When she thought of retirement, she could only think of Florida and golf—both of which depressed her greatly. Margaret was the sort of person who rarely prayed about anything, except a quick and painless death before infirmity took any kind of hold, preferably at the exact moment Terry suffered a similar demise. John, she recalled, had sent his wife into tears when she brought up retirement a year or two back. So Margaret was perfectly content keeping her mouth sealed on the matter now.

As the city unraveled sixty miles on, central and western Illinois looked charmed in the overcast Saturday morning half-light that muted whole fields and pastures, towns, and the large patches of forest, creeks, and rivers that came between. The landscape felt concentrated and intricate, a place you drove *through*, not *over*. At the far edge of the state, the Mississippi was thick and murky. From the bridge, they could see a few casino boats pushing up the river, no matter the hour. They both knew the names of the boats from the billboards that had begun inside the city limits and continued for the next hundred and twenty miles: *Mistress Luck* or *Mississippi Belle* or *Lady Jackpot*. Because gambling was illegal in both Illinois and Iowa, the tables and slot machines did not open until the boats pulled away from the docks, out into the no-man's-land that was the river. For three hours then, a boat would push upstream and float down, up and back down, as if pacing.

Margaret went to the *Mistress Luck* with her father several birthdays ago. Her mother said she'd heard the boats were filthy and refused to go but her father was intrigued, had been since they started up ten years ago. When he asked Margaret if he could take her to the boat for her forty-eighth birthday, she agreed. He sent her a bouquet of stargazer lilies at work, her favorite, and kissed her on the lips with a loud smack and a pat on the bottom like she was a kid when they met in the parking lot. They partook of the all-you-can-eat prime rib dinner at fifteen dollars a head and she had lemon meringue pie, with a slightly chemical meringue, for dessert, no candle. He was a surprisingly good craps player—he knew all the hand signals and played with the quiet confidence of a real gambler. He said he learned in France, Monte Carlo, when he was one-fifth his present age, in the Army just after World War I. "Craps doesn't change much," he said. "And you don't lose any talent for it, if you have it in the first place." Margaret tried to imagine him on the Riviera, with his straightforward, quiet, gentle face and his casual country-boy posture. He won $185 in the first half hour.

BOTH JOHN AND MARGARET thought it unlikely that their parents would drive off the edge of the quarry a bit beyond the farm, even if they could get to it, although boulders and an old abandoned refrigerator meant they could not. It wasn't their style. But the young deputy thought it would be a good idea, so on Thursday a couple of state police had come up with thick diving suits and an underwater light and nets. They found some new stuff—a golf cart and two motorbikes—but no bodies. No real gravel had come from the place for probably twenty years. When they dragged the pit once before, in the early seventies when a young kid had, in fact, died there, divers found a 1945 Studebaker, with a rusted cubic zirconia tiara in the glove compartment, or so the story went. The police never figured out where the car or the tiara came from, and the kid was a fifteen-year-old boy who got drunk and went swimming alone.

The Friebergs, who lived just to the northwest of their parents and who'd never had particularly good taste or manners, went out to spectate the quarry dredging on Thursday with some coffee and donuts, according to Officer Sargent. John imagined they took folding lawn chairs and probably their yellow and black Hawkeye football wool blanket, too. They were the same age as the senior Guttersons, both over eighty years old, and still they carried on like that. Mrs. Frieberg called John at his office in Evanston afterward—Margaret would shut her down; she was quicker and blunter than John. Mrs. Frieberg told him that the sheriff said he knew they'd never find anything. "He said your parents were too reasonable for such a thing," Mrs. Frieberg reported. "He said that if your parents wanted to kill themselves, they'd likely do it in an airplane. He said that seemed a more fitting way for Henry Gutterson to go down."

They did not yet know that one of the elderly Guttersons had, in fact, been flying again after all these years. And it wasn't Henry, the old Air Mail pilot, one of the first of his kind, when airplane wings were made of linen treated with gasoline stretched over wood skeletons, resembling maple seed wings. Angry and sad as he was when the FAA took his license away in 1976 because his blood pressure and his vision got too bad, it was Ruth last month climbing in behind the controls, alone. She took off from the Iowa City airport on October 13, flew a perfect twenty-mile triangle, out to Kalona, over to Lone Tree, and back, kissing the earth on landing as if she herself were the plane. This was what the flight instructor at the airport said anyway. "Oh, she could never get her license, no, and probably if the FAA got wind of it, I'd be in trouble for letting her go up alone at all. But she was so good, so competent in her lessons, and she begged to go up, just once." When he saw the news report that Henry and Ruth had been missing since the Saturday after Thanksgiving, the instructor had called John and explained. "I wasn't even going to call the police and tell them what I knew," he said, "except I was afraid they'd figure it out from canceled checks, and then, well, it would look suspicious if I hadn't called. Right?"

John was surprised, not just at the boldness of her flying, but also because his mother had deferred most passion for flying to her husband, after a certain point anyway. Early on, flying seemed his mother's greatest love; John was even envious sometimes, and she would seem to forget him, leaving him behind on Saturday mornings with his grandparents so she could go flying with Father, climbing into the plane right there in the cornfield, turning around only to wave dramatically from the cockpit. When they came home, it was his mother's exploding, contagious happiness that made the whole house feel like a circus. She would describe what they'd seen—a riverboat with everyone waving handkerchiefs at them, the state fair in Des Moines, a huge barn on fire that you could see for thirty miles, and another plane—a big silver thing with three motors! And they'd all cook dinner together, John helping to mash potatoes, and sometimes they'd dance or sing until well past his bedtime. He could still remember the photographs of the time before he was born, of their wedding, his mother's flushed cheeks in a lacy gown and his father's proud grin and his dark suit, flowers pinned to both of them, and they stood in front of the tan Jenny, which had JUST MARRIED painted on the side and two interlocked hearts with an arrow through them. Mother looked like a beauty queen, except happier; Father looked like he had just won a sweepstakes; and the Jenny looked massive, her two wings framing the picture, the writing along her side as big as Mother's torso. There were other pictures, too, with the de Havilland and the Argo and the Jenny, again, the Swallow with crop-dusting barrels attached to her belly, John being held in Mother's arms sometimes before these planes; but none with Margaret.

As for her, Mother's flying lessons felt spiteful. When John called to tell her, she immediately thought of being fourteen and her father wanting her to start going to Iowa City, learning to fly for real, not in his lap, and getting her license. "I figure it's a good summer for that," he had said. But Margaret balked and developed a sudden and all-consuming passion for 4-H, even though when raising a calf the previous year she'd been neither successful nor amused. But when faced with a whole summer at the airfield, away from her friends, plus her mother's certain, smothering attention, like when Margaret wrote a report on Amelia Earhart and Mother insisted on driving the whole family to Earhart's home in Atchison, Kansas, and then begged Margaret to take her own flight helmet and goggles to school as part of the report, even though no one else did such a thing; no, she couldn't endure a whole summer like this, and so Margaret had seized upon the idea of foaling her grandparents' only mare.

When she explained her plan to her parents, her father

looked hurt but he kept his voice even. "You tell me when you're ready," he said. He was confounded, primarily, and Margaret hoped this would ease a little bit of the hurt. Her mother, on the other hand, was offended.

"You shouldn't turn down an opportunity like this," Ruth said, her voice going low and husky and dark with frustration and disbelief. She looked straight at Margaret and made her daughter meet her clear brown eyes, unblinking, unwavering, fierce. "Most boys would kill for such a chance and most girls would not even be allowed to dream of it. Do you want to simply be like everyone else? Do you want to become a farmer's wife who never sees any of the rest of the world? How can you not want to learn to fly?"

There was no good answer to this question. Margaret couldn't say, *No, I have no interest in flying* because clearly that wasn't acceptable. She also couldn't say, *I'll die before I let myself be a tedious Iowa farmer's wife*, because if that description did not partially fit her mother, then what did?

No, Mother's lessons weren't surprising in the least. They were just a good fifty years late, and their dangerousness, and the extent to which it seemed Mother was saying, *See?*, defiantly, like a child, made Margaret ache.

"I wish you had known her when she flew," John said quietly to Margaret that day as they left the bridge over the river, riding up the hills of Iowa like waves climbing a shore, and the beach they met was a thick, unbroken spread of corn that made one feel held, nestled, and secure.

"Oh?" Margaret said, listening.

"The flying lessons would make sense to you."

She nodded. "Well, they already make some kind of sense

to me. All those scrapbooks about the aviators, and how defensive she was of Amelia Earhart when the papers were saying it was her fault. And how angry she was when I didn't fly. The lessons do make sense to me."

"But she used to fly. Long before now."

"I know that, John," Margaret said, testy. "She was Dad's navigator."

"Yes, but I remember it," he said, firm yet warm enough that Margaret backed off. John's wife, Susan, had told her just the night before that John forgot his Monday breakfast meeting that week, the meeting he'd been going to for eighteen years. Same place, same time, same people. "They all thought something awful had happened—the only time the meeting was canceled before was when Jim Sheridan's wife was in a car accident," Susan had said. "Anyway, it's killing him, your parents' being gone, but he'll not say so."

Margaret hoped he'd say something to her in the car that day, and she was quiet enough that he might've. But as she watched the methodical rows of corn click by outside her window, he remained silent.

~

THANKSGIVING DAY, ten days ago, their parents seemed fine. After a rousing game of dodgeball with the children, Great-Grandpa Henry made his special hot cocoa and Margaret kept imagining his arthritic hands dropping the teakettle and scalding young and old socked feet. She was a catastrophist, as Terry frequently said, and this was another good reason they'd never had children themselves; Margaret would have stayed two steps behind them, murmuring, *Be careful*, their whole lives.

Father wore the new cashmere vest Margaret and Terry had bought for him last Christmas and he talked about the reunion he was planning in Miami with the Frenchman who taught him to fly after World War I. "His sight is as good as ever and the FAA won't let him fly," he told Margaret in the kitchen before dinner. "The bastards."

"He's blind in one eye," her mother said from the sink.

Father raised his hands and rolled his eyes toward Margaret in impatience or conspiracy. "He's always been nearly blind in that eye and he's been flying for the better part of seventy years," he said. "Some young upstart who's younger than the jet engine is telling him he can't get up in his Piper Cub, which, frankly, your dog Fern could fly half blind."

Margaret laughed and Mother conceded the point.

Everything was mostly in order by two, and Bloody Marys were made while children changed into nicer clothes and the turkey finished cooking. They sat down to dinner, fourteen of them, at four o'clock.

Friday, they went down into the city, braved the crowds at the Field Museum with the grandkids, and had bratwurst and one beer at the Berghoff. Her mother said she was thinking of doing an Elderhostel trip to Italy with her walking friend, Jeanie Cooper, and a woman from the church chess club, which her mother had started a few years back. "Your father says he doesn't want to go with all the old people," she said. "But I don't see him organizing any grand plan for us to go alone, so until he does, it's Elderhostel." She even brought the brochure so that they could all look at the map and itinerary together. Margaret had been expecting the trip to be overpriced and dull, but it looked good and she told her mother this.

Nothing seemed wrong, for sure.

Looking back on those three days, time and again, as everyone couldn't help but do, the only discernible clue was this
comment of her mother's: "I'm just ready to travel for a bit.
I've worked hard all my life, so has your father. Now I think
we should do things together. For us."

Margaret started calling the farm every half hour once it
got past seven on Saturday and no one had heard from them.
Henry and Ruth had left John's in Wilmette around noon.
Usually they did the trip in four hours, tops, with a couple
rest stops for the bathroom and one can of Pepsi, which they
passed between them like it was moonshine. The 230 miles
between Wilmette and Cedar Bluff was not so far in a
Cadillac on four- and six-lane highways, a sixty-five-mile-an-
hour speed limit, and her father driving beyond it.

She barely slept for fear she'd miss their phone call
Saturday night; when Sunday morning came and still there
was no word, she began to believe the worst. Even if the car
had broken down somewhere or they got home to some dis-
aster, they would have called by now, she kept thinking, to let
someone know they were fine, to tell the damn story, as
Mother so loved to do. By Sunday noon, when they had been
missing for twenty-four hours, Margaret called the police.
"My eighty- and eighty-seven-year-old parents disappeared
on the way home from Thanksgiving," she said. She gave
their physical descriptions, the car's, and told where they had
been headed. She answered the nasty questions about fights
they may have had or medicine they might die without or suf-
fer dangerous side effects from; she dutifully reported that
her mother carried nitroglycerin because she had angina and

her father was on Furosemide for his blood pressure. The police also wanted to know their financial details and any business partnerships, soured or not, that existed.

The trooper hung up and then called back around three P.M. She was drinking a glass of wine by then.

"Mrs. Donnelly, are you forgetting anything they told you?" the state trooper asked.

"Like what?"

"Like plans to go away, I don't know, something mostly secret that one of them might have whispered to someone. This happens all the time, by the way," he said. "People get so caught up in planning and preparing sometimes that they forget the obvious things."

"Like telling their adult children they're going away?"

"Yes," the trooper said, waiting for a more considered response.

She thought about it, but came up with nothing. "No. They talked about going to Italy in May, but that's it. My father might go to Miami around Eastertime. Look, my mother cooks and shops a lot for Christmas and basically begins the Monday after Thanksgiving. She wouldn't have taken a trip during this time. And there's one other thing—icing the leftovers. If she'd been sure they were going to be more than five hours between refrigerators, she would've gotten more. She became very sick from rotten meat once, so she's fanatical about keeping things cold."

"They could've got ice at any gas station," the trooper pointed out.

"Right. Well, you asked. That was the only detail I could think of. That, plus the fact that she said she was hoping to walk with her friend Jeanie if the snow was cleared from the sidewalks when she got back."

"Have you spoken with Jeanie?"

"Of course I have," Margaret said. She tried her best not to be riled by his condescension.

The state trooper said he'd be in touch and hung up.

Terry came home with a stack of movies, but all she could do was keep moving, and no amount of wine seemed to touch her. Cooked a pot of soup and baked a loaf of banana bread, even though the freezer was already bulging with food since they had about three pounds of leftover turkey and Tupperware spilling over with stuffing, sweet potatoes, peas, mashed potatoes, and beets. Next she consolidated pickle jars and mustards—regardless of the fact that some were dill, some were sweet gherkins; some had horseradish, and some were French Dijon—to fit everything in. Finally, she cleaned the oven and the floor.

She called John every hour.

～

THEY WENT TO work Monday morning, and the Cedar Bluff police took over. On Tuesday, Officer Sargent called her around ten in the morning and she got John on the phone, too, and they learned that their mother had made a $2,500 withdrawal exactly a week before. The bank teller who processed the cash said her mother had commented with a smile, "Christmas shopping starts Friday."

"Well, that could make sense," Margaret said. "She has a lot of people to buy for, and Dad likes to travel with a lot of cash, no matter how much we discourage it, right, John?"

"That's true."

"And she always pays cash," Margaret continued. "Usually we go shopping on Saturday and they leave Sunday. This year they left on Saturday because they said they were scheduled to take the gifts up at Mass on Sunday morning, ten A.M. But, way back on Tuesday, Mother maybe forgot this, or maybe she didn't even know, and was thinking we'd shop like we always do."

The officer said he'd call the church and look into it. Then he told them that Jeanie Cooper said her mother had recently been talking a lot about California. And Martha who worked at AAA said she had come in recently and picked up some maps and travel books. Given all this, the officer said, foul play was looking less and less likely, and the "secret vacation" scenario was gaining credibility.

"But it's just not like them," Margaret insisted.

"Well," the officer said, and coughed. "We do value your opinion, Mrs. Donnelly." He told her that the whole of I-88 and I-80 and nearby secondary roads between Chicago and Cedar Bluff had been swept. No accidents were found; no tow trucks had been called to a white four-door Coupe de Ville.

"So, what's next?" John asked.

"We're going into the house tomorrow and we should have credit card and telephone reports by then."

"Yes, well," Margaret jumped in, "my father hates credit cards and he more or less refuses to have them unless it's an emergency."

"She's right," John said.

"We'll monitor them anyway," the officer said, without any tension or aggression.

"And if you find nothing?" John asked.

"We wait."

"For what?"

"For something to turn up on their credit cards, for them to turn up in a bank or a hospital, or for a policeman or trooper to spot them."

There was silence for a moment. "Sounds like a needle in a haystack to me," Margaret said. "There's got to be more you can do."

"We'll enter them into the missing persons bank and every local and state police station in the country will receive their picture. But you must understand—we can't suddenly pursue them like they're wanted fugitives. They may be causing an undue amount of concern, but they do have rights and there's nothing to suggest that they are dangerous to themselves or anyone else—"

"Not a danger to themselves?" Margaret burst out. She couldn't believe the cool nonchalantness that seemed the tenor of this search for her parents. "They're almost ninety goddamned years old! And they've disappeared! If they've done it themselves, they are a danger to themselves—they've lost their minds. You're trying to tell me that's not dangerous?" Margaret was breathing hard. She knew she had crossed a line, she knew the police weren't to blame for any of this, but it still felt good to yell a little bit. Maybe she should've done it sooner. John closed the conversation neatly, erased as much tension as he could, and the officer hung up.

John was taking it all very calmly, as if performing a complicated surgery. "I understand your frustration," he said to Margaret when they were alone on the line. He was standing at the window of his office in Evanston that looked out over a broad, tree-edged lawn, now white and perfect as if a giant wool blanket had been drawn across it. "But maybe this Officer Sargent is right—maybe they're in Vegas—maybe they just didn't want their overcautious children to know, so they just took a lot of cash and went. What about the bank withdrawal, Mom's AAA visit, the car being checked, and whatever this Jeanie Cooper is reporting?"

"You'd think they'd call, John. Don't you think it's rude, at least? They must know we're worried."

"Oh, I don't know," he said. "Of course I'm concerned, but it does sound like they could be playing a game. A stupid, selfish game, admittedly, but a game. And the police are right— until we have evidence or barely a suggestion of foul play, there's nothing we can do."

"I think you're a little too calm about this, myself," she replied, standing up from her desk on the seventy-sixth floor, turning, leaning close to the huge window behind her, looking out at the clumps of wet snow that were swirling down in between the skyscraper she was in and the one facing her. Then she sat back down. "Your eighty- and eighty-seven-year-old mother and father have disappeared without a trace and you're making jokes about Las Vegas as if they've done this before—as if we're even sure of where they are, which we don't actually have the slightest clue about."

"Oh, come on," he said. "Mother's always done these spur-of-the-moment trips. Remember when they took us to Niagara Falls? It was completely unplanned. She just herded us into the car and we went. And there was the trip to Amelia Earhart's house. She *loves* to do things like this."

If, indeed, John believed that they were just playing games, why didn't he feel as angry about it as she did? She couldn't let go of being hurt and offended by their actions, like her parents were taunting them with carelessness. John and Margaret switched supporting roles quite a lot, such that if one of them was needy or hysterical, the other stayed calm and rational. When he was twelve and she was eight, he crashed his bike into a fence post. The barbed wire cut his head, not too badly, but still, right behind the ear and it bled all over the place. Mom and Dad were gone someplace so Margaret called Grandma and John lay in her lap on the front porch as she held a towel on the cut. The washcloth absorbed blood as it kept spilling, all over her legs and into her socks, and there was water, too, as the ice melted and her tears fell on him. John was very scared, in shock probably, but she was the one who cried. She sobbed the entire time it took Grandma to get there, not very long, and then the drive to the hospital, and it worked: Margaret did all the crying and John stayed calm.

With her parents' disappearance, she didn't think that one of them needed to stay calm while the other was upset. She realized, this time, she needed him to be upset, too. "Why doesn't this bother you more?" she said. Her secretary's voice came over the intercom then, telling Margaret the scheduled conference call was waiting.

"Don't tell me how much this whole thing does or doesn't bother me, Margaret," he said. "We'll hear from them in the next few days, I'm sure." He thought his parents' actions strange and frustrating, but he assumed they were fine, off on a whim somewhere, as the police said. He had always believed—and gerontologist friends said so—that any independence his parents claimed as they aged was a good thing, given they were healthy, which they were. He had told himself this throughout his fifth, mostly sleepless night.

"If they don't call tomorrow, to see how your lecture went, will you be worried then?" She signaled to her secretary, who was now at the door, that she needed two minutes.

John sighed. "I'm worried now. I wish you'd stop telling me that I wasn't. I'm just trying to be reasonable about this—"

"Even though I'd feel a lot better if you weren't so reasonable?"

"Yes, even then," he said. He was now officially tired of speaking with her. He knew she was curling, then flexing her toes inside her shoes—or maybe they were off—as they talked. This was her nervous tic. She laughed about doing it sometimes in important meetings—slipping her shoes off where no one could see and flexing, curling, pointing. It calmed her, who knew why. In his head, John wished his "little" sister a pleasant afternoon of toe curling, and when she was ready to be an adult again, could she call him back? They had things to talk about. "Call me later," he said aloud, simply. "I've got to run."

She apologized, thanked him, stared out at the snow for one more minute, and then turned back to her notes and picked up the conference call.

But Margaret couldn't get herself to feel calm or patient. She kept imagining her parents out on the side of a back road somewhere, bleeding, crying, hoping someone would stop for them, but their windows were fogged up so no one could see in; no one could see they needed help; no one stopped. Her mother's white hair was down because she took it down out of the bun and twisted it around her whole hand when she was nervous. Maybe her father had a heart attack or maybe just a little stroke or maybe their car was broken down and it was too cold to get out and walk.

And what if they did take a plane up and crashed it way out where no one would see them? She tried to tell herself that air traffic control was too exacting for a plane to just disappear without comment, but she wasn't sure of this. She kept seeing them slip out from under the radar's swoop, escaping a single tower's notice, and click, they're gone. But why?

FOUR DAYS LATER, coming into Cedar Bluff, they passed the tiny, private cemetery nestled into the corner of two fence lines defining a smallish pasture now next to the new post office. Some of the headstones were broken in half, some were leaning against a fence post, and in the very middle, one small, faded American flag such as children wave in Fourth of July parades stood at a slight angle to the ground. Turning down Main Street, they saw that the antique stores were doing well, as was the grill-your-own-steak place. The ice-cream stand boasted year-round hours and there was a new restaurant, with a sign in the window proclaiming, VEGETARIAN SPECIALTIES AND FISH. Must be some alums from the university, Margaret thought, living the idyllic country life. John turned right at the Sunoco station at the end of town, headed straight on, about three miles, until the jokey twenty-foot-high "airmail" box. MR. MRS. HENRY GUTTERSON. RR 46. And the white Prarie-style farmhouse with a deep front porch, green shutters, and the oak tree in the side yard.

Grandpa had given sixty of his seven hundred or so acres to his daughter and new son-in-law as a wedding present and then twenty acres to John and Margaret on their first birthdays. At first, Father didn't farm the parcel—he used twenty acres for a landing strip, and in what sounded like a standoff, the remaining forty were left fallow. Margaret imagined Grandpa was convinced Father couldn't resist the temptation of free land, empty and rich, and that he would certainly give up flying to take over the whole farm. When ten years passed and the farmers in town began to say the men were both fools, Grandpa Paul planted those forty acres and began working it again.

His final tender was the house, as if giving Father the farmer's house would tip the scales, once and for all, and convince him to be a farmer. Father took the farmhouse when Margaret was five because his family was too big for the tiny house up the hill and because Mother insisted, but he stuck to his flying lessons and crop dusting—and perhaps this was disingenuous, because Grandpa Paul was furious. "Waste of a house," he said one day when he finally realized Father was going to do exactly as he pleased, which didn't include taking charge of the whole farm. "I should give it to the hired hands that help me. The output on this farm could double soon, and you'd rather be shooting around on the breeze." As the story goes, Father told Grandpa he had a singer's talent for words and Grandpa swung at him right across the cheek. But things got better as everyone got older and Father helped the farm plenty, both in dusting and spraying the fields with his planes and contributing his income to upkeep, and it was Father who found Grandfather dead out there next to his tractor one day.

John shut off the car and they climbed out. On the porch, the old swing did a slow, constant to and fro in the wind as the chains groaned weakly against the hooks set in the ceiling. John had dug up a key, although Officer Sargent was there, too—he had to be, he said, apologizing—and he had a key if they didn't. The house hadn't been locked more than five times in her whole life, Margaret figured, but with all the publicity around the case, looting or robbery was a possibility. The screen door slammed shut with a large metal *thwack* behind them and the old smells washed over her, flowery hand soap and furniture polish and a salty food smell she could only nearly identify as chicken broth. It was warm, as if her parents were just out for a few groceries, and she made a mental note to turn the heat down at the end of the day. Margaret saw that her mother had already put up the clear plastic draft insulation in the windows. In the kitchen, the Metamucil and vitamins were lined up between the sink and the coffeemaker, along with a spare traveling pill container. There was a half month's worth of frozen food in the freezer. All seemed normal.

They set to business right away, exploring the two-drawer file in the pantry, which held all bank account records, land values, house and equipment appraisals, health records, and birth certificates, including Ruth Anne's, which surprised both of them only because their parents so rarely mentioned her. There had never really been pictures of the baby, as if any memory of her were meant to be erased, any public memory, anyway. Margaret didn't even know about this older sister until a Christmas or Thanksgiving dinner when she was ten or twelve years old, and they went around the table saying whom they wished especially to bless. It was Grandma who asked to bless "those who have gone before us." And then, moved by some very strange mood that never came again in the same manner, Margaret's mother said, "I'd like to bless all three of my children. John Henry, Ruth Anne, and Margaret Elizabeth."

Margaret had never, ever heard Ruth Anne mentioned directly before, although she'd always sensed somehow that there had been a third child. Still, she had enough manners and apprehension of her mother's strange mood to stay quiet at the dinner table and to ask only John later when he was reading a magazine in bed: "Who was Ruth Anne?" She whispered this.

John had replied as if he, too, were afraid of mentioning it, even though he was a teenager, nearly a grown-up. "She was the baby who died before you were born, I don't remember how," he said, anticipating her next question.

"But where is she buried?" Margaret replied—he hadn't guessed this one.

"In the north field," he said quietly. "Beneath the boulder."

As an adult, Margaret could still remember how much this revelation stunned her—she had played around that rock sometimes. There was a wild rosebush nearby, right up against a fence post, but otherwise there was no indication that the rock was there on purpose, that a baby lay beneath it. Why wasn't she in a cemetery? Margaret had always thought the boulder marked only the beginning of Father's landing strip, the highest point on the farm. Hearing this news, imagining a body up there, was grotesque and sad enough that

Margaret never, ever asked anyone about the baby again. And then came *this* day, her parents missing and Margaret pondering her own retirement in idle times, and certainly beyond confusion over such old news; but with the birth certificates and the mood and state of affairs as it were, she was curious and confused all over again and—this was new—annoyed.

～⌐

THEY HEATED SOME of the frozen dinners for lunch, drank some tea, and afterward, they climbed into the attic. In between the stacks of boxes, piles of old, disassembled furniture and slipcovers, and rolls of insulation, murky light stroked the floors. The square windows on each of the four walls had cobwebs spanning their panes. The air was surprisingly cold and fresh—and then they noticed the window on the south side of the house, overlooking the backyard, with a broken pane in it, inviting a breeze in. "Maybe a heavy bird or a branch from the white oak," John said, and Margaret nodded, made a mental note to patch it before they left so that nothing could get in, take up residence there. They set about going through the boxes that were stacked neatly and labeled in too-faded ink, not necessarily expecting to find anything relevant to the present situation. They found tea sets and trains, old photographs, school projects, and correspondence between their father, uncle, and aunt in Wisconsin, and with Philippe DeBreault, the Frenchman who taught him to fly, who lived in Miami. And postcards from all over the world, Tangiers, Rio de Janeiro, Reykjavik, written by Philippe and other flying buddies.

In their pictures together in France, Philippe and Father

and their friends stood with arms slung over one another's shoulders. They stood before open-cockpit bi- and tri-wings, half smiling at the camera, or grinning from ear to ear, looking over their shoulders at the plane with eyebrows raised, as if to say, *How about that!* They were great, ecstatic pictures, full of a youth that was decades away.

Their father had never talked about France too much—there were stories, certainly, but you had to ask. This Philippe, although they'd gone several decades without seeing each other, was Father's closest friend, the kind of friend only a few people have.

"I think we should call Philippe in Florida," Margaret said as she closed the box and opened another. "Maybe he's heard from them."

"I did call him," John Henry said, opening another box and finding Christmas decorations. "I called Wednesday."

"Oh," Margaret said, surprised and annoyed. "Why didn't you mention it?"

"He didn't say anything—he's very surprised and concerned, too, and concerned that their reunion might not happen. I think I upset him by calling," John said. "He does not sound very well. A lot of dementia, or even medication of some sort. It took a while for him to understand who I was and why I was calling. So much so that I told Officer Sargent not to bother. Why—do you think we should call him again?" John asked.

"Not necessarily," she said, looking at a few baby pictures. "Who's this?" She held up a picture of an infant in a christening gown. She moved closer to John so he could see the picture. "Is it Ruth Anne?"

"I don't think so," he said. "I think that's you. You're too old—Ruth Anne only lived, I don't know, a month or so. This one looks older. It's you."

"What about this one?" she asked, showing a small picture of Mother holding a newborn, seated in the living room, and Father behind. There was snow piled up on the windowsill behind them and on the tree visible through the window. The baby was wrapped in a couple blankets.

"I think it must be," John said. "Ruth Anne was the only wintertime birthday."

"Could've been a rogue October snowstorm," Margaret suggested. "It's not that unusual, which could make the baby you or me."

John took the picture and looked very carefully. He tilted it this way and that in the poor attic light. "I think it's her, yes," he said. "I'm pretty sure."

Margaret nodded, took it back, blew some dust off it, looked again. "Well, there she is. I don't know that I've ever seen a picture of her."

"Is that so." John opened a box of scrapbooks.

Margaret continued looking at Ruth Anne, who was small and indiscernible, really, under so many blankets. How many pictures could there be of a baby who only lived so briefly? How did Mother and Father look? The same. Nothing surprising there.

"You're going to call Philippe," John said.

"Maybe," she said. "Does that bother you?"

"You're Margaret; you've got to do it for yourself," John said, without edge. "And it's probably a good idea."

"Thanks for the endorsement," Margaret said, moving on,

into the cedar chest, which contained antique tablecloths, lace, and her mother's wedding dress, with its doll-sized shoulders and waist. It looked familiar despite the fact that the only wedding picture of her parents that she knew by heart was the one of them wearing their flight clothes, not this gown, in front of the Jenny. Why in the world do people save such things? she thought. Her own gown was boxed away somewhere, where it would certainly stay for decades yet. We leave these things, she thought, until someone else decides what to do and tells us—or just does it.

By about four in the afternoon, they both began to feel the weight of their eyelids and the age of their knees, which had been asked to bend and rise too many times for one day. They were perhaps most exhausted by what they now saw as the nostalgic purposelessness, or at least fruitlessness, of the afternoon's work in the attic. They had found no clues there whatsoever. They would drive home that night—both wanted to sleep in their own beds, with their spouses, and take the Sunday to rest. The sunlight was waning and one side of the attic, which had been dark in the morning, was now illuminated. She noticed, while taking one final look around, a dead sparrow, with its wings tucked at its side, in a corner that had been lifted out of shadow. Perhaps this bird had broken the window, and if so, had it been killed on impact? Or perhaps the window had already been broken—from a storm or tree branch—and the bird had flown in, surprised, and never found its way out again. Maybe it finally died trying to get out to the light and air and open sky, trying to find the perfect spot in the tempting invisibility that had beckoned it, *Come.*

Next to the sparrow in the newly lit corner, there was a typewriter on top of an old metal milk crate, a Royal, with a locking cover, which was clean and dust-free, perhaps because of the breeze from the open window. Margaret went to the typewriter, lifted it, and saw the crate beneath was full of papers, the top ones not particularly old or yellowed. Margaret picked one up. It was dated just few weeks before. She bent down, thumbed through a few of the pages, and they all bore the same address, so she returned to the top one, the only one with little red pencil edits on it. She straightened and read.

November 15, 1987

Anne Morrow Lindbergh
c/o Charles A. Scribner and Sons Publishers
Fifth Avenue
New York City

Dear Mrs. Lindbergh,

It has been nearly fifty-four years since my last letter to you. It was 1933, the year following the one in which each of us lost infant children. I am sorry that I did not write to you when Colonel Lindbergh died in 1974, but I thought much about you.

He was a great, great man and you don't need me to tell you that. But he was a person who lived by his own convictions and never by what others wanted or expected of him. If only we could all live so truly!

It seems to me that lives grow and change in infinite ways and at different rates—and it is still funny to me that my husband Henry and your Charles started at about the same place—in the northern Midwest, flying for the Air Mail Service. Since the last letter you had of me over fifty years past, Henry and I have not moved from our farm in Iowa, nor have we become important people in any sense. What we have done is raise two fine children—one a doctor and the other a lawyer—and we have stood by and watched as the single-engine biplane spawned the Tri-Motor, then the DC-3, and now all the jets. I wonder how many Curtiss Jennies—remember the original mail plane?—could fit inside this new monster, the 747!

My daughter tells me women still do not have exactly the same choices as men in this world—we never will because we are such different species, men and women—but so many things have changed since our youth. I wouldn't trade anything that I have had for something that I haven't, however. Of course this is not to say that I haven't had my unhappiness, my disappointments. This is only to say that I don't believe life has been unfair to me. Fairness, of course, is never something God bothers to explain to us, does He? But still, I am at peace. I have lived a full life.

I do wonder what you would say to me if you were to respond to one of my letters, just once. Probably you have never gotten a single one of them. Or maybe you've gotten a few, and, having decided that I was completely crazy, you have disregarded all the others. I cannot say that I would blame you. I am very sorry if I ever disturbed you. That was never my intention.

After all these years, I got back up in a plane last October. Henry helped find me an instructor who thought the both of us to be legends after he stumbled upon some old pictures in a deep, dark archive at the University of Iowa library. Pictures of Henry and me flying the mail together back before 1928 and John's birth; pictures of us with John after he soloed; pictures of Henry in front of twenty different planes over forty-odd years. This instructor was a real nut for history and he wanted to hear all about our lives, everything.

"You'd think we were the Lindberghs!" I said to him once when he was asking so many questions. "You might as well be," he said. Next, he agreed to take me up in his 172, see if I couldn't solo at long last. And I did. I won't tell you what it felt like because you know. You know the ecstasy, the physical and spiritual sensation of lifting from the earth and entering that space that scientists quantify and only pilots swim in. The feeling of being pulled up above the audience as if on a wire, a great wire that will let you go where you want, a wire that you trust as you trusted your mother's hand on your shoulder or your knee as she read to you or showed you how to cook an egg. The world takes on a different property—namely of being separate from you, a feeling of pure detachment, a feeling of power, as you say, "the glaze on life."

Henry and I are about to do a bit of traveling just now— perhaps I'll send you a postcard!—and when we're finished, I suppose we'll finally settle into the rest of our lives. I have a feeling that everything has happened to us that's going to happen, and my feelings like this are usually spot-on. We're 80 and 87 years old, after all. I suppose it's about time to face the curtain's fall. Henry will probably live until he's a hundred and ten. He has that feel about him. He seems vaguely middle-aged to me even though he's been napping in the afternoons many years longer than I. As for me, I don't expect I'll see 85.

You've been a good friend to me, Mrs. Lindbergh, whether you know it or not, whether you care or not. Still, you would have liked me, I think. We would have been great friends because at one time we had a lot in common; and always, I believe as much as I believe in flight itself, have we been similar women. It is too bad that you have never known me as I have known you; you have certainly had the chance. And perhaps, after all, you have read every one of my letters and perhaps they have seemed as close as diary entries, as your books sometimes seem to me, and perhaps you have never known how to respond, that it was not by choice but by inability. But, you must know, I love and admire you no matter.

Your friend,
Ruth Gutterson
Cedar Bluff, Iowa

Hardly aware of her own breathing, her head oddly thick and dull, Margaret began to unpack the crate, setting the hundreds of letters carefully on a box nearby. When John came over to see what she had found, she handed him the top letter without a word. While he read, she reached the bottom of the stack.

April 1920

Dear Dr. Emily Blackwell,

I am 11 years old and live in Cedar Bluff, Iowa, which is a small town near to Iowa City, where the university is. Several years ago, my school teacher, Miss Isabelle Jenkins, gave me a magazine about you and your sister Elizabeth and the New York Infirmary for Women and Children, and I liked you so much I wrote a letter to you—my teacher didn't tell me you were dead! I wish you were still alive—I would so like to meet you! Instead, I'll practice writing you.

The other day, our neighbor, Mr. Cilek, hit himself in the head as he was splitting some logs. Something distracted him, a dog running across the yard, his wife calling him, he doesn't remember, and the back of the axe came right into his head. He's pretty lucky, of course, that he got away with just a great big lump and some sutures. If he'd turned an inch more, he would've taken it on his brow. Old Dr. Fischer came out and spent a good several hours with them. He was afraid, I guess, that the injury was worse than it looked. And when I asked, he let me watch while he stitched Mr. Cilek up. You wouldn't think there'd be fat in a forehead, but that's what the doctor said I was seeing. I wonder, have you ever touched a beating heart? I mean a real, beating heart? I wonder what it must look like, or feel—how warm?

I wasn't squeamish in the least about Mr. Cilek's head and I thought it was great how Dr. Fischer could help. Which gets me thinking. Maybe I'll go to college one day be a lady doctor, too!

Sincerely,
Ruth Sheehan
Cedar Bluff, Iowa

THREE

Love letters will be carried in a rose-pink aeroplane
steered with cupid's wings and operated
by perfumed gasoline.

—*Headline of the* New York Telegraph *ridiculing the launch
of the U.S. Air Mail Service in 1918*

*R*UTH WAS ROLLING out a piecrust in the kitchen when she saw her mother turn off the water and lean forward, squinting out the window. "What is it?" Ruth asked.

"It's that Air Mail pilot again, I think."

Ruth rushed forward. "Where?"

Elizabeth pointed to the southeast. "There."

"I see him," Ruth said, trying to temper her voice. How could he be landing in their field again? Ruth wondered. Was it possible? She could barely get the crust out, her hands were so unsteady. Then, sure enough, twenty minutes later her father came in with his arm slung around Henry's shoulders. Henry was wiping water off his face—he had washed the dust off at the old pump by the barn before coming to the house.

"Look what dropped from the sky," Paul Sheehan said with a wide smile, which told Ruth he was pleased by the pilot's return. "Can we give this boy some supper?"

"Hello, Miss and Mrs. Sheehan," Henry said, bowing slightly. "You don't need to go to any trouble for me. I just thought I'd say hi. I saw your corn wasn't quite up yet—I could still get my plane down here without hurting any-thing."

"Hello, Captain Gutterson," Ruth said. "I'll just be setting your place at the table now, that's all the trouble there is."

During dinner, Henry told them the story of his family in Wisconsin, of his twin siblings, Noelle still farming and Jack at law school in Madison. "We are blood relations, of course," Henry said, "but you couldn't find three people more differ-ent in their interests than the three of us. I couldn't farm to save my life, and Noelle is afraid of heights—she even has a hard time getting up in the hayloft, let alone an airplane. Jack, he just wants to be in a city, in a courtroom or in an office, surrounded by books. He likes a three-piece suit and a leather briefcase."

Paul fixated on Henry's statement that he couldn't farm to save his life. "About you farming," Paul said. "I thought you said you worked your grandparents' farm for a little while."

"Oh, I did because I had to. But I have no talent for it. I'm like my Uncle George. Animals just don't like me. They decide something—I don't know what it is. Horses run from me; cows only barely let me milk them. It's like I have a scent. The Army had me running the stables over there in France. And I tell you, if you've never seen twenty-five equine types frown and sigh in unison, you've got to walk into a horse barn with me. I'm sure your own horses here that have already gotten together to pass around the skinny on me. They just know."

Ruth thought this funny and charming, but she could also see the horror in her father's face.

"So don't farm cattle," Paul said. "Stick to corn. You can never have too much corn." Paul was pleased—if surprised—by the pilot's return because he seemed kind enough and he was serving his country and it was flattering that he'd come back, put a plane down in the field again. Tom Cilek would be talking all over town about it. Also, it had occurred to Paul that this Henry was someone who might turn Ruth's sights off nursing and college and onto settling down into her own family on the farm. Paul had seen the two of them chatting way out the drive by the road; he'd known how long they were there and he'd seen Ruth's face after the pilot had left— Henry got to Ruth, somehow, like no boy in town had yet. And all this, right around the time Paul found the letters from the colleges in the trash. To be honest, Paul worried that she might run away, like poor Dean Cilek, who had good cause. Ruth didn't have good cause, but Paul still worried because she was so unhappy, so full of disappointment—he worried she might do something drastic. He and Elizabeth, they couldn't bear to have her go away, and they couldn't afford it, either. Ruth seemed to think they were merely being cruel, holding on to her, and for the life of him he didn't know how to make her understand, how to see it from their place. If Paul suspected his daughter's affections after Henry's crash-landing, he was quite sure of it on this second visit; Ruth looked alive, her face smiling, excited, for the first time in weeks.

Paul felt that finally something good might be happening for Ruth, for the family. He planned to encourage the pilot as much as he could and he figured his approval was all that was needed; his daughter was beautiful as well as being sole heir to some six hundred acres of the best farmland in the country. Regardless of what the pilot was now saying about his lack of talent with farm animals, Henry assumed he would eventually put his plane in the barn and take to the land, which could be his someday. All that land, *that* land—no man would turn it down.

Paul advised: "Stick with corn, my friend, and you'll have no problems."

Henry did not want to anger or disagree with his host, Ruth's father, but he also did not want to deceive him about his inclination to farm, given the obvious development of a courtship between himself and Ruth. "I've got a vocation for flying, Mr. Sheehan," Henry said. "And I have great respect for people such as yourself. It's hard work, farming is."

"It sure is," Paul said. "You got that right."

Ruth asked about France, then, and Henry told them about the great men he had known or seen from a distance as they went into the officers' club. There was the American Edward Vernon Rickenbacker, the "ace of aces," who downed twenty-six enemy aircraft in the waning months of the war—from March 1918 to the November Armistice, and about the Canadian Billy Bishop, who scored an incredible seventy-two victories and lived to tell about it. "And of course you know about the famous Kraut, Baron Manfred von Richthofen—the famous 'Red Baron.' He was so good and so mean," Henry said, slowing down for emphasis "that he engraved silver cups with the name and description of each of his victims. In April 1917 alone, the Red Baron shot down twenty-one enemy aircraft."

"What do you mean 'so good?'" Ruth asked immediately. "How come you call the Red Baron 'good'?"

"Because he was an amazing pilot. The odds of living through just one dogfight are pretty slim," he said. "So the fact that the Red Baron lived through over a hundred is pretty incredible."

Paul, his fork suspended in midair as he watched Henry tell this story, grunted a kind of approval when it was over and Elizabeth nodded, her eyebrows furrowed. Ruth felt like she had stepped into someone else's life: This pilot was there, talking to her about the *Red Baron*—was she Ruth Sheehan?

June 1924

Dear Ruth Law Oliver,

My father won't let me go to college in Iowa City and my dreadful teacher, Miss Jenkins, who said she would help me, will not. The sisters from St. Catherine's wrote to me and said they couldn't take indigent girls. Orphans, yes, but indigents they simply cannot afford. And what could I do? Miss Jenkins, who went to St. Catherine's and had given me hope that they would admit me, didn't say a word about the letter. She just gave it to me, the skin of her hand cracked and red as always, I can't believe she's never found a salve to help her, and she didn't say anything but "Go on home, Ruth. Go home and take a rest and you'll feel better." How I wanted to slap her, to sink down to my knees and wrap my arms around her and beg her, beg *someone,* for help. Shall I stay here for the rest of my life? I wondered. I'd rather die.

I asked if we could telephone them, to explain, to talk to them, and Miss Jenkins said, "Ruth, it's a party line. Your father would be humiliated."

So I walked home, what else was there to do? I walked, feeling as sorry for myself as I could, thinking that I would write to you and ask if you'd help me get to a flying school. I could work off my fees, if only you could advance me the money for a train ticket. I would pay it back to you as soon as I could earn it, I was thinking, even though you only know me from the one letter I sent before—you sent me an autographed flyer from one of your shows. Thank you.

But then, as if God himself heard me, a pilot came straight down from the heavens and crash-landed in our cornfield and when I walked home that day he was standing at the end of the driveway, waiting for help. He must've had wings, leather perhaps, folded up under his flight suit; maybe he didn't have an airplane at all.

And then, he came back! My father invited him back for dinner after the first landing, though I didn't believe he would come, but there he was. He is a small—medium height but very thin—and quite handsome man, and he is kind, too, and he listens to what I have to say. He's lived in France! I can't even imagine it.

I feel certain he'd help me, and I may ask him if he comes again, but I'm not at all sure that he will. But maybe he'll be *sent* back to me, and when he comes, I'll see if he'll teach me to fly.

And if he doesn't come back, I'll write you a real letter and see if there's anything you can do. You're my last resort, or maybe he is. Captain Henry Gutterson.

Sincerely,
Ruth Sheehan
Cedar Bluff, Iowa

⸺◦

HENRY RETURNED FOR Sunday supper again a few weeks later and it gradually became a biweekly affair. As it was acknowledged that they were courting, Paul and Elizabeth let them go off on a walk after supper until nearly five o'clock. It was mid-June and daylight was already stretching toward eight.

Ruth was always asking for stories and Henry described ancient monks jumping out of towers with fabric wings roped to their arms, about Otto Lilienthal's superb gliders, about the Englishmen who, in the course of the first piloted balloon crossing of the Channel, had stripped their vessel of every ounce of weight—including their clothes—to keep the balloon aloft. When they landed in France, Henry said with a laugh, they were naked and cold as plucked chickens.

"And of course there's the crazy Alberto Santos-Dumont, the very short son of a coffee plantation owner," Henry said. "He landed his balloon outside his apartment on the Champs-Élysées regularly and had his tables built eight feet high, as if he believed that balloons would be adapted for use inside the home. Until then"—Henry laughed again—"old Monsieur Santos-Dumont had a lot of work to do to get to his *déjeuner*."

Ruth laughed, too, thinking of *Alice in Wonderland*, and

they walked in silence for a while, each enjoying having the other there. The road was damp and slightly mucky in parts from the spring rains. Ruth thought about her hopes to go to Dr. Blackwell's school and become a nurse and she thought about nursing a pilot who had been shot down by the Red Baron. She wondered what a pilot who had been through something like that would look like. She mulled this over for a few moments and then decided she probably didn't ever want to see a pilot after he had hit the ground in his plane, and, shocked as the thought occurred to her, she hoped she would never, ever see Henry that way.

"What are you thinking about, sweetheart?" Henry said, his arm reaching across her shoulders tentatively, with "sweetheart" said gently because it was so new in his mouth. She didn't seem to be objecting, which Henry decided was good, and his arm relaxed on her shoulders. The sun was sliding toward the top of the trees on the horizon and Henry knew he would have to leave soon. Ruth didn't answer, so Henry asked again, "What's going on in that head of yours?" Ruth sighed and decided not to tell him that she'd been wondering what a Red Baron victim looked like. Instead she said, "Oh, nothing."

"Well then, why don't you tell me a story?" Henry said. "I don't want to bore you with all my flying stories."

"But I love them. I could listen to you all day long. I don't have a single good story to tell." Ruth looked to the other side of the road, across the Cileks' land. Their farm was just slightly smaller than her father's was, but she knew this wouldn't be the case for long. Her father came home from the store the other day with the news that Cilek was buying another hundred acres to the east, which would make his farm fifty acres bigger. Her father had said it didn't bother him—that he could never farm eight hundred acres by himself anyway—and Ruth knew, although he didn't say it, that he meant Ruth should find a husband so they could buy more land and together farm a great big farm, bigger than the Cileks'.

"I don't believe that for a second," Henry said. "I want to hear one of your stories."

Ruth laughed because she could not think of anything to say. She didn't want to talk about her games in the pine grove, her father's fear of grasshoppers, little Deanie Cilek, or about her plans to go away from there. He knew too much of the world to be interested in such stories. "Please just tell me one more story," she pleaded. "Then I'll think of something. I promise. Oh, I know," she said with a jump and a smile. "Tell me about those cubs again."

Henry smiled and sighed. He began, for probably the fifth or sixth time, to tell Ruth about the two lion cubs named Whiskey and Soda that William K. Vanderbilt had sent as mascots to the Lafayette Escadrille, a group of American pilots who volunteered to British and French Air Corps when they were restlessly waiting for the U.S. to join in. They fought at the Battle of Verdun on April 16, 1916, and scored a total of thirty-nine victories against the Germans, losing one-third of the group in the effort. A few of the Escadrille had come to Henry's air base just once for an honor ceremony, but he had no real personal acquaintance with any of them. A few Sundays back, Henry had brought Ruth the picture he'd clipped and saved from *Le Monde*. There were sixteen men standing in front of a Nieuport *bébé* and Whiskey and Soda were stretched up on their back paws, nibbling on pieces of meat held above them by two pilots.

Ruth loved to hear these stories and it never mattered to her that Henry had not been in any dogfights himself—it didn't taint his heroism in Ruth's eyes. Just to have been there, just to be a pilot, made Henry remarkable. As they turned in the road and started back—dusk was coming soon—she knew she owed Henry a story, so she decided to recount the time she almost took her head off with her father's rifle. "When I was seven I decided I wanted to hunt like my Uncle Matt's boys, who live down on the Iowa River near the Missouri border," she began. "They've been hunting from about the time they were weaned, or nearly. So I got ahold of my father's rifle and decided to shoot a bird, any bird. I went over to the creek on the south end of the farm and pointed the gun at a flock of geese. I pulled the trigger and the recoil sent me tumbling backwards and the nose of the rifle became implanted in the soft ground of the creek bank. I got myself together, figured out I wasn't hurt except for a good bruise coming up on my shoulder and arm, but the gun was messed up, and I decided that the best way to fix it was to shoot it again."

Henry laughed, confident that the result could not have been too bad, since Ruth was standing there, whole, before him; he was surprised and not surprised at the story she was telling.

"That second time, the recoil sent me back fifteen feet, into a tree, where I cut my head and fainted clean out for three minutes. When I finally stumbled back into the yard, I guess there was so much blood on my dress and in my hair that

Father thought I shot myself. He said, 'You're damn lucky that barrel didn't explode on you. You should be glad you decided to play with my best gun. If that barrel had exploded, you'd be dead now.'" Ruth lowered her voice, squinched her eyebrows, and dropped her chin to her chest in imitation of her father, and she and Henry both laughed.

Ruth quit the story there—where it was mostly still funny. She didn't tell Henry that she had watched her father for hours that evening as he sat on the porch with an oilcloth and ramrod, cleaning the gun of the dirt and gunpowder Ruth had infused the thing with. She watched him from the hayloft, where she climbed after milking the cow, Annie, because she couldn't stand the angry, disappointed looks both her parents kept giving her. The hayloft smelled wet and dirty and dry all at the same time to her and she was always afraid—even if it was irrational—of the snakes she felt certain must live there. And so lying up there the night she almost killed herself with her father's gun was like hiding, but it was also penance, to her. She watched his small, thick hands slide and crawl around the rifle. He was sitting on a bench on the back porch and the nearly full moon made it seem as bright as early, early dawn. She could see the blue-gray of his pants and the early white in his blond hair. He was smoking a pipe, which he only did when he was very, very tired and deep in thought.

Ruth also did not tell Henry that the rifle she had almost killed herself with was, in fact, the rifle that her grandfather had propped under his chin and triggered with his toe twenty years prior to her own nearly fatal spring. And she certainly didn't tell Henry that her grandfather's other son, besides her father, Uncle Matt, had followed in his father's footsteps and thrown himself into the Mississippi with sandbags tied to his feet only a few years back. If she told him, Henry might start to think such actions ran in the Sheehan family, and maybe they did.

Ruth sometimes tried to picture her grandfather with the gun, even though she didn't even know what he looked like. His shoes had to have been off, and maybe he was in his nightshirt, in the dead of night, since no one was able to see what he was doing and stop him. The dead of night with a full moon, and he sat on the porch for a very long time, with his wife and three sons sleeping in the house behind him. Then, just before dawn, she imagined, he set up the rifle just to see if he could do it, just to see if the rifle could be propped up and if his toe could really trip the trigger. And then it did, whether or not he really meant to, how could you really mean to?, and he was dead.

When her father finished cleaning it, the rifle went high over the doorway, where it would stay as protection for the rest of her father's life, or as long as she could remember anyway. He oiled it periodically to be sure it worked if they needed it, but Ruth, in thinking back, was fairly certain they never did.

After Ruth told Henry the shooting story that day, they arrived back at the house and Henry gave the Sheehans all the proper thank-yous before heading out to his plane. Ruth watched him go, as she always did, and she wondered how long she would have to wait before he would take her up there with him, cursed herself for not asking this time. Next time, she resolved. Next. As for Henry, he wondered how long until he could have this lovely, smart, funny, mercurial girl all for himself, and if he could ever have her all for himself, and what marriage might be like.

~~~⌒~~~

As SUMMER TURNED to fall, the fury of summer heat mellowed, and Henry got used to landing on the road, since the crop had come in and there'd been no landing in the cornfield for several months now, Ruth finally told Henry of her futile hope to go to college, to become a nurse, to see a world beyond Cedar Bluff, even if she was destined to return. And would he take her flying, even teach her someday?

He didn't say anything at first—just listened, considered, and wondered what the right response was. "Well, I would like to take you flying someday soon, Ruth," he said. "And that's a world beyond Cedar Bluff, for sure. I don't know what to say, to be honest with you, about nursing or college. I myself don't have my high school diploma."

"When can we go?" Ruth asked eagerly. "How?"

"Let me think about it," Henry said. "Let me think. Next time I see you—I'll know."

Ruth thought he sounded hesitant, so she kept quiet, waiting for him to say something else, something better.

"It's just—I need to be sure your father doesn't find out, Ruth," Henry said, thinking he'd like to wait until they were married, because what could Paul do then? But if they flew now—and if he found out about it—he could refuse to give Ruth's hand. Already, Henry knew, Paul was feeling a little nervous about the question of his flying instead of farming; Henry's reception by Paul had noticeably cooled since the spring. "I'll think about it, Ruth. Trust me. Just give me some time."

When Henry came to see her those Sundays, she would feel her life start anew every time; he arrived, bringing his kind, handsome face, his gentle laugh, his polite ear, and his stories, and she hooked into a universal hum that she had never known before, a greater resonance, louder, better. Then he would leave, and always she was falling from a higher precipice, always barely keeping herself from running in the opposite direction, down the field, away from her father and Henry and all of it. He promised to take her flying—but then he seemed to back off. And did she trust him? Did she trust anyone? He would say goodbye, he would take off, and she would stay frozen there, watching, trying to believe she was there with him, going away, too, not being left behind. She shaded her eyes to the light and she could barely make out his figure on the horizon. What could he see from where he was? How much farther could he see than she could? Still, she always wanted him to come back, to come back and stay, she never didn't want that.

But he came through. One October afternoon, Ruth got her father to let her go to Iowa City and see a film with her friend Mary, so long as they picked up some of the new fertilizer on their way home. Instead, Mary drove Ruth to the airfield, where Henry was waiting, and she climbed into the front cockpit of a red Argo and it all seemed like pretend, like a vivid, late-morning dream, until the noise of the engine seeped straight through her sternum to her spine and down her tailbone, then all the way to her toes. Her eyelids, even, seemed to be fluttering in time to the buzzing slap of the propeller against the wind, and dust, too; she felt like an insect. And then they were moving and Ruth kept her eyes straight ahead as her goggles were pressed tighter and tighter into her face. The world shifted and slid so that she was above and everything, everyone else, was below.

It was several minutes that they were up there, Ruth staring straight ahead, not daring to move because she thought shifting her weight might upset the plane like a canoe, but Henry pounded on the body between them to get her attention—which first made her think they'd hit something, a tree branch, a bird—and she realized it was Henry and she turned her head cautiously, leaned up in her seat so she could see better, looked around, and there it was, the rest of the world, cracked open for her like a geode, and there was Henry behind her, nearly smelling her delight, feeling the tightness of her ecstatic cheek, tasting that smile.

November 1924

Dear Ruth Law Oliver,

I've been flying!

Henry took me up in his Argo just a few weeks ago. My father thought I was at film in Iowa City, of course. But I slumped down in the cockpit in case anyone looked at us too closely as we took off.

Oh, I'll never forget that feeling when we first lifted off. I'm not sure how anyone could. But it was a day of good weather with some bold clouds—great big puffy clouds that make you want to reach out and grab them. The ones that look like cotton puffs. They look like a child's heaven—when I was young I imagined that heaven must be in a cluster of those lovely clouds.

It was a dry summer here, so Henry said we didn't have to worry about clods of mud sticking to the wheels and flying up into the prop. He did advise me to wear a scarf about my face because the dry ground meant dust. And I could probably gag on the exhaust coming off the engine, too. So I wrapped my face in a scarf and I was glad, too, because when we landed in Iowa City, all I could smell and taste was dirty engine fumes and the scarf was covered in a fine silt of dirt.

My stomach lifted with the plane and suddenly I feel as though all my insides might just float away out through my mouth. I am almost dizzy for a moment, but I am watching so much and Henry's such a good pilot that the horizon—a lovely white where the blue sky meets the flat green and brown Iowa prairie and farmland—is always steady at the end of my yellow-scarfed nose. It is heaven, pure, lovely, amazing, heaven. I feel like I've never lived before this very moment. I don't know how the horizon gets that whiteness—but it's always there. A silver-white humming where the land releases into sky.

How could you possibly have given this up? I am confounded!, & quite sure my life will never be the same again.

My friends tell me Henry will propose to me, but I can't believe it's true. Didn't I tell you he was an angel sent to take me flying with him? All my life, I've been waiting for him, I think, and I knew it from the moment I first saw him. When he came for suppers this summer, walking from the de Havilland in his dark brown helmet and jacket and the perfect robin's-egg-blue sky behind him, and the creamy tan plane against the green green fields—

I think every girl in America would've fallen for him like I did. He's handsome, wise, and kind, and loving.

Sincerely,
Ruth Sheehan
Cedar Bluff, Iowa

In the living room after supper, January 1925, when Ruth and her mother were washing up, Henry cleared his throat and said, "I'd like to know, sir, if I could propose marriage to your daughter."

Paul, on a brand-new pale violet sofa, raised his eyebrows and reached over to the side table for his pipe box and tobacco. He had anticipated this evening for a few weeks now. He filled the pipe and lit it. Ruth had rarely looked as happy in recent years as she looked when Henry came around. Paul couldn't deny this. He liked that Henry made his daughter smile, at a time when Paul himself was at a loss for her. He was eternally grateful and warm to Henry for this. Paul did have a few concerns—some of which he'd resolve in time; some of which would simply have to be solved straightaway. He thought these over in his head before speaking aloud to anxious Henry. Ruth was young—he'd like them to wait a year and a half to get married, when she'd be nearly nineteen, but that delay seemed unlikely. She was young, but there was something old and wise about Ruth, too, probably from being an only child and being around adults so much. Second, but really primarily, Paul worried about the flying—he wanted most of all for Henry to quit flying the mail and work the farm.

"Well," he said, after what had seemed like an eternity to Henry, "I think you know that I'd appreciate any help you saw fit to give the farm. But I'll leave it at that."

He puffed his pipe once, twice, so that Henry asked, "Is that all?"

"No," Paul said, in his own time. He couldn't force Henry to change his work, not right now anyway. But there was a bottom line he could, and would, draw. "I'd like it if you had your house in Cedar Bluff, Henry. We built that little house up the road from here just two years ago. There's tenants in there now, but I can get them out and you two can live there. "

"Yes, sir, Mr. Sheehan," Henry said, nodding politely. "I understand what you're saying."

"Let me just be clear," Paul said after his third puff on his pipe. "I don't want Ruth to live anywhere else but in Cedar Bluff. Not in Chicago so you can be closer to your airfield. Not in Paris, France."

"Yes, sir," Henry repeated.

Paul continued: "And I'd like it if you quit that flying and worked the farm with me. There's more work than I can handle and some land to be bought to the south of us, if you like."

Henry thought for a moment. "I can agree to the first," he said, choosing his words very carefully. "But I don't know about the second, to be honest with you, Mr. Sheehan. As I've said before—I have no talent or inclination with the farming. I'm a good pilot but a terrible farmer. I think a man should try to do what he's good at."

But this was what Paul had expected. In time, he was confident, the young man would agree to the second, too. "Just think about it," he said. "That's all I ask."

"I'll do that sir." Henry allowed himself to sigh a little in relief.

Paul stood, extended his hand to Henry, who shook it, and then Paul went to the porch to finish smoking his pipe. Elizabeth hated the smoke in the house. Once settled out there, he resolved to let Ruth know, too, what it might be like to marry this pilot. A kind man, for sure, but didn't she want someone who'd be on the farm with her, not up in the air?

As Henry flew home that night, he was both relieved and a little sick to his stomach. He loved Ruth and liked Paul Sheehan, whom he would not like disappointing, as he suspected he would.

⁓

A MONTH LATER, right out in the clear field, it was sunny but bone-cold. The ground was frozen, hard as rock, and Henry had barely been able to keep hold of the stick for the pain in his wrists, broken two months earlier on a rough landing. He had brought to rest his boss Oswald's big red Argo, in which Ruth's first flight had taken place, and Ruth was there, all wrapped up. He didn't even wait until his hands and his jaw had defrosted enough to work properly. He climbed out of the plane and he stepped down and patted his chest. He took Ruth's hand and patted it against the pocket where the box lived, had lived for the whole two weeks' interim since he'd last seen her. She reached in because he couldn't and she had to know what it was, yet she was still surprised when she opened the royal-blue velvet box and saw the ring there.

It was ten minutes before Henry's mouth could actually speak the words, "Will you marry me?" and by then she had long since said, "Yes."

Tears formed in the corners of her eyes, while they simply froze on Henry's icy cheek. Ruth took her gloves off and Henry slipped the ring on her warm finger—on the stinging-with-cold finger that felt warm to Henry. He kissed her, long and carefully, on the mouth, and she wrapped her arms around his neck and stayed there for a while. The simple diamond and platinum ring was shiny there in the cold, flat February light and the gray fields with flecks of snow. He was hers; he could go now, he could go and she could be sure of his return, to her.

ONE THING PAUL SHEEHAN was dead right about—four months was a short engagement. Everyone still got a chance to get to know Henry and Henry got a chance to get used to the idea of living out there on the farm, and to set it up so that he could keep his route. And Elizabeth had a chance to get Ruth's dress, once Elizabeth's, ready. The lace was so delicate; some careful repairs were needed and Ruth wanted the sleeves changed a touch, which required an order to come in from Chicago.

In May 1925, then, the whole town of Cedar Bluff came to the wedding, as did the boys from the Iowa City, Moline, and Des Moines airfields. The cream-colored lace dress that came with Elizabeth and her family from Ireland had a high collar and three-quarter sleeves and there was a veil to match, which her father lifted from her face at the altar with shaky, callused hands. Paul Sheehan was still a little unsure of the match he had endorsed, but Henry had agreed to make their home in the house up the hill on the north side of the farm and this was what he thought most important of all.

After the ceremony and Mass, there was a big dinner. There was a pig on the spit and the town band plus Mr. Gustafson, with his shiny steel banjo. The cake stood three tiers tall with gleaming white icing that curved and crested like the edges of snowdrifts. Seeing Ruth in her wedding dress, Henry felt as if he were meeting her for the first time. Near the end of the reception, he caught and held her hand, pulled her in front of him, and they stood with the party going on around them, with his chest not a full breath away from her lace-covered shoulder blades, close enough that the space between them was more electric than touch.

Ruth changed clothes around four P.M. and by five they were climbing into a Curtiss Jenny, now fully his, theirs, which he had unveiled, with JUST MARRIED and two inter-twined hearts scripted in red on the side, to great applause. Even Paul Sheehan looked almost thrilled with the couple's departure from the new twenty-acre strip, created out of their sixty-acre wedding present. He enjoyed the happiness in his daughter's face, her whole being. Henry's brother Jack propped the plane and Ruth gave a thumbs-up. They bounced twice on the way down the strip and then the Jenny lifted off. They were headed south to the Des Moines River and the town of Keokuk. From there they would turn slightly west. There wasn't a single cloud in the sky and the Jenny's wires hummed in perfect resonance. Ruth stretched up and looked over the side, back down at Cedar Bluff and the crowd they had just left. She took a picture, just barely catching the side of the Jenny at the edge of the frame.

The wedding guests looked like saplings swaying in the wind, with hats and ribbons trailing off behind them. Pale upturned faces stood out against the dark, rich field. At the edge of the frame was the house and the tables set with tablecloths in the backyard. Also, there was Elizabeth's special decorative touch—multicolored paper lanterns strung along the clothesline, which would be lit when the party carried on into the darkness, long after Henry and Ruth had left.

They could see the Iowa River snaking its way downstate through the endless squares of fresh brown soil with little dots of green. Ruth felt the little food she had eaten shift in her stomach as final nervousness ebbed and pure happiness, pure excitement, set in. Henry smiled under his goggles as he watched Ruth, his wife, in front of him. He patted the side of the plane affectionately, thanking her for delivering him to Ruth, for keeping both of them safe, for the future the three of them, together, promised. The wires sang, the air was warm, even a thousand feet up, and the clear, sure sun, slanting west just over the wing, promised a safe flight the whole way.

Henry turned a perfect twenty degrees farther west at Keokuk and an hour and a half later they spotted the Lake of the Ozarks, huge and blue and welcoming, bigger than any lake Ruth had ever seen but not nearly as big, Henry reflected, as Lake Michigan. They flew to the east side of the lake as they had been instructed. About two-thirds of the way down, near the train station, Henry spotted the grass field. He flew low overhead to signal his arrival and then banked back to land to the northwest. The wings shook and rattled a bit and Ruth laughed out loud because the other times she flew with Henry she had been afraid of all the rattling. It had felt as if the plane were falling apart. This third time she knew the rattling and shaking was a good sign. Besides, she told herself, Henry had done this a hundred times, maybe even a thousand. A few moments later, they were lined up with the runway and then Henry floated the Jenny down just perfectly. She took one, then two slight bounces, and she was good. They rolled to a stop in front of the tiny shack that was an office. It was just seven o'clock and Ruth stepped out of the cockpit feeling as fresh and relaxed as after a long evening walk.

FOUR

Night flying. At first, thrown into a bowl of darkness,
starred top and bottom, the same consistency all around.
Stars over and under you. Gradually two darknesses appear.
A black bowl of velvet, brightly spangled below—the earth; a dark
blue bowl, lightly pricked with stars above. . . . Reaching for one
beacon as you let go of the one behind—stepping stones,
signals just for us as the lighted cities were, too. The sense
that the whole world was made for us, for flying.

—*Anne Morrow Lindbergh, April 4, 1933*

*H*ENRY WAS VERY handsome when he was young and
first married, sugar-cane-brown hair that stayed straight
against his head, green eyes, light skin, broad shoulders, and
a square, deliberate chin and jaw. As he became a husband, a
father, and a good pilot for the United States Army and then
for the Boeing Company, he only seemed to grow more dis-
tinguished-looking and gentlemanly. He noticed women on
the streets of Chicago and Omaha watching him, catching

his eye, and then looking away. Sometimes, with a new, vague curiosity, but no true desire, he wondered what it might be like to have one of them in his arms. Mostly, however, when he closed his eyes and was lonely, it was the feeling of Ruth's fine hair at his neck that he imagined, her hair that fell all around her face in lovely honey warbles. He imagined his eyes opening in the middle of the night to see her long, sleeping eyelashes bathed in the brassy streetlight flooding over his cot. Ruth was beautiful, to him, to everyone, he assumed. He liked the way she smelled; and he liked looking forward to, craving, both her touch and his touch on her, at week's end, and he wished he could do it every day, although he did not consider how these everyday things might ever happen. There was his mail work and there was his wife.

He didn't tell Ruth half of the things that happened to him on a weekly basis: how much blind flying there was; how many times in five days he thought, Well, I might not make it home this week; how many accidents the company logged per day; how he had tried to buy life insurance but was laughed all the way out of the office by the agent. She didn't know that Henry himself had already cracked up ten different planes, in rain and mud and ice and snow and in the clearest of blue skies and green grass; or that he'd watched two people who flew the Chicago–Cleveland route burn to death in the Junkers that they called Flying Coffins for good reason; or that he watched two other pilots crash into each other during takeoff, the impact killing both.

These things were a regular part of flying the mail and Ruth didn't need to know, not when she was home alone. But there was also no question of "too dangerous" for him; flying was his life—it was who he was, what he did.

With his pilot friends, he freely argued over who had the most forced landings in a single flight—Otis won, with twenty-nine between Chicago and St. Louis during a spring hail and electrical storm. They argued about who had bailed out the most times—Slim Lindbergh had the record among all pilots with five, but Henry'd bailed twice—and they argued about who'd walked the farthest to a phone after coming down in a dark, snowy place. Jackie O'Hara said he walked twenty-seven miles once and they all laughed themselves to tears—Jackie flew Chicago–Cleveland and there wasn't anywhere along there that you could walk more than ten or fifteen miles—let alone twenty-seven—and not run into somebody or something. Unless, of course, you were walking in circles, of which they all admitted Jackie was capable.

Generally, Henry flew home Friday evenings in time for dinner. Ruth had gotten so that she could feel his plane humming and popping through the air before she could hear it, no matter what she was doing—getting supper ready, tending the garden, helping her parents, or walking home from town in the late afternoon sun. By the time she walked to a place where she could see the landing strip that her father still hoped would entice Henry to farm for work and fly for fun, there was her husband, the OX-5 engine sputtering for water since the radiator always was less forthcoming than it needed to be. He landed, coasted to a stop, and staked the plane, and she would be there waiting for a sooty, gritty kiss. She took his elbow and they walked slowly home, Henry's body still shuddering in time to flight.

He bathed and she sat next to him, telling him of her week, asking him questions about his flights, about Chicago, the other pilots. She soaped his back for him and warmed more water when the tub ran cold. The sun was down by the time he climbed up out of the tub, weary, clean, relaxed, and Ruth looked down, away, demurely, as she handed him his towel. They were physically similar in slightness and proportion. Ruth's hips were not much bigger than Henry's, although that would surely change in time. Both were powerful and lean as athletes. She loved the spot on Henry just inside his hipbone, where there was no hair, no roughness, just a perfect porcelain smoothness—yet she could not get her eyes to settle there in the broad light of the bathroom. Henry put on some clean slacks and a shirt and shoes and Ruth splashed her face with some of the warm water from the kettle. She dabbed perfume behind her ears and lower on her neck, in the slight gully behind her collarbone. She neatened the front of her dress and tied back a few renegade hairs. They sat down to properly eat their dinner, if they didn't find their way to their bed, to the beautiful and affectionate other, first.

Saturday or Sunday mornings, Ruth would beg to go up in the Jenny. They'd fly east to the Mississippi and Ruth would hang over the side with her new camera. She took pictures of the chessboard Iowa countryside, the great sweeping green or brown or blue river, the marshlands and Fox River swamplands that marked the west coast of Wisconsin, and the riverboats of Henry's childhood. She looked so hard sometimes, for so long, at all these things, trying to imprint them on her brain as if she held a photographic plate there, that her eyes would be sore for a day afterward.

Though he did love to watch pieces of Ruth's hair escape from her helmet and dance in the wind, sometimes Henry pounded on the cowling and pointed to something that wasn't there—just to get her to look back him, smile, even in question or confusion or concern. Otherwise, Ruth loved flying so much, she might not show Henry her smile once, as she would be so engrossed in looking, seeing, watching everything that went on around her. Henry loved her passion—and he thought, sometimes, that flying was how they best understood each other. Because they shared this passion, in all its isolation, they were ultimately together, there, in the air. Although Henry felt somewhat jealous when Ruth seemed to forget him while they were flying, this forgetting also told him that they were cut from perfectly matched cloth.

Once, they both squeezed into the pilot's seat so that Ruth could have a chance at holding on to the stick. They took off on a sunny day and did one nice circle over town with Ruth's hands over Henry's, feeling how firmly he had to steer and hold to keep the plane steady. Eventually, he slipped his hands out from under hers and Ruth held the plane even all by herself, which impressed Henry, since the Jenny was only naturally as sturdy as a small shell in the surf. Henry controlled the pedals but Ruth held on to the stick with two leather-gloved hands and every move she made was careful and calculated. This was life for her; it was life the way she had always hoped to live it. She could feel the whole world spread before her. Horizons were infinite and in their wondrous, beautiful spread of infinity, she could steer and float and swim in it. She found a certain religion there, a certain nourishing faith.

She loved this whole procedure, having him drift down to

her from the heavens every Friday, giving him up Sunday evenings; and in between, the giddy weekends of flying and fishing and eating and coupling—at night, in the morning, after lunch if they could be sure Ruth's parents weren't coming around. It was all so new, so wonderful; she was only thankful, never greedy.

June 1926

Dear Ruth Law Oliver,

For nearly a year now, I have been Ruth Sheehan Gutterson, and it suits me better than I once would've guessed. Henry is still flying the mail—he goes up to Checkerboard Sunday evenings and returns to me on Friday as soon as he can. In the summertime, it's dusk; in the winter, it's nighttime and I must go meet him in Iowa City, as, without any lights, he'd be a dead man to try and land in a pasture or on one of the roads around here.

We have supper and sometimes see a picture after he comes in. After he cleans himself up, that is! Wash off as much oil and dirt and gasoline as he can and get him in a fresh shirt and pants. Although he's probably craving home-cooked food by Friday, he's also just out and out hungry, and it's nice for me to get out some. There's one place right on Clinton Street that serves a good pork chop at a fair price and we tend to go there. He's even taught me to drive and we have a little Ford.

A few weeks back, I took a job at the post office two days a week. It's funny to see the occasional letter stamped AIR MAIL and to imagine that Henry might have carried it in his plane, right beneath or behind him. Mr. Johansen is the postmaster in Cedar Bluff, and he does most every-

thing, but he's been ailing, his back, and it's nice for him
to have the rest. Mary Hitchens calls me Air Mail Ruth,
or ARM for short, somehow, because of first Henry and
now this work. She comes to see me both days I'm there,
when it's slow, after three o'clock when most folks have
gotten their mail and the outgoing sack has been picked
up. She likes to do impressions of Cedar Bluff people—
like our friend and classmate, ever so serious Alice Jaczys,
who's smiled about twice in her life, stooped Mr. Gray at
the grocery who can't help but say "Yep" and nod his
head, all the time, whether he's in a conversation or not,
and even Mrs. Cilek, with the giant, meaty mole on the
side of her cheek, which Mary pretends—too meanly, I
think, Mrs. Cilek has never had it easy—weighs that
whole side of her head down. Sometimes I wonder if Mary
never dreamed of being an actress in the theater, but she's
always seems perfectly content with her life—she's never
one to complain, which I must say I envy.

I'm trying to convince Henry to take me up flying with him
more—I do love it so—I tell him he should just pack me
away in the second seat—I can hardly weigh more than an
extra bag of mail—but he just laughs and promises to take
me the next day. Sometimes he tells me stories that I think
are meant to scare me—like landing in a complete cloud of
fog, never being sure when or how soon the ground would
come up to meet him. He told me how hard he has to pull
on the stick sometimes. "Your arms feel like they're breaking," he says, and once, for real, wrists did break, on a very
hard landing. In another bad storm, his altimeter said 3500
feet, but he ripped some of the linen on the Jenny's belly
when it brushed across the tops of some trees! Once he put
a DH-4b upside down in the mud along the Mississippi. In
France, he crashed upside down in the Alps!

Still, I'm not afraid. Every day, it seems, I want to be up there more, with him, where the world is bigger, sharper, and full of power. And every time he takes me up there, I'm not sure I can bear to come back down. Henry's been lucky, but he's also a good pilot and I pray to God every day that neither his luck nor his skills change. I don't think he could give it up and I don't want him to. If someone asked *me* to stay grounded, I couldn't do it, either, I'd be—like a rabbit caught in a trap, trying to chew my leg off, to get up, away, *up there*.

And you? Where have you been flying?

Sincerely,
Ruth Sheehan Gutterson
Cedar Bluff, Iowa

Barely a year in, something changed, the novelty of marriage wore off maybe, and Ruth found herself thinking her father was right—that she had been crazy to marry the pilot. It was September, and one of the first truly cold winds had worked itself up to blasting the windows so hard they rattled. She was lying in the dark, having just read about one of Henry's colleagues crashing in a lightning storm in Ohio, and she imagined being alone when someone from Mr. Boeing's office came to tell her. Her father had meant "trouble" as coyotes or running out of coal or her falling someplace and having no one there to find her. That sort of trouble she did not fear, could not even imagine; but her sort—the fantastical, wicked sort, Henry's possible death, every day—perfectly stunned her. It was too cold to get up and ring the phone downstairs; and she didn't know how to find Henry, anyway, even if she needed to, even if it was an emergency.

Although she had willingly forfeited her nursing college dreams when Henry proposed to her, she still longed to see the world—more of it than Iowa, even Iowa from the air— and hadn't he promised to show her? He was home so little she couldn't even get enough of the world *through* him. Well, she told herself, she would become more accustomed to it, to all of it, and life was constantly changing. So much was still possible with Henry. As for her fear—she had never before been afraid of him flying, maybe this was simply overdue, and worse for it. One look from her mother when Ruth spoke to her told her this. *You made your bed,* the look said. *You made it.*

Henry gave her phone numbers in Chicago and Omaha, promising to call when he could, even if it was expensive— and this, plus her work at the post office, and Mary Hitchens, maybe it all helped a little. Yet still, more often all the time, in the darkest hour of the night, even if she was exhausted, with another busy day ahead, she thought constantly about flying, as if it were music playing too quietly somewhere that she couldn't make louder so as to hear properly, nor could she turn it off. And so she feared the future, relentless and urgent, and a nescience of joy returning from the days before Henry. Again, the maws of time were so wide, descending, and she couldn't put a mark on them, couldn't anticipate them; she couldn't begin to mold a life as she wished, couldn't decide what it was she wished for anyway. She felt absence— Henry's, her own—like a needle at the base of her spine in the billowing black night. She was nearly nineteen years old—or still only eighteen, depending on her mood—and a wife already, and she felt fifty years old and she felt eight years old. Weary. Afraid and unconfident. Nothing was *light* to her anymore. Nothing charming. Except Henry, whom she didn't get enough of, and flying, though she was not a pilot. But she was not a farmer, either; she was hardly even a wife and she didn't want yet to be a mother. That left Ruth. Just Ruth. And what was Ruth?

MARY HITCHENS WAS always talking about her diary, but Ruth felt awkward when she tried to keep one. "Dear me," she'd begin, but she'd get no further. She liked the letters, though, and started writing to some of the pilots she'd been reading of in the Chicago and Omaha newspapers. Amelia Earhart and Jacqueline Cochran and Mr. Wiley Post and so many other pilots, men and women alike, although she preferred the women. She read the articles, clipped them, reread them, maybe twice again, and saved them, folding them up and stacking them under the laundry table on the back porch. Gradually, these famous people were *real* to Ruth and she wrote to them as if they knew her as well as anyone. No one wrote back, of course, at least not after a preliminary autographed picture or something of the sort. Still, the stack of her copies of the letters grew in an old stationery box, and the clippings reached near the top of one milk crate.

Then the clippings blew away one day in a summer storm, which had seemed so apt to spawn a tornado that Ruth moved a chair by the cellar door and sat and watched. When the newspapers began to tumble and float out from under the table, over the porch railing, and into the backyard wind, she had first dashed out, into the rain and curious, amber gray light with her hands outstretched, as if the papers were twenty-dollar bills, to gather them in to her, to take them back inside to shelter and possession. She got three, before so many of the others blew out into the cornfield, and the hail started, a splutter of rocks on her head, and she ran inside, her face a mess of rain and tears and total, vacuous panic. She held three sopping newspapers in her hand and sat down in the chair, and it hailed and blew like hell, but no tornado came, and it was a good thing because Ruth might not have moved.

Afterward, she laughed at herself. How could she have cared so much about the silly newspapers? Oh, it wasn't the papers, she told herself, it was just being so afraid of the storm, afraid of being alone there, who would find her in time if the house blew in?

Thereafter, she carefully cut each article out of the paper with scissors and she kept them in a folder in a drawer, and then in a crate in the attic, where no wind could reach.

~⌒⌒

"Henry," she said to him one late fall weekend when they were fishing from a flat-bottomed boat on a little lake north of town.

He looked up from the spot in the water where he had sunk his line. "Yeah?"

"I get scared sometimes now, at night."

"What of, sweetheart?"

"Oh, I don't know. It's silly. Criminals, maybe. I'm lonely."

He laughed gently. "I thought there weren't any criminals in Cedar Bluff."

She shrugged, embarrassed, and adjusted the brim of her

hat so that the sun wasn't in her eyes. She wouldn't tell him
how she was worrying, about him, and how she wanted to be
in whatever plane might take him down. She reeled in her
line and cast again, trying a different spot, the little wooden
flat-bottomed boat rocking with her movement. The previous week's rain and an unusual warmth had inspired a
strange, very late batch of mosquitoes. So they wore their
long-sleeved shirts and stockings or socks, no matter how nice
it would be to feel the fresh air on their arms for the last time
before winter took hold. "How much longer are you going to
have to be away like this?"

"Ruth, it's my job."

"I know, but—I—"

"What would we do for money?" Henry asked

Before she could think, Ruth had blurted, "Can't I come
with you sometimes? The de Havilland has two seats, just
like the Jenny."

"They put mail in the second seat, you know that, not
wives." He attempted a smile.

"I'm serious. This time, Henry. Honestly."

Henry did not show surprise by dropping his jaw or turning his head quickly or starting forward. Instead it was his
silence and his curious stare that told Ruth that he was very
surprised. "Why?"

"The post office—well, Mr. Johansen—*needs* me, that's
true, and it's nice to help, but that's not *doing* anything—
that doesn't *make* me anything," she said quickly, looking
down and smoothing her skirt across her lap with one hand.
"I need something to do," Ruth continued. "Something to
learn or be."

Henry considered this. "Your father would hunt me down," he said, laughing.

"But he stopped being in charge of my life when I married you."

"He hates me, doesn't he?"

"No. 'Henry's a good man,' he said on our wedding day. 'Good-hearted, intelligent,' he said. He just thinks you're crazy for flying."

"And for leaving you all alone at home."

"That, he blames me for. It was I who chose to marry you, not my father."

"He thinks I'm going to quit and farm with him."

"Well," Ruth said. "He has ideas that have nothing to do with you."

Henry reeled in his line. He took the worm off the hook and laid the pole in the bottom of the boat. He said he'd talk to Oswald, ask him, but he wasn't very confident. He feared, frankly, that Oswald would say he was crazy. "Don't get too hopeful, now, please, Ruthie," he said. "Please don't get too hopeful."

"But you're going to ask? You'll try?"

"Sure."

Ruth dropped her fishing pole into the water and lurched across the boat to hug him. Henry met her halfway, held her, as he reached into the water and snatched the pole out. The boat rocked so much that the pail with two fish in it spilled into the lake and so, almost, did they. As they rode out the tumult, Henry imagined asking Oswald—prayed that he wouldn't be laughed out of the hangar. No other mail pilot that Henry had ever heard of, anyway, needed any sort of copilot, and no one else flew with his wife. Still, it seemed to matter a whole lot to Ruth and he *would* enjoy seeing more of her. She was already a very good navigator, with a jar-tight memory, good care for detail, and perfect math. She was curious and fearless and confident and strong and she loved to lean out the side of the plane and look way out. He was thankful, at least, for the mail's and thus his recent transposition from the military to private contractors, via the Kelly Bill. Uncle Sam would never have let Ruth onto any field; Henry'd find out soon enough if William Boeing was any different.

Oswald did nearly laugh him out of the hangar. But then he said yes, on condition that they would, indeed, start a family before too long and her flying would end there, and on condition that Henry never said Oswald okayed it—Boeing would fire him for sure, he said—and on condition that if Ruth ever delayed them, she'd have to stay back. Henry did not thank his boss for this because he knew the man—who had burned his neck and back badly in a fiery crash over German lines in 1917, and who persisted nevertheless in smoking cigars near linen wings doped with gasoline—would assert that he hadn't done or given Henry anything.

On her birthday a few weeks later, a Saturday, he set a box on her chair.

"What's in the box?" she said as she handed Henry a piece of pie and sat down. She took the box on her lap, staring at it without untying the cherry-red ribbon.

"Well?" Henry said with his fork poised over the pie. "Aren't you going to open it?"

She smiled and tugged on one end of the bow.

"There," he said as the ribbon fell away.

The brown leather jacket, thick and tough and official with a sheepskin lining, was folded as perfectly as possible and the helmet lay neatly on top of it.

"I don't know your numbers well enough for a flight suit," he said. "But I wanted to surprise you, so I got the jacket. It's the smallest they come. There's no customizing."

She didn't say anything, just stood up and set the box on her chair and tried it all on. She touched her arms, patted her front and her head. The coat felt thick and heavy, reassuring, like a hand on her shoulder, and the helmet was snug and warm. She put her arms out and twirled around for Henry to see.

"It's perfect," he said.

"Yes," she agreed, wondering if she'd ever received a better present, hoping it meant what she thought it meant.

"We'll have to wait for spring," he said. "It'll come fast."

She stepped slowly toward him, leaned down, as he was still sitting at the table with his pie, took his face in her two hands, and kissed him.

March 1927

Dear Jacqueline Cochran,

I've just returned from my first trip as a navigator with my husband, flying for the Boeing Company. Henry listened to me, at long last, and for my 19th birthday, surprised me with a flight jacket, custom-made in my size. I don't know how he got it right—his own clothes barely fit him half the time, before me and my ungainly stitches get to them, anyway! But he did get it right. It's beautiful. Most of the time, Henry picks me up and drops me off in

Iowa City, so at least the boys in Chicago don't know, because Oswald, our boss up there, says they can't know, even though they're going to figure it out sooner or later. All these boys talk. Sit around the fields and talk. In Omaha, I slip out of the plane right away, so that I'm out of sight by the time the line boys come to refuel and the mail is retrieved. I never knew how big Omaha was. Bigger than Des Moines, even, and different! More cattle there and not as much corn, and trains everywhere. There are *cowboys* walking around, which you really don't see in Des Moines. To think, just the other side of the Missouri, just the other side of Iowa, and that much different, a gateway to the whole West. How much different, then, someplace as far away as California or Paris must be!

I am alive, reborn, even. Henry and I, up there, together, a king and queen of the air. Soon, I'll be good enough that they'll hire me, and we won't have to sneak around, and I'll be the first female employee for Mr. Boeing's airmail!

Sincerely,
Ruth Gutterson
Cedar Bluff, Iowa

Henry had been right about navigation coming easy for her—she was good. His trips became very efficient because he could focus on how the plane felt, with only half an eye to their course, as he could count on Ruth to point one direction or another when necessary. She always knew where precisely they were going and how—she even saw through storms and cloud cover better than Henry did. Perhaps best of all, she was never afraid. Henry had been certain that their first storm—when the plane shook and jumped so much that he left the cockpit bruised and achy—would make Ruth a fair-weather flyer. But she wasn't even fazed by one real doozy of a thunderstorm with driving rain and pitch-blackness and strong winds, which sent them down to land, to try and wait it out, about six times between Iowa City and Omaha. The trip took more than twice as long as usual and they arrived soaked to the bone; even Henry was a little rattled. Yet Ruth was fine. She did not complain.

Over about fourteen months, they got to know Omaha and a bit of Chicago—the times when Ruth begged, successfully, not to be left in Iowa City, which she knew to do both rarely and well. They had their favorite restaurants and hotels; they listened to music and walked along the lakeshore or the river. Much as Ruth loved what she saw and experienced in those cities, she also came to appreciate the beauty and good fortune of Cedar Bluff and her family. She told her parents about music and the food, but about the dirty streets, too, and children playing in them; about the great billows of smoke coughed out of the factories and the noise of streetcars and buses and car horns. "Although they are fascinating, and alive to me, because they are different," she told her father, "I cannot imagine hearing that, breathing that, all my life. I would miss the Iowa air too much."

Paul, who resented greatly what Henry was doing with Ruth and considered it in violation of the promise his son-in-law made to him not so long ago, took her words, at least, as a good sign. "So we shouldn't be looking to rent that house out again soon?" he said, looking at Henry.

"No, sir," Henry said, shutting his mind against Oswald's recent proposal that they live in Chicago, so that Henry could take on more responsibility. He hadn't planned on taking the offer—there was, after all, the promise to live in Cedar Bluff and he meant to stand by it the best he could. But he was surprised to hear Ruth say the things she was saying about the cities. Whenever they had free hours, which was very rare, she wanted to go downtown and shop or eat or simply look around. She seemed to come alive in a city—her whole face widened and lit—with all the people and noise and energy. Yet she was professing the opposite to her father, probably to reassure him that they weren't leaving Iowa on any permanent basis. Henry understood the gesture, but wondered whom she was deceiving.

The men at the airfields gradually figured out what Ruth and Henry were doing, and whatever teasing they began stopped as word of Ruth's abilities and their perfect, fast record together spread. She began flying to Chicago with him Sunday nights, and flying whole months, not just two weeks at a time, as earlier. She was still paid nothing, but was treated with respect. After they landed, chocked the plane, and gathered their delivery, they walked to the field offices together to sign in. Ruth was never allowed to sign her name, but often Henry allowed her to sign his. One young pilot in Chicago looking for a permanent job asked her if she knew a faster way to get to Cleveland, and she had to tell him she'd never been there. "I just heard you were a good navigator," he said. "That's all."

Ruth blushed deeply and felt the compliment in her toes. "Just between here and Omaha," she said. "Illinois and Iowa."

Even Oswald acknowledged privately to Henry that Ruth was "a very smart girl," but he still disliked the arrangement and wondered aloud to Henry when "Juniors" would be about. "We're coming up on a year," he said. "Remember what I said? She's good, I know. She's a novelty, too. And you're still fine without her."

Henry heard all this, but didn't exactly listen. After all, imagining a way to stop Ruth from flying with him now felt like imagining a catastrophe. What in the world could he say to her?

But he didn't have to think of anything, because in October 1928, a year and a half into their flying together, when Oswald was genuinely displeased in part because Boeing had become United Air Transport and there was talk of bigger planes and passengers and Ruth, then, would simply have to stop—in October 1928, Ruth, nearly twenty-one, discovered she was pregnant. Neither one of them had meant for it to be, but they hadn't not meant it, either. There was no discounting the doctor's advice that flying might not be good for the baby. She only needed to think of the bounce she sometimes had to endure on landing, or in a good gust of wind, to realize that no pregnancy should be carried during flight.

Now she lay awake, feeling the spreading of her abdomen, the pressure of a life there. Or maybe she was imagining it, the baby had to be so small yet. She wondered how much she would like being a mother, how good a mother she could possibly be, and what it would be like, now, to stay home alone, if she would be better at it than she was before. Once, she turned onto her shoulder, propped herself up on an elbow, and watched Henry sleep. There was moonlight coming in the window and his face looked pale and so relaxed, dead, even, that she found herself putting her head on his chest to be sure of his heartbeat. When she had told him of the baby, he looked all over her, face, shoulders, body, face again. He had touched his fingers to her collarbone and probed the dip there; then he ran his hand behind her neck and pulled her toward him, his eyes watching her face all the while. He whispered, "It's wonderful, Ruth. It is." And it seemed, for one fleeting moment, that he was trying to persuade her of this.

That Henry was happy about the baby she did not doubt. But then again, Henry was happy about most things. Hot biscuits, good fishing, sunny weather, rain, too; sleeping and waking and walking to the plane across a warm, soft field. He was easy. She needed this ease; it was the quality she loved most in him, but also the one she hated most. She wondered how to upset him, how to frustrate him, how to move his face into anything more or less than careful, controlled, and understanding. He slept soundly as she touched his face, pulled his lip and cheek all the way back until she saw his back molars, exposed them like an animal's teeth. He couldn't possibly know what it felt like to be her.

June 1929

Dear Mrs. Lindbergh,

I must say that I am delighted by, proud, and envious of you! Congratulations on your marriage to the great Colonel Lindbergh, and I read that you are navigating for him, which is impressive, indeed. My husband started as an Air Mail pilot, just as the Colonel used to be. (Since the Kelly Bill, he's been with UAT.) And until last fall, when I discovered I was pregnant with our first child, I navigated for my husband as you navigate for yours. When this baby is born and then grown reasonably, I'll climb back into the seat with Henry. Who knows—maybe someday I'd be good enough—a pilot—to enter one of those contests like the Bendix.

We live in Cedar Bluff, Iowa, which falls about fifty miles west of lady Mississippi. I know the Colonel is from Little Falls, Minnesota, which isn't too far from here. North, certainly. But with Little Falls and his years of flying the Chicago–St. Louis route, surely he's never been too far from Cedar Bluff. I think the Colonel's dignity and humility tells a lot about where he's from. My Henry was born just across the river from the Colonel—near Prairie du Chien, Wisconsin.

Henry is sure he met "Slim" Lindbergh a couple of times in Chicago before '26. But they weren't close acquaintances. Henry sure is proud of your husband, though. Maybe someday they can sit down and swap stories of those old Liberty engines on the Jennys which liked to quit as they pleased. Henry told me that once when his plane stalled, the Colonel bailed out without fully cutting the engine so that as he sailed down through the clouds with his parachute, he could hear the plane sputter back to life and circle around near him before it finally sputtered into the ground about a hundred yards from a barn full of sheep and cattle!!

I do worry that these new planes are not getting safer, just shinier and faster. Especially with these passenger planes crashing and sixteen or twenty people being killed in one fell swoop, like that TAT plane downed in California. And they say that pilot crashed simply because he got confused about what was the ground and what was the horizon! Henry says there's no excuse for being out in weather like that. None at all. Mail pilots can be stupid, but then it's just his own life and a bag of letters he's risking.

If Henry hadn't gotten a job with Mr. Boeing for the Chicago–Omaha leg of the Chicago to San Francisco route, he might've flown for Transcontinental Western Airways, as you do. Can you believe all these coincidences? Maybe it could've been me and Henry that were the great Lindbergh duo, and you could be us! Of course, not really, because Henry isn't interested in setting any records or anything. He just loves being up there, hearing the wind "whistling through the wires," like they say.

If you two ever come through Iowa, you must stay with us and have supper. We won't tell anyone you're here— we'll keep those newspapermen away. Just a couple of pilots and their navigators having some supper together! Imagine that!

It was very nice to meet you, Mrs. Anne Morrow Lindbergh. Perhaps you'll even reply to me.

Sincerely,
Ruth Gutterson
Cedar Bluff, Iowa

The nine months passed in a flash, aided in part by Ruth's sleeping about fourteen hours of every day. There were things to do, too, preparations. Her parents were thrilled and her mother relaxed with each passing month that the pregnancy proceeded without problem or incident. It would be a healthy baby, she said. And indeed, John Henry was born in July 1929, beautiful and pudgy, and he was *hers*, she had done *this*. The first three months, she could not imagine being anywhere else and she watched him with an intensity that suggested a fear of his disappearing if she looked away. In the nights, she was always listening for his cries, for his steady breathing. Time disappeared before and behind her like a fog burning off at noon. Awake nursing him in the middle of the night, rocking in the ash chair that had been Henry's mother's, she looked over the top of the dogwood tree and into the yard, where she imagined John Henry would be chasing a ball before she knew it. She imagined the two dogs—Henry'd gotten them back in the winter, for company—sleeping, stretched out like fallen dinosaurs, in the sunshine. The baby sucked on her breast in even rhythms without any of the desperate, luxuriant squeaking and grunting of the little girls who would follow him. Once full and tired, he gradually let go of Ruth's nipple, his mouth still shaped to suck but his tongue stilled, his eyes closed, his body motionless in the utter abandonment of sleep. The moonlight came into the window and Ruth looked at her breast, the color of beeswax, and at John Henry's pinker face, pure and forthright as water in a stream. From time to time his hand, flung out at his side, hanging over Ruth's supporting arm, would flutter, his fingers moving one by one as if waving through water, through memory.

Gradually, during some of these dead-of-night feedings, Ruth could feel her whole heart and stomach turn on itself as she contemplated, feared, her love and attachment to this child, who would take his first language, balance, and confidence from her; this child who needed her beyond expression and comprehension. She would lay him back into his crib, cover him carefully with the thick blanket her grandmother had knit for Ruth when she was a baby, and she would slip downstairs, lighting only a candle, to write a few letters, telling them about the Gypsy Moth Henry was thinking of buying and where their first flight would be when the baby was old enough to be left alone for the day. Canada, maybe? They'd never been so far before, but they should celebrate, shouldn't they? They had a son!, she wrote.

ON SUNNY, WARM DAYS toward the end of that first summer, Ruth walked all over the fields with the baby in her arms. She watched the sky, pointed out cloud formations and weather patterns, and explained how crosswinds would make Daddy's landing difficult. She licked her finger, held it up, and announced where the wind was coming from. And she told him that Grandma and Grandpa's house was south, the Cileks' farm was east, and that north and west were the opposite directions.

They always stood and listened, then watched Henry's approach. "Just a mile north-northwest now," she said to John Henry. "Pull back a bit, Daddy." Then she took his tiny hand and pointed it up at the plane. "See?" And when Henry flew right over them, as he did sometimes just for fun or because he overshot the runway, he rocked his wings back and forth in a giant wave and Ruth leaned far back and held the baby up to feel the wind and noise.

But one afternoon, tiny, wordless John Henry got a terrible sunburn. Elizabeth scolded Ruth, shaking her head slightly.

"The baby's got to come first, for a while, Ruth. Children are a miracle. If you don't think so, you don't deserve to have them. What were you doing out there?"

Ruth knew about her mother's miscarriages, something close to a dozen of them, and herself the only "miracle." Still, Ruth said what she said: "I don't think deserving has a whole lot to do with it." She gingerly took John Henry from Elizabeth. The baby smiled up at both of them as he passed from one to the other, as if they were two planets that shared a moon. Ruth shrugged, looked at her mother, who had begun peeling apples, and said, "Anyway. John Henry likes it outside. Don't you like to walk with Mommy?" and he laughed a short, piccolo laugh.

"I get antsy, Mother," Ruth said.

Elizabeth nodded, and Ruth thought maybe, maybe she might have something, some reason, some comfort, from her mother.

Elizabeth said, "You'll learn. You'll get used to it."

And Ruth looked at her, wanting more, recalling the one memory she had always kept to herself like the shame of her first bleeding—the memory of her mother gone missing two days and nights one summer when Ruth was nearly nine. Elizabeth had kept her tongue that time and never said another word about the coyotes or a lock for the defenseless chickens, her prized chickens; she had swallowed the fury at her husband, though this fury drove her from her home and family for two whole days; she had swallowed it, come back, picked up where she had left off.

Then, as now, with Ruth grown up and tiny John Henry

between them as they dabbed calomine lotion on his cheeks
to ease his sunburn, Ruth wished her mother would say *something,* tell her what was going on inside, tell Ruth that she
knew this feeling of going crazy, with the house and the
trappedness and the long, straight, flat life that spread out
ahead of her, every morning without end. Ruth didn't understand it, plain and simple, didn't understand why she felt this
way and how it would end, and she would have given anything, anything, to hear her mother, someone, say, *Me, too,
Ruth, me, too.*

October 1929

Dear Mrs. Lindbergh,

Do you ever wish your mother would speak to you honestly—have you ever felt like her holding her tongue has
made things more confusing for you, when they don't
have to be, when you don't have to be alone, feeling such
a way, because you *know* she's felt the same way, only she
won't say so, and why?—there's no good reason.

She scolds me for being antsy, as she calls it, for my wanting to fly with Henry, for wanting to do things besides
mothering John and keeping the house clean and perfect.
But she understands, I know she does. She used to take
great pride in her chickens—they were about the only
thing that was *hers* on the whole farm, besides the kitchen
and the washing machine. She loved them, but once when
I was about nine, we had some coyotes get in to them,
twice, and the second time, as my father had refused to
listen to her and buy a lock, mother was furious. So furious that she left us, for two whole days and nights, and to

this day I have no idea where she went. And I was the one who first saw bloody feathers in the dirt on my way to milk the cows.

At suppertime, she told my father, "A lock would have cost nothing compared to those dead chickens." "Since when are you tracking figures," was his reply. "I'm the one figuring the farm here, Elizabeth. Who told you to put your head to it?"

A little bit later, she told me she was going to town to buy fabric, since I was outgrowing my dresses at the time faster than corn was coming up. "Don't worry yourself about the chickens and the coyote, Ruthie," she told me. Then she walked out of the backyard, around the house, and down the road. And we didn't see her for the next two days. At first, my father suggested she'd gone to visit her sick aunt in West Liberty. And when the bread ran out, he made jokes about how hungry we were getting. Mostly, we played a lot of chess and didn't talk much. She finally came back just after breakfast on the third morning, as I was leaving the barn with the first two pails of milk.

When it was all happening, I just wanted it to be over and it was enough that she came back. Now, ten years later and a mother myself, I can't help but think of that time, especially when she counsels me to "Settle down, give in to being a good wife, and you'll find you enjoy it." "Settling down" seemed like it nearly killed her, if you ask me.

Have you read this essay Mrs. Sanger published in the newspaper a few years back? Don't mistake me—I don't support her "procedure," but she has some interesting things to say. "Women should not have children until they're 23." "Couples should be married for two years before having children." We did the latter, but not the former. I wonder what my mother would say, if she read it. Though I suppose I can guess. It's Mary Hitchens who gave me a copy, although she had her first one before her first wedding anniversary even hit!

I don't think that being a good wife means that the person you were before you were a wife goes away. And before I was a wife, I had hopes and dreams about going places and doing things besides staying on this farm forever. I love this farm, I love Iowa, don't mistake me, and I'm grateful for all the advantages I have—a healthy son and a good husband who loves me, my parents, too, and good, prosperous land all around us—but those hopes and dreams are still there. My mother must understand this, she must know the feeling, but she'll never say so. I feel sure your mother must be different—she couldn't possibly have raised three such smart, talented girls otherwise.

I'll be up there again. If not, I may just turn into a plane. Sometimes I feel my head spin around like a propeller and my arms stretch and go broad and flat. My ribs are wires and my belly is soft and greasy and warm, from the engine and the friction of the air. My feet are rudders and there I go. I try not to be too anxious for that sky, that feeling again, the sound of Henry's voice trying to get over the hum, the creak and moan of the wings, the sheer scream of wind up there, but I'll admit, it's very difficult sometimes. I do love it so.

Sincerely,
Ruth Gutterson
Cedar Bluff, Iowa

The letters, the blessed letters, for which no one could scold her. Because no one, not even Henry, knew. The pilots and aviatrixes knew, of course, though they might as well as not know—they never wrote back and probably threw her letters out. Still, she wrote. And she read more and more about this Anne Morrow Lindbergh, the Colonel's wonderful girl and his navigator, too, Ruth found herself writing nearly every day. Mrs. Lindbergh was a pilot's wife like Ruth and she was small and looked so kind that Ruth dreamed about what good friends they could be. She felt such kinship toward Mrs. Lindbergh and she thought of her all the time, wrote to her almost as much. She'd put John Henry down for his first nap, take a clean sheet of paper and her best pen, and, with clean hands and forearms lest they smudge the page, she wrote. She wrote to Mrs. Lindbergh and she flew high above Cedar Bluff, high above the farm, her life; she flew away.

She devised a system so that perhaps Mrs. Lindbergh might write her back. First, Ruth restricted herself to mailing one letter a month. She'd write as many as she liked, decide which one to send at the end of the month, copy that one until it was perfect—keeping one of the marred copies for herself—and stack all the rest to be burned. When she had time, she went to the incinerator in the backyard and ignited the letters one by one, watched them curl up at the edges and dissolve into bits that floated away, up into the air. Whole, pleasant mornings were spent this way. Burning the letters meant she didn't care too much, she wasn't losing herself, or reality; writing the letters and she was finding, had found herself, all along, all all along. Dear Mrs. Lindbergh: it sang like a whipporwill, sometimes like a lullaby, and sometimes like a breeze, in her head. Absent the cockpit and Henry's strong, guiding hands, and the rush of air and oil fumes and cold against her face, she was transported by these simple words, this incantation: Dear Mrs. Lindbergh.

In the process of setting the record altitude flight of
33,000 feet, Captain Rudolph Schroeder passed out due to
oxygen starvation and carbon monoxide fumes in the open cockpit
of the airplane. At about the same time, the intense cold froze the
moisture around his eyes. With Schroeder unconscious, the plane
plummeted earthward in a six mile dive; Schroeder recovered at
an altitude of 2000 feet and somehow managed to land
despite blurred vision and bleeding from lacerations
caused by tiny shards of ice in his eyes.

—*Roger E. Bilstein*

WHEN JOHN HENRY was just over a year old and weaned from his mother's breast, Ruth begged her mother to watch him a few Saturdays a month so that she and Henry could fly together. Elizabeth reluctantly agreed, sighing and not saying that she looked forward to it. The first day, they flew down over Missouri, retracing the initial leg of their honeymoon flight to Lake of the Ozarks. Early in the flight, Henry spotted a silver flash of light below them that he initially believed was a perfect clear stream reflecting the sun back at them. When he looked again, however, he saw that the stream was moving at nearly the rate the plane was. He squinted far enough ahead that he could see the end of the stream, and before it, a long spurt of track stretching into the future. It was the Zephyr, shooting toward California. Henry reached forward and pounded on the cowling until Ruth looked back at him. Then he pointed down, to the ground below. Ruth looked, maybe she thought it was a stream, too, then she looked again, and finally she smiled and mouthed, *Zephyr*.

Henry pushed the stick forward and the plane slid down toward the ground. He leveled out above the train and flew right with it until he saw two porters smoking cigarettes in between cars. One man saw Henry and Ruth in the Jenny and nudged the other and together they leaned out to the side and waved their handkerchiefs while they squinted up at the plane. Henry reached the locomotive and then passed in front of it. Next, he banked up and flew back, until he had gone behind the train. Again he lined up and slowly passed above. By now, passengers had opened their windows, four porters were standing on the caboose, and everyone was waving white handkerchiefs. At the front of the train again, the engineer pulled the horn once, twice, and reached his own hand out the locomotive window. Henry waved the plane's wings and continued west along the empty tracks. The beautiful Zephyr beneath them, waving to them, mustn't it be, Henry thought, a good portent? Other times, they flew east to Gary and the Lake Michigan dunes; southeast to Galesburg; north to Minnesota.

Early the next year, 1931, Henry bought a decommissioned Swallow from the company when he was offered a good deal on it. The Swallow was a nearly new, lovely plane, more stable and sophisticated than the Jenny, sturdier, too, and, Ruth thought, not quite as exciting. She didn't dare tell Henry she preferred the Jenny. Nevertheless, the Swallow offered her a chance, Ruth started thinking, to learn to fly herself. Three years had passed since navigating for Henry and she had no illusions about returning to that role soon—she couldn't be a mother and a navigator, after all. One had to make choices, and although she hadn't *consciously* chosen to be a mother instead of a navigator, her and Henry's gentle, impulsive couplings in the nights, yes, did constitute a very clear choice. She was a mother first, but that would not change by her learning to fly the Jenny solo.

She told Henry this one Sunday on the way home from church. "I could learn to fly and then you can rest when we go up. Or—imagine!!—we could take the two planes up together!" she said. She was bursting at the thought of it, but she checked herself to gauge Henry's reaction, which seemed to be total surprise. There was more to say, more persuasion to issue. She smiled and tried to be light, not too desperate or too exuberant, both of which she felt: "I wouldn't really fly when you're not home. That's not the idea. I mean, on a very rare occasion, perhaps. And then I wouldn't travel *far*— I'd just go up there, and up and around." She paused; he was still watching her, not ready to speak. She bit her lip, tried to wait for him but couldn't. She blurted, "It would make me so happy, Henry, you know, just to be able to get up there sometimes and not have to ask you, to wait for you. I don't mean to go anywhere, really. Really, I mean it. Just to fly."

But now Henry's face darkened and Ruth knew immediately that his response would not be what she had hoped. He was measured in both his silence and his words. He said she needed to be with their son, not playing around in the Jenny. "What I do, Ruth," he said, "is my job, not play. And yes, I love it and am lucky, but Ruth—you shouldn't be putting yourself in danger like that. I lost both my parents and can't you see I'll never let that happen to John Henry?" Henry shook his head, shifted his grip on the steering wheel as they bumped through a pothole in the road. "Isn't it enough that we fly on the weekends?"

Short of breath, she couldn't even say, *No, it's not.* Instead she looked down at her feet, one crossed over the other on the black floor of the Ford. She spoke with barely any sound: "I know I can't fly with you every day—I don't want that, or no, I do want that, but it's more important to me to be a better mother to John Henry. And I believe I'm doing that. I just thought—we have the Jenny and the Swallow. I thought I could fly the Jenny once during the week while you're away. I don't see what the harm would be."

"The harm would be—that I want my son to have two parents and I have to fly because it's my job. I love it, yes, I do. But it's not a game, Ruth. It's not a pastime. Not for me."

Ruth looked out the window of the car at the other people driving into town or driving home, all Sunday bustle, to rest. Nearly-two-year-old John Henry slept in the backseat. She would say nothing more, nothing about her father having given them sixty acres and being willing to give it all to them if only Henry were willing to farm it; nothing about it being disingenuous and simply untrue for him to say that he needed to fly for the family, that it was their only possible work, nothing about how wretched his words made Ruth feel. She loved Henry because she trusted him, and she trusted him because he was, she had always believed, an utterly honest and unselfish man. Now, suddenly, she felt her world spin, and she felt an anger toward Henry that she had never before experienced. And yet she also felt like a child who had been corrected—angry as she was, she also knew, somewhere, that he was wiser and more reasonable.

As for Henry, his hands sweated as he drove. He knew what he had said hurt Ruth and he felt badly for this, but also nervous. Teaching her to fly—it just seemed dangerous. And yet he felt like he was killing something by refusing her. Her asking, the urgency, the wordless need that he didn't know how to answer—he felt completely powerless and trapped, with no good way out. Ruth wept silently, tears dropping off her jaw and onto her hands in her lap as she faced the window, and Henry noticed the tiny slap of each drop. He thought of how to please Ruth, how to make life good for her, happy. They could move to Chicago, where he'd be with her much more often, he considered, but then he'd break her mother's and father's hearts as well as his promise. He could quit working for the company, but then he'd break his own heart. If Ruth were to fly with him, John Henry would be *like* an orphan, if not, eventually, an actual one. And this made Henry angry, because Ruth knew the stakes. He kept the stories, the crack-ups, from her, but she read, she knew. She knew about the first forty Air Mail pilots in 1918, of whom only nine were left alive seven years later. She knew.

The sickness, the panic he was feeling reminded him of the day Philippe begged him, one last time, to stay in France. He had come to Henry's quarters with the Gershwin albums held tightly under one arm and an umbrella held in the other, pushed against the wind and rain. Rain was blowing sideways and a few drops ran down his nose. His hands were wet, too. As Henry took the umbrella, Philippe dried himself off, the records, too, and a mysterious, flat package, smaller than the records and flimsy, wrapped in brown paper. Then he collapsed on the bunk, looking up at the bed over him, keeping his glance there, away from Henry. "So you're leaving," Philippe said. "It's okay. I do understand your reasons." A smile crossed his face, but a bitter, sarcastic tone crept into his voice: "You go back, you find a woman to marry, and you grow some children."

Henry didn't correct him; nor could he hide his smile at Philippe's awkward English, but his friend was not looking at him. "Why don't you come live in America?" Henry said. "There's plenty of flying to be had there, you know."

Philippe blinked once, slowly, and the grin came across his face again. "You don't really mean that." His eyes, still and unfocused, looked watery, like a birdbath with a blue-painted bottom. "You don't mean it the same as I do, anyway."

Henry watched his friend's sadness and near-anger and he couldn't explain, exactly, everything that was going on. It was confusing. Philippe seemed to be listening, waiting, and he seemed to hear Henry shrug his shoulders and drop his hands. What to say—even if he wanted to stay on, with Philippe, it wouldn't seem right. He should go home. He was an American.

A moment passed and Philippe swung his legs over the side

of the bed and stood up. He took the brown package from the stack of records and gave it to Henry. "Be sure you tell everyone back in America that a Frenchman taught you how to fly," Philippe said.

Henry held the white silk flying scarf up to examine and Philippe took it, and began wrapping the garment around his friend's neck. He took such care in doing this, and was so serious, Henry was utterly quiet. When finished, Philippe looked at Henry for one brief, suspended moment, then turned on one heel, reached and lifted his umbrella, and walked back into the furious, endless brown-gray afternoon rain and wind. Henry stood in the doorway, the rain on his own face now, watching until Philippe was gone, curious if he would look back, and he did not.

Henry had not known what to say then, and he did not know what to say when Ruth asked to fly the Jenny by herself. In both instances, there seemed some danger, a forbidden territory, and no good route in or out. But at least with Philippe Henry had been sure his friend would find his way.

March 1931

Dear Mrs. Lindbergh,

I write to congratulate you on your lovely little boy, Charles Lindbergh Jr.! I suppose you must give up your navigating now to be a mother to Charles Jr. Trying to be a mother and a pilot is just too much, plain and simple. The risks one must take in a plane—well, I don't have to tell you about it. Sometimes I think it would be okay— but Henry and my mother remind me that I need to be home for John Henry, and they're right.

My advice to you, if I can give it, is not to despair too much. Just make sure your husband takes you flying every so often. I have missed flying quite a lot—as much as one might miss a sister or a limb or a sense. I even miss the fear that grips you when you're about to touch down, or when you're dropping down through fog and rain and you can't see the ground and all you can do is close your eyes and hope your husband does not close his. It's a different scare when you think that you have a young son who would be orphaned if your husband happens not to see the ground. But then, you trust him and you get to the ground in one piece and all is well or, no, it's better, because you've been *up there*.

In any event, you, too, will understand these frustrations, I am sure—maybe you already do! Just remember that you are not alone. Flight is sometimes a dangerous opiate to we female pilots with children.

Flying is like a sixth sense to me—and I only need to remind myself that we're only born with five senses so that's all we should need, right? Five senses are enough to enjoy anything.

But, the first time back up after spending days and nights with the new, helpless, innocent little John Henry and his eyes which at first seem afraid of seeing the world, they just squint out at you. Getting back up in the sky and seeing the farms checkerboarded into green and gold and brown beneath you, and the muddy rivers after a rain, and the sun shooting through the wet air. Watching the world tilt as you bank into landing. This is like opening your eyes, your mouth, your ears, everything, for the first time again. I'm not even sure holding my own brand-new, pink, and howling John Henry after he was born is equal to it!! It's a close contest.

Apart from writing to congratulate you on the birth of Charles Jr., I wanted to write today with a suggestion. I wonder what you think about starting a husband/pilot-wife/navigator club? We could have meetings. I bet there's more lady navigators than just you and me—maybe there's even a lady pilot with a husband navigator. Now, that would be something. We could put a notice out and see who responded.

Would you write back and tell me what you think? I think it's a good idea. Good luck with Charles Jr., and again, many congratulations, to the Colonel as well. He must be so pleased with a boy.

Sincerely,
Ruth Gutterson
Cedar Bluff, Iowa

Then she was pregnant with their second child. She was mostly glad, a diversion after the awful fight with Henry that still seemed poisonous several months later. She wondered if this one would be a girl, if she would be as easy as John Henry. She also feared that someday—perhaps after everyone knew and decided that this would be the baby to settle Ruth Gutterson down, at last—she feared that she might feel more trapped than ever. And it was this rare but loud fear in her that kept her from telling her husband about the pregnancy. She told herself she just wanted to be sure, to give it a few more weeks, but really, she simply couldn't say it out loud yet: *We're going to have another.*

She was standing over John Henry, putting his undershirt on, combing his fine hair with her fingers as he stood perfectly still under her touch, then letting him go, and for no reason she remembered about Mary Louise Swift and the doctor she saw after the farmhand climbed in her bed one night and put his hand over her mouth, made her promise not to scream. Ruth was thirteen when this had happened, and all the mothers and fathers in the area had locked their daughters' bedroom doors for a year afterward. Ruth had not been as scared as she was interested to know if the doctor had done anything to make sure Mary Louise didn't carry a bastard child. Mary Louise's mother had told some of the ladies in town that Mary Louise, wasn't she lucky, hadn't been pregnant after all and that they simply went to the doctor for a checkup and then stayed away for some rest. But Ruth didn't believe it. Especially because she saw Mary Louise's face one of the days after her return. It was not a face of relief but rather one of weariness, grief even. Flat, erupted beyond spark.

Maybe it was fear or the other changes wrought by pregnancy itself that made Ruth think of Mary Louise; or maybe there wasn't any reason for her thoughts to go there. Still, it was the case that John Henry shocked her out of thinking about the poor girl—he ran back to her where she was standing, threw his arms around her legs, and exclaimed, "Let's go fishing, Mommy!" with his *sh*'s not yet perfect, so that it became *fithing*. Immediately Ruth felt guilty; immediately she loved her son infinitely more than she'd ever loved herself; and immediately she vowed to overcome her own desires for flight, the world, with devotion to the next child.

She pressed her hands gently around John Henry's head.

She stroked him once, twice, and leaned down to kiss him. She said, "Soon, John Henry, soon."

That very night, while Henry was helping her with the dishes, she told him of the new baby. He put his arm across her shoulders and kissed her on the cheek, on the nose, on her ear. "It has to be a little bit like flying, mothering does. You never really know what lies ahead of you. You just have to keep yourself steady and take the weather as it comes. Hope for the best."

"And you count on being a good pilot," Ruth added, letting her head fall forward so that Henry could rub her neck.

She thought of all the beautiful late summer and fall Saturdays to come that she would spend on the porch swing, in the car, on the grass, away from the Jenny and the Swallow, rolling marbles in the dirt with John Henry, touching, singing silently to her abdomen. And much later, during the dead, black night-morning hours, she climbed out of bed and wrote seven letters, burned all but one before sunup with a single white candlestick over the stove, and returned to bed before anyone, even Henry's arm, which was still extending as if holding her, took notice.

In something like a blessing, John Henry talked—to the extent he could—constantly about the little sister or brother he would have on Valentine's Day and he helped Ruth as much as she would let him during the mornings when she was sick. She found him once in the kitchen, trying to loop her apron around his neck twice. "I was gonna make oatmeal," he said when she found him.

"Stay away from the stove, John Henry," she said. "You're not tall enough yet."

Having seen his father touch Ruth's belly sometimes, and listen to it, John Henry took up these gestures. "It's a baby," he would say with a broad grin on his face.

One Wednesday in the middle of December, Ruth was sick with the baby all day and wondered if the labor wasn't starting early. As the day went on, she knew it wasn't labor, just very late in the term, and she took John Henry into town for a newspaper and some sugar and oleo. The fresh air and the diversion of an errand helped temporarily, but then, coming out of the store, Ruth felt her throat gag. She held on and managed not to throw up. With her throat burning and aching and her head spinning, she got John Henry in the car and started driving, away, not exactly sure where, just *away*. She was suddenly racked with something like claustrophobia and this increased at least twofold the nausea and listlessness.

She drove north for two hours, stopping once at a Sunoco station for a tank of gas and a bathroom break. When John Henry asked why they weren't taking the normal way home—he was only two and a half but he noticed such things—Ruth had merely laughed a fun laugh and told him they were taking a surprise trip. He fell asleep.

Two hours later, he awoke in tears. "Mama, I want to go home. I'm hungry."

"Almost home, John Henry," she said, turning west on some road or another. She gave him the buttered roll she'd bought back in Cedar Bluff to chase her nausea.

But John Henry kept crying and agitating on the seat, sliding down to the cold floor of the car, repeating that he wanted to go home.

She kept reassuring him, reminding him that big boys

don't cry and how good the air would feel when they were there. John Henry would like it, too, she was sure. They turned east, then south again, and when she found they were driving along the edge of a lake, she thought perhaps they had arrived. It was so pretty. They took a road that traced the perimeter of the lake and John Henry said he had to go to the bathroom. There were log cabins, fishing cabins, and white clapboard summer cottages, all so pretty, just as she imagined Little Falls, Minnesota, would be. She strained to see lights, a flagpole, and smoke coming from a chimney. She would tell John Henry, *Just go knock on the door. Ask for Mrs. Lindbergh, Colonel Lindbergh's mother. Tell them I'm a friend of hers and I wanted to visit. I'm gonna make us some sandwiches while you're gone. Just knock and ask. They'll be real friendly. It's okay. Mommy'll be right here.*

And then he was crying again, afraid-crying, not tired-crying, and he had wet himself and maybe it was the smell that finally brought her back, maybe it was hunger, or maybe just pure luck.

They arrived home halfway through the night to find the loaf of bread she'd left in the hot oven disappeared into ashes.

Henry called every day now and when he hadn't been able to reach her, he told himself not to worry. If the baby had come early, he reasoned, someone would've called him. And if she still wasn't home in the morning, he'd call her parents. And if they didn't know where she was, he'd put the plane down in Iowa City on his way back from Omaha and he'd find out what was happening. Even with this plan in place, he barely slept, and he allowed himself to pick up the phone once the clock struck four. Ruth answered, not sounding asleep. She had, in fact, only been home for an hour. "Where you been, Ruthie, I tried to call you all night long. I was worried."

"Oh, we were driving," she said. "It's been so pretty lately."

He said, "You were driving all night long? I called several times. Past midnight."

"Yes, past midnight," Ruth said, as matter-of-factly as she could, without laughing. She did think the whole experience was quite funny. What pregnancy could do to a person!

"It's ten below in Iowa, Ruth. Where in god's name did you drive all night?"

Ruth announced, "Little Falls, Minnesota, to see Colonel Lindbergh's mother. We bundled up and there were blankets in the car," she lied. "John Henry loved it."

"But she lives in Detroit now. You know that. You're the one always clipping articles about them."

Ruth didn't respond to this. "How's work?" she asked.

Henry said he had to go and he'd be home soon. Hanging up the phone, he stood chewing his thumbnail, wondering how he could stop in Cedar Bluff without delaying the mail— or whether he could ask for a holiday. He'd never known any-one to do it. The field manager called to him, and Henry went to his plane.

December 1931

Dear Mrs. Lindbergh,

I have not heard from you yet about the pilot/navigator couples club, but I found an article about other hus-band/wife teams out there and I think I will write to them proposing what I proposed to you. I am sure you have been very busy with the new baby, but I would still like to know if you are interested in joining. I have been reading of your travels to China and South America and such. You are a rare and fortunate woman to have both your children and your flying. As you know, I have not been navigating for Henry since John's birth two and a half years back. I thought mine should be every woman's lot who wanted to be a mother and a pilot. I thought everyone, such as I, would have to choose between the two. You have proved me wrong, of course, and I would thank you for setting a good precedent if I weren't so terribly envious!

I myself miss flying so much I try and forget what it's like in hopes that somehow I can miss it less. Of course it might be easier to convince myself to jump off the roof than to forget about flying. I dream I am flying sometimes, a pure, perfect feather of a Jenny, and I am going forever, I'm never coming down, and then I wake up. Sometimes I think about getting up there by myself. I've been so many times with Henry, I've got to be able to do it myself. I know exactly what he does, why couldn't I?

I am thinking of writing Mr. and Mrs. Omlie of Louisville, Kentucky. Apparently Mrs. Omlie has been a flying instructor since 1920! Also, there's Mr. and Mrs. William Marsalis of Long Island, New York, and the O'Donnells of Long Beach, California. The St. Louis Haizlips and the Thadens. I think this is quite a good beginning and if we can convince this group to join together, certainly they will all know more flying couples. I read that the Thadens have a little boy who regularly goes up flying with them!

We took John Henry up for the first time in October and oh, did he love it. He kept wanting to peer out to see the whole world below him. But I, of course, was panicked about lifting this little guy high enough in the seat to look out. He is quite steady on his feet, but of course you know they're so fidgety and scrambly at this age, boys in particular. Henry was good about turning frequently so that we could see out the side without too much leaning. John Henry didn't like the noise too much—he clapped his hands over his ears much of the time—but other than that he had a big grin on the whole time and his eyes stayed wide and he just kept looking around, at everything, including at me while I held him. I couldn't have been more proud. When we finally landed, he just laughed and laughed and laughed. He didn't want to get out of the plane and when his daddy finally wrenched him free of me, who got out last, he pronounced, "Again, Daddy— again, please!" I think that planes will be so sophisticated by the time he is old enough to fly them himself—he'll barely remember this old Swallow biplane, which is of course brand-new to us now.

I hope this letter finds you all in good health, with especial blessings to Charles Jr.

> And you, what were you?
> I must have been a bird before this life, an eagle
> it is the very essence of life itself
> Flying is living.

Henry said nothing about her drive during Friday dinner because he didn't want to upset or anger her, but when they climbed into bed, he held Ruth close to him, massaged her neck, and kissed her spine through her nightgown. Then, out of the silence of a moonless, windless, dead-of-winter night, he said, "Do you want me to quit flying and be home with you?"

Ruth sighed, barely. She knew he wasn't really offering her this. Instead, it seemed he was daring her to ask for it. She was silent, still.

"But you're miserable."

Ruth closed her eyes, needing to contradict this. "I'm pregnant. It's a little uncomfortable sometimes." Why not tell Henry what was wrong? It seemed to simple so say, *I miss flying*. But also like an indictment of everything she was doing instead of flying—namely, mothering. She said nothing.

From Henry at her back came a whispered plea: "Well, no more midnight drives to Minnesota, okay?" He wanted to sincerely believe that she did not want him to quit his job and instead to farm. But in truth, he did not know what to think. He did not know what she wanted, what her dreams were that were so clearly being disappointed. It couldn't be that she simply wanted to fly more.

The next morning, a bold sun bloomed and warmed the air above freezing, if only barely, for the first time in weeks. After breakfast, they went out with the baby to find a Christmas tree; in the afternoon, they left him napping with Elizabeth and took a walk through the woods along the Cedar River, near where they fished in the summertime. Henry walked with his hand at the small of Ruth's back, barely discernible beneath her heavy coat, in case she lost her footing. There had been little snow that year, and the forest was dry and winterized; no green anywhere on the skeletal trees or on the dormant forest floor. Sticks and leaves cracked and disintegrated under their feet, which was the only sound apart from their breath—small huffs that swam white in the air.

They stopped to watch two deer ahead of them, a doe, and

a stag with the beginnings of antlers, drinking, and Henry asked if she thought it was a girl, the baby.

Ruth nodded, looking away from the deer.

He smiled at her with his head tilted slightly.

There was a grassy spot in the sun and they took a moment to rest on a fallen tree. They ate some of the chocolate bar that Henry carried in his pocket.

"I had another idea, Ruth," Henry said suddenly as the idea, the desire, finally crystallized in his mind, before he had time to think it through and consider whether it was good or ridiculous.

Ruth listened.

"Let's move to France."

"We'll be the king and queen, I presume?"

"Philippe was always saying that there were plenty of flying jobs there."

She waited to see what else he had to say before she reacted. "Well?"

"There's work for pilots here, too. You do have a job here, and a house, and a family, remember?"

"But you'd like it. I've never taken you to Paris and didn't I promise that I would?"

Ruth laughed, and felt irritated. Once, yes, this would've been a dream. Now it seemed crazy. Which was frustrating in and of itself. "Oh, Henry," she said. "Sometimes."

"It's not a bad idea."

"I don't speak French, Henry. And you don't, either."

"We'll both learn, together," he said, but he could tell the suggestion had angered more than excited her. "Say we just went for one year, for a change, and then came back—maybe we'd stay on the farm then. I'd give up flying. That'd make your parents happy enough maybe they wouldn't begrudge us the year away." He looked at the river and the perfect circle spreading near the bank where a fish had surfaced or maybe an acorn had plunged from one of the many oak trees leaning out over the water.

She watched another deer approach the water's edge upriver, catch sense of something, the intruders, his own image in the unusually still water. He dashed off with almost no sound. Ruth said, "You'd learn French because you'd be out working and talking. I'd be home with the children, singing to them in English. I would be lonelier than I am here. It would take us a year to get anything like settled, and then we'd be leaving."

"And what if I could get something that would bring me home at night?" Henry said, bewilderment and frustration burbling up inside him.

"You could do that here."

He put the chocolate back into his coat pocket and drew his hand across his mouth. He sighed. "I just thought you might think France was exciting, that's all."

"I'm not French," she whispered. "I'm not Philippe. I'm not a pilot and I'm not exciting and I don't know much about the world."

"Oh, Ruth," Henry said. "I didn't mean anything like that and you know it. I thought you really might like France, or you might like the change. That's all."

"Okay," she said, and looked down at her hands, not having the energy or the inclination to fight with her husband.

Henry continued, "I've already talked to Oswald about

being with you during the week, maybe managing things in Iowa City."

Ruth's head snapped up quickly. "I didn't ask you to do that."

"I wanted to."

Ruth's glance went back to the river.

Henry let her look; he waited for her to say something.

Finally, he sighed and said, "Do you hate it, Ruth? Is that what it is? You hate being a mother and my wife?"

"Of course not."

"Then what is it? How can I make you happy?" He jumped up, grabbed her hand, and he was angry, but he found himself pulling her up next to him, putting his hand around her waist, forcing her into a waltz despite the large mound of baby in between them, and neither one of them was sure what was happening. They danced. Two full turns, and then he stopped. "I just want you to be happy, Ruth," he said. "It's what we all want." He started the waltz again, and she went right with him. Her head was up straight, almost defiantly. He loved the feel of her belly against his. He loved how far away she had to stand to make room for the baby. They kept dancing and he could feel Ruth relaxing. He became sure that he'd said the right thing. He thought of her belly, how big it was, and he couldn't help but grin. Happiness, relief, anxiety.

"The baby—" he said. "Your belly feels—" He almost let himself laugh then, because he was so sure Ruth would join him and it would be a very good thing for them to laugh together while they danced along the river, in the warm December sunshine that seemed a custom-made reprieve from bitter winter.

But instead of laughter, her stern face broke into tears and she had to stop dancing, and they sat down, first on the tree, then on the ground. He'd never seen it before, her crying like this. Desperate and yet consistent, with a cadence. She curled up like a child with her head in his lap, and continued to cry, albeit softer now. He wanted desperately for her to speak, to explain it all to him, and she would have said something, if she had any idea where to begin, how to describe what she was feeling, but once again, she did not. She wanted to say how much she missed him and how much she missed flying with him, missed seeing a further, broader horizon than anyone else. How much she wanted to do something more. And it wasn't France and maybe she didn't know what it was. She only wanted to feel the world fall away below her, to feel the land flatten out and spread, to have it stay there. Henry stroked her hair and her tears wet his pants legs and there was the dry, vacant smell of the wintering Cedar River all around her. She felt overwhelmed and still and speechless.

After a time, Henry leaned down and kissed the bridge of her nose. "I'll tell Oswald yes, Ruthie. First thing Monday. We'll go home now and tomorrow we'll have a little ride. It's supposed to be lovely and warm again and the air will be still. Iowa City's just filled in some holes on their strip—it's smooth as glass. Can't hurt. And after the baby is born, we'll fly more. I promise. I miss you, too, Ruthie. I miss you, too."

Feeling the steady rise and fall of her breath and seeing the slackness of sleep settle into the corners of her mouth, Henry reached back into his pocket for the remaining chocolate. He ate two more pieces, careful not to drop any on Ruth's forehead. He looked out over the river and imagined his father's boat there, tossing up a mist as the little paddle wheels spun on each side, and his mother standing on the dock with three children hopping up and down to see their father. What he would give for his childhood innocence returned, for the absolution of the unhappy creature who lay in his lap, whom he loved beyond reason. With one clean finger, he pulled back a strand of Ruth's hair, which had come out of its tie and was blowing across her face in the new breeze. For the absolution of his resentment for this interminable, maddening sadness of hers. The absolution of his powerlessness.

SIX

I followed him down, yelling at the top of my voice,
imploring him to wake up.

—One fighter pilot describing a partner pilot
blacking out from hypoxia and hurtling
his plane into the Black Sea

*R*UTH ANNE GUTTERSON was born late in the afternoon of January 14, 1932, a few weeks earlier than expected.
The delivery was easier for Ruth than John Henry had been,
but the baby was only four pounds or so and a little blue. The
doctor, Dr. Greene, new to town from Chicago, stayed
overnight with them at the hospital in case there were diffi-
culties. In the morning, however, when the nurses brought
the little bundle to Ruth, she saw a beautiful little girl with
pink cheeks and Henry's high forehead. They would call her
Anne, for Henry's mother and also, although Henry didn't
know it, for Colonel Lindbergh's wife.

As the little girl squawked in her mother's arms, Ruth's

heart felt as if it would burst with love and fear—she refused to let the nurses take Anne away that entire first day and the baby slept on her mother's breast, at home again near the heartbeat that was the only thing she knew thus far. Ruth vowed that she was going to raise her daughter with strength and courage and fearlessness. The doctors said she had a slightly irregular heartbeat but that those things could correct themselves in time.

"When do I get to see Mommy and baby Anne?" John Henry asked morning, noon, and night.

Elizabeth, too, was pleased to have a new little girl in the family, although she noted the baby's small size with some concern. "I hope she eats well," Elizabeth said as she rocked the crying baby in her arms. "She needs to grow and be stronger, this one."

The first weeks flew by and occasionally her cries in the middle of the night were strange and weak and Ruth would find the baby's breath raspy, but she didn't think anything of it because once the baby was in her mother's arms again they were both at peace. This baby needed her more than John Henry had—she wailed more, it seemed, in pure fear of the world than in any demand or pronouncement of hunger or discomfort. She was like a tiny little bird with a broken wing and Ruth rarely set her down.

When Henry took off for Chicago the Sunday after Anne's birth, Ruth watched from her bedroom window. She imagined exactly what he would be feeling—bumping down the frozen winter field, lifting up with the wind hopefully beneath and behind, the engine crowing, and sunlight angling over, around, and then behind as he turned due east in the

January early dusk. But Ruth did not feel left behind. Anne was asleep in her arms; John Henry sat next to her on the bed, staring at his favorite page of the atlas—Greenland and the Canadian Arctic. Ruth was exactly where she wanted to be.

Henry had told Oswald the month before, as he promised Ruth, that he'd take the manager position in Iowa City, but then the young pilot who could've taken Henry's route got himself killed falling off a streetcar, which left them with no one. "Just hang on with us until spring, when we can find someone else," Oswald had said to Henry. "I did you a favor once—now you can do me this one."

Henry agreed and went to Ruth about it, who said she'd never asked him to stop flying in the first place.

When the Lindbergh baby was kidnapped in early March, Ruth moved both children into her bedroom. She didn't really think that they were in danger, and yet having them there made her sleep better. The kidnapping was so shocking—to Ruth, to everyone. Putting a ladder up to a nursery, *that* nursery, and taking a baby, not even able to talk yet. None of the twenty-odd family members and staff heard or saw anything, not even the girl who wished so much she had that she poisoned herself. It was beyond comprehension. Ruth could only think of the wide frozen cornfield beyond their home that any malcontent could walk his way across with both of her children in his arms, their cries swallowed up by the wind. She locked her doors and windows, even when Henry was home.

To Henry, the Lindbergh kidnapping made the world seem wrong somehow. If such misfortune could befall so great a man and his wife, then what was in store for the rest of them? Henry asked himself. He didn't say anything about

Ruth's moving the children in with them—one of his friends said his wife did this, too, except they had four children! And there was baby Anne's health, too, which meant Henry felt a little better having her right there even though the doctors said she'd get stronger.

March 1932

Dear Mrs. Lindbergh,

I can't believe the horrible, godless act of someone taking your Charles Jr. Now I keep imagining your little blonde curly-haired angel in his crib, making a quiet sigh as he falls into lovely dreams. I refuse to imagine a man standing at the window on a ladder, or gloved hands reaching down into the crib, as I'm sure you, too, try to refuse imagining. You probably are not even opening your mail; there must be so much of it and you must be so weak with fear. But still, I hope somehow you know that I am so very, very sorry for you and your family. And I hope you know that I believe your little angel is alive and well somewhere. I read in the papers that since the whole thing seemed to be so professional, Charles must be in the hands of a good nurse. These horrible people know what they're doing— and they must know that it would be terribly foolish to let any harm come to your son.

A baby is a thing of joy and of beauty. We have a brand-new infant, Ruth Anne, who was born in January. She has not a single hair on her whole head and I always slip a hat on her which is no bigger than the end of one of Henry's wool socks. It's cold here in Iowa—ten degrees below zero for the last three days! We are going through coal very fast. Ruth Anne's middle name comes from you, Mrs.

Lindbergh, although my husband thinks it's for his mother's sister. It's for both, I suppose—but you know, he wanted a family name and I was lucky enough to find an Anne in our very own family!

Ruth Anne's minuscule mouth and ferocious cries of fear and hunger pull me to her from any distance. I don't believe girls are weaker than boys, Mrs. Lindbergh, no matter what my doctor and my own mother tell me. So far, in fact, little Ruth Anne sleeps better, eats better, and cries less than John Henry did. Sometimes I just stare at her. I watch her watching the world, taking it all in, deciphering it. I say to her, "You can have it all, little Ruth Anne. You can go and do and be whatever or wherever you want." She smiles when I say this. She knows that she'll grow up to be in a better world than this one. She wraps her tiny, doll-like fingers around my one giant adult finger and she squeezes it, hard. She hangs on. She's very strong.

I just know that your baby will be returned to you in good health very soon, Mrs. Lindbergh. I can understand that you'll never rest until he's back in your arms. I'm praying day and night for you and the Colonel and of course for baby Charles. I think people all over the world are. As far I'm concerned, God must hear all these prayers. If he answers just one of them, you'll have your baby back. I'm not a very religious person, Mrs. Lindbergh, but I believe he'll answer. We must simply wait and trust. I myself have not had a night's sleep since Charles's abduction. I stand watch over my own children, my windows, my own too-terrified heart, which whispers, *This can't be.*

Sincerely,
Ruth Gutterson
Cedar Bluff, Iowa

Once Henry awoke and Ruth was not there. He looked in on John Henry, back in his own room, sleeping soundly. But Ruth was gone from the bed and little Ruth Anne was not in her cradle. Henry felt scared. He checked the toilet. He checked John Henry's room again. He looked to see that the attic stairs were up—it made no sense, but he wanted *any-thing*, any sign of them. He went downstairs, aware that he could hear his heartbeat in his ears and his hands were sweating. No one in the kitchen, nor the living room. He began to turn all the lights on, no longer concerned with waking or disturbing anyone. Illuminated, the rooms were more devastating; there was no corner they could lurk in unseen, and they simply weren't there. He looked on the floor behind the couch, under the table, anywhere they might not be in plain sight. He ran back upstairs, breathing hard now, and turned the light on in his room, and, ridiculously enough, fell to his knees and looked under the bed. He opened the cedar closet, then John Henry's closet.

And then he was outside—where was the car—had she gone driving? In the garage, where it belonged. The door wasn't even open. He walked around the house. Once. Slowly. He called to her, but got no reply. It was a still, too-quiet, nearly full-mooned night. The lack of wind meant it wasn't too shocking to be outside in nothing more than pajamas, until the cold underfoot began to burn into his toes. Standing out there, straining to hear something, anything, the baby's cries, Ruth singing to her, he remembered the cellar. He ran around to the back of the house—the bulkhead was closed, padlocked since the Lindbergh kidnapping—and so he ran inside, down the stairs, turned the switch to light up the space.

Nothing. "*Damn* it," he cursed, loud enough that John Henry would've heard him if he was awake.

Even with a bright moon he could not see into all the yard's shadows. Should he take the truck out and drive in widening concentric circles from the yard, into the fields, until he found her? Should he drive into town? Head out on the highway and call the police? No, he didn't think she'd meant to *travel* anywhere. She was just *out*, he felt. In the middle of the night with the baby. He could call down to Elizabeth and Paul's. But no, waking them wouldn't help yet. He was thankful, for a split second, that the fields were yet empty and so she couldn't be out among the rows of six-foot corn. *Think*, he told himself.

And then he knew—had he known this all along, would he have realized it if he'd slowed down sooner?—they were out with the planes.

Later, long after, he would be very surprised that he knew this, and that he was correct.

He gathered blankets, as many as each arm could hold, climbed into the truck, backed up, then forward, and squeezed through the gate and onto the field of mostly ruts, going slowly enough that if he came upon them, heading out or in, or, just sitting and looking up at the stars on this forty-five-degree night, he wouldn't endanger them. Yet he had to drive quickly, too, to get there. And there was the Jenny, at last, and swathed in bright moonlight, Ruth in the cockpit wearing only her nightgown. He couldn't see the baby. The Swallow sat beyond the Jenny, slumbering through the night in her shadow. Henry turned off the truck and got out.

"We're off the beam," Ruth called. "Off the beam?" And

she listened for a moment, then called out, "Altitude!"

The baby—where was she?—was silent—asleep?, Henry prayed.

"Altitude!" Ruth commanded again.

"Okay. Altitude."

Ruth did not take note of his voice, but just continued. "Contact, damn it!" Ruth's parents were nowhere to be seen. How couldn't they have heard her? How long had she been there? Her lips were quivering, barely.

"Ruth," he called softly, calmly.

She did not turn.

"Ruth, let's go to sleep," he said, and lifted the blanket toward her. "Do you have Ruth Anne?" he asked.

She looked at him blankly at first. Then she lifted the baby from her lap, up into Henry's sight, and held her to her breast as if coaxing Anne to nurse, and she began rocking gently from side to side. The baby was not crying—she was not making even a single sound. She was wrapped in her sleeping blanket but nothing else. How long had they been out here? He was both eased by and afraid of the baby's utter quiet.

"But we're not tired, Henry," she said. "I'm not tired."

"Let's go, Ruth," Henry said, just firmly enough that fear and confusion came into her blank stare. Suddenly she stood up in the cockpit and extended the bundle of baby to her husband. Henry took it, held her tight to his chest and kissed a cold, dull forehead. Henry's chest constricted as he held the baby tighter, felt nothing, and knew. He looked into Ruth's face, and she was still blank, completely ignorant, and at last he understood why.

A few seconds passed and Henry thought that he would

like it to be a year later, immediately, or a year earlier, ten years, sometime far away from *right now*. Because *now* was suddenly unthinkable, indescribably wide-mouthed and help- less, out of time, so strange. His throat hurt, his neck, and he thought he might vomit. He squeezed the baby more tightly, as if she would object, wail aloud suddenly, fight back. He pinched her gently, then harder, at the back of her neck, and his eyes blurred with tears, and he felt his gut wrench one huge, coughing sob. He was ready to run, away from this, away from Ruth, where he could cry loudly, where no one would hear or see.

But Ruth's blank face, and her hand, reaching out to him only for the assistance of stepping out of the plane, kept bring- ing him back, and he swallowed once, twice, pushing the cry- ing back down. He raised his arm to her while clasping the baby—lifting her so that her head was in the crook of his warm neck—with the other arm. *There*. Ruth climbed out, her thin nightgown billowing in the breeze, and he supported her at the waist with his free arm as she climbed down next to him.

"There you go, sweetheart," he said, preparing himself for her to collapse into him when she got there, to lose herself with him. But she did nothing. They stood there, side by side, doing, saying nothing. Finally Henry went to the truck and opened the door and Ruth got into her seat. Henry walked around to his side, opened the door, and put the keys into the ignition, still holding the baby, as Ruth did not reach for her. She looked straight ahead with the blank and adamant stare that Henry would never, ever forget. He drove back in silence. Such a cloudless, bright shiny night, and they were aware of how nice it would be for flying.

Back in the garage at last, Henry took the baby from his shoulder and cradled her in both his hands, as if she were brand-new again and so fragile. Ruth began to laugh, looking at his feet. Henry was disturbed and angry.

"What is it?" he said in a voice no louder than a whisper, since he could hardly stand the sound of his own voice.

"You're without shoes. You went out and forgot your shoes."

"So did you."

For the first and last time in a long while, Ruth looked at him straight on, at Henry with the baby, and then she looked down at his feet again and tears started falling down her cheeks, hitting her hands in her lap, but she made no sound, and this made Henry angry. He wanted her to rage, to let it out, to be *there*, where he was, with the baby. Instead, the awfulness of her behavior, whether she could help it or not, made him furious.

Henry tried, but could say nothing. He turned away from her and went inside to their bed. Ruth followed.

Of course, he didn't know what had happened, whether Ruth woke up with a mother's sense and found Ruth Anne silent, unbreathing in her cradle, or whether something happened out there in the Jenny. It was easy and right to deduce the former, but the mere possibility of the latter haunted him.

Ruth followed him into the room and climbed under the covers and turned away from Henry wordlessly. Both his feet and hers were filthy and caked with cold mud from the field. The ticking of the cuckoo clock downstairs in the kitchen was audible.

Henry lay there, stroking Anne, not lifting her from his chest, not wanting to look at her, only to feel her, sometimes mistaking his own heartbeat for hers, until morning light. Standing up out of bed, he watched Ruth for a moment and tried to know what was the best thing to do. He wasn't angry right then. Her eyes were closed, though he couldn't be sure she was sleeping. He reached out and tucked a strand of hair out of her eyes, behind her ear. She didn't stir, and he left. He drove into town, woke young Dr. Greene up, and left the baby there because he didn't know what else to do and Dr. Greene was kind enough to keep her. He would be out later in the afternoon to see Ruth, the doctor said. Henry nodded and stumbled to the car. Driving away, Henry felt like he was doing the worst, most hateful thing of his life, but he couldn't keep her back at the house, especially not when John Henry would be up and around.

He was due in Chicago that afternoon, a Sunday, but he drove to the post office from Dr. Greene's and rang Oswald. There was an emergency and he wouldn't be flying, he said.

"It's the baby," Henry elaborated. "She's died."

Oswald said he was sorry to hear it and to call as soon as he could get back. They could make do until Tuesday or Wednesday at the latest. "But again, my condolences," he concluded.

It was the first time Henry had missed his route entirely. When he got home, he found John Henry at the kitchen table, pouring milk over cold oatmeal and all around it, too, on the table. He had a giant soup spoon next to him. Henry looked around the kitchen and pantry and back porch for any sign of Ruth.

"Hi, Daddy," John Henry said. "I was hungry."

"I see that. Where's your mother?"

"Still in bed. I'm an early riser like my daddy."

Henry went over and kissed the top of his head. "You're a good boy," Henry said. "If you want to put that bowl of wet glop out for the dogs, I'll fix hotcakes in a minute or two."

"That's a deal," John Henry said. He dropped his spoon in the glop and it caught a spoonful of milk before it flipped backward on the edge of the bowl and threw the liquid all over the table. Henry was almost angry and then he laughed. John Henry was afraid for a moment, waiting for a scolding, and when he saw his father laugh he started laughing, too. Henry picked up a dishrag and tossed it to his son. "Clean that up before I come back."

"Right-O," John Henry said.

Henry walked quietly to his bedroom and looked in to see Ruth sprawled out across the bed, belly down. She didn't move when the floorboards creaked under his feet and he felt sure that she would've heard him in the kitchen. So it seemed that she was asleep. He sat down on the bed and pushed her hair off her face and over onto the pillow. He watched her back rise and fall, and it seemed too fast for sleeping. He was frightened. "Ruth?" he said. "Are you awake?"

She feigned a sleepy groan and turned her face away from him. She didn't say anything.

"Ruth?" He waited. "John Henry's up feeding himself and making a mess of it."

Ruth said nothing.

Henry waited and realized he felt freer to talk without Ruth Anne in his arms. "Why were you out in the Jenny last night?"

Still, nothing.

"What possessed you to take Ruth Anne out to the Jenny at two A.M. and keep her there while you pretended you were having an adventure? What in god's name were you thinking?" Henry knew how cruel this was but he couldn't stop himself. He wanted to hear her say something, to tell him what happened, to say *anything*. Tears ran down his cheeks and he was afraid of what was happening to Ruth, angry, again, but at his own helplessness, angry that he hadn't woken up last night. He wished he hadn't taken Ruth Anne to Dr. Greene already. He would've held her then, sitting in the chair next to the window where the morning sunlight fell.

Henry moved over to her and her whole body throbbed with crying. He kept thinking that if he had woken up when she first did last night, if she had awoken him—why didn't she?—he could've held her as she found the baby's body still, in the cradle. He could've held Anne and maybe Ruth wouldn't have run away from him to the Jenny, where she still seemed to be. He told himself now, and began to trust it, that the baby had died in the crib—from Dr. Greene's reaction ("She never got over that weak heartbeat") and from his own instinct. It had to have happened this way. He stroked her shoulder and she seemed not to notice and long after he thought she would stop crying, she kept crying and so he lay down next to her and pulled her toward him and tried to form his body to hers, as if to ease the nightmare from her body and into his own. Then he heard John Henry's voice coming from the doorway. "Daddy, what about the hotcakes?" he said.

Henry looked at John Henry's face, which was awash in concern and nervousness at his mother, who was facing away from the door, not moving or speaking. "I'll be right there," Henry said, getting off the bed and going to his son. "Did you give the oatmeal to the dogs?"

John Henry nodded and stared at the floor, every few seconds sneaking a glance at his mother's form.

"Mommy's okay," Henry said. "Now go downstairs and I'll be with you in a moment."

"Where's Anne?" John Henry asked, looking to the cradle at the end of the bed.

"Go downstairs, John. Now."

John Henry obeyed, his thumb in his mouth, shuffling out of the room.

Henry took a deep breath and told himself just one moment more. He kept remembering the moment when Ruth handed him the baby—her body had posture for the first time, too early; for a split second, he thought maybe it was new strength in her, maybe his little girl was growing and getting stronger, since everyone was always talking about how she needed to; but then he realized, of course not. And that moment, the feel of her whole back under his hand, was what would stay with him most clearly, from here on, just as the densest memory of his own mother was the feel of her cheek against his ear, smooth and warm, and her saying, "There, there it goes," and laughing. They were flying a kite, and she was wearing a yellow dress and his father was watching from the shade of a tree.

Ruth hadn't moved or turned. With his eyes, Henry traced the profile of her body, still on its side, and then he went back to her and stroked her exposed arm one more time, and leaned over and kissed it. He left her and went into the hall, where John Henry was waiting, never having made it too far away from his parents. Henry lifted his son up, surprised at how light he still was, and kissed him on the cheek. "Anne is at the doctor's," he said.

They started down the hall, downstairs, back to the kitchen, and Henry tried to set him down so as to cook but the boy clung to his father's neck and squeezed his little legs around Henry's middle. "No. I want to stay here."

Henry sighed and pulled a chair out from the table and sat down with John Henry still clinging to him. "You're a big boy now, John Henry. You don't need your daddy to hold you."

Still, his son held on and Henry let him because he understood his fear and confusion. In fact, he shared it. He didn't know what to say or what to do. He didn't know how to reach Ruth, or where, exactly, she was. What was going through her head? The situation seemed worse than he'd imagined it to be, if that was possible. As he sat there with his son, he felt such weariness, and apathy, too, that he wanted to join Ruth and crawl back into bed without any promise of coming out.

He looked around the kitchen and imagined that Ruth was still pregnant with Ruth Anne; as if it were November of the previous year and Ruth was morning sick, as she had been throughout both pregnancies. He and John Henry had spent several weekend mornings together making hotcakes and playing ball outside. But this wasn't one of those pleasanter mornings. Little Anne was at Dr. Greene's and Henry couldn't get his mind around what was happening. It refused to seem real to him.

"But why?" the boy said into his father's collar.

"Why what?" Henry said, pushing the boy away a little so they could look at each other.

"Why is Anne at Dr. Greene's? Is she sick?"

Henry sighed. "Yes, very."

They made hotcakes and they ate until Henry leaned back in his chair and groaned and John Henry did the same. Ruth still had not come out—had not moved, even, from what Henry could hear. He did know enough to get John Henry out of the house, get him down to his grandparents, whom he realized could be kept out of this no longer.

As they descended the slight slope of the field to the white farmhouse which would be his own in a few years, Henry was grateful to see his father-in-law's truck gone from the driveway. They had never gotten along superbly, but as the years went by and Henry continued to fly, Paul Sheehan had less and less to say to him. His mother-in-law did not seem as angry, but she had never been particularly warm to him, either—although she wasn't warm to anyone, he reminded himself. That Sunday, he found her on the back porch, taking things out of the washer.

"Hi there, Grandma," John Henry said.

She looked up. "Hello." She wiped her hands on her knees. "What brings you down?"

"Oh, we just thought we'd say hello," Henry replied, meeting her eyes and hoping she understood that he wanted to talk out of earshot of her grandson. "John Henry," he said, "why don't you go see how the piglets are doing? I also hear there's a new calf been born since last week."

Elizabeth nodded. "I'll give you some stale bread to toss

the animals," she said to John Henry. "You can feed them if you like. We've named the calf Ozzie."

"Ozzie, that's a funny name," John Henry said, following his grandmother into the kitchen, where she handed him a couple pieces of bread.

When John Henry ran out, Henry decided to be direct and quick. "Ruth Anne's passed away in her cradle and Ruth won't get out of bed. Or speak."

Elizabeth stopped as she was reaching for two glasses. She put her hands back on her hips and took a deep breath as if to steady herself. "Oh, Henry," she said, turning to him finally. "I'm so sorry."

"She's been in bed all morning," he said.

Elizabeth nodded. "When did this happen?"

"Last night."

"Anne was a weak little thing, Henry," she said, reaching for glasses once again, then filling them with water from the pitcher. "We were all afraid for her from the beginning." She handed him his glass and gestured to a bench where they could sit and see John Henry near the animals.

"Dr. Greene said she was weak, too," he said, "but I never felt that way."

Elizabeth nodded again and patted Henry on the shoulder, then let her hand rest there a moment. "Babies die like this," she said. "It happens. And if she was to be sickly, it's better now than later."

Henry nodded, not feeling anything positive, that anything was "better" at all. He knew Elizabeth had had numerous miscarriages before giving birth to Ruth and that she had almost died in her one and only delivery. He understood

where her wise perspective came from—years of bitter disappointment—but he felt none of it.

Later, Elizabeth would tell him that it was a mother's intu-
ition that had woken Ruth up in the night so quietly, and a
mother's grief that had driven her to the fields, crying for
hours with the dead child in her arms. He told her about Ruth
being in the fields with the baby in the night, because
Elizabeth had asked, when she saw Ruth later, why Ruth's
feet were so dirty. But Henry would never tell her, or anyone,
where Ruth actually was, in the Jenny. He was trying to erase
the Jenny from his memory. He was trying to forget Ruth's
stare, her calling, "Altitude," his calling it back to her, and
above all— All of it.

They talked for a few more minutes, and then he said he
wanted to get back to Ruth, could John Henry stay there for
a while? Of course, Elizabeth told him, and when Paul came
home, she'd have him take the boy to look at new tractors and
then perhaps for ice cream. They would enjoy it equally, she
said with a tired sigh. "I'll not tell Paul until later, when he
comes back with John. Otherwise, he'll be no help."

Henry said all right, vaguely impressed by the amount of
will and control Elizabeth, quiet Elizabeth, exerted when she
wanted to. "I'll be up just as soon as I can," she said, patting
Henry on the back as he stepped out the door.

Back home, he looked in on Ruth, who was still there, still
the same, for what, six, eight hours now?, and then he went
out and sat on the back porch and rolled himself a cigarette
from tobacco so old it tasted of mothballs. He waited for
Elizabeth to come, and maybe an hour passed, maybe two.

"I'll go in and see her?" Elizabeth said when she arrived,

standing right before Henry with a basket of what looked like soup and bread.

Henry nodded, started up the steps after her, thinking he'd call Dr. Greene. He heard his mother-in-law's steps above him, and then she called out. "Oh, Ruth, Ruth look what you've done." Then she came to the top of the stairs, although Henry could hear her perfectly from where she'd been: "Henry—bring me some clean towels and washclothes, some warm water, and clean sheets," she said.

So he did. He went to the linen closet and extracted the white washcloths they'd received as wedding presents, and a towel and sheets, too. He got some water from the kettle, which wasn't warm but wasn't cold, either. He went up to the bedroom as if sleepwalking. Elizabeth had pulled covers off the bed and balled up one offending sheet. The mess was all over Ruth's nightgown and he choked on the stench. Ruth was curled up in a ball, rigid, faced away from her mother. She hadn't been sleeping these several hours—none of them, Henry realized—and he had left her all alone.

"There, there, Ruth," Elizabeth was saying, as if talking to the baby. "Henry," she whispered. "Go over and get her to sit up. Help me anyway, get the bottom sheet off." She stroked her daughter's shoulder, the only part of her back which wasn't smeared with feces, and whispered, "Oh, Ruth. I'm so sorry." Ruth stared into nowhere. Her pupils were glazed and her whole face was slack, forfeited, which made it seem as if she had borne the tragedy her whole life, and the life before. Elizabeth knew something of what her daughter was feeling and she knew that there was nothing to say or do except to let time pass and, she hoped, to have another child. She felt Ruth was lucky to have John Henry already. He would be as great a comfort as anything. Still, she feared the Sheehan blood in her daughter, the blood that had seen two suicides in as many generations. Elizabeth took the sheets downstairs to wash, and left Henry with his wife.

"Hi, there, sweetheart," Henry said as he knelt down next to Ruth, who continued to stare, blinking slowly. But she didn't see him, just as she hadn't seen him the night before in the Jenny. He thought he wouldn't be able to stand it, that he'd have to leave or cover her eyes with his hands. He couldn't stand her staring through him like that, and he couldn't stop looking at her, hoping something would change in that stare. But then she squeezed her eyes shut tight like a child putting her face in water.

Henry gently went to Ruth's ankles and started lifting the nightgown off her. She let him, she even raised her hips a bit and then her shoulders and head so he could get it off completely. She kept her eyes closed the whole time, although they were not squinched tight anymore. When it was done, she lay naked on the mattress pad and he saw her beautiful woman's body—hips still a bit thicker than usual from the pregnancy, her belly, slack now, and her breasts, so full of milk that they wet the fabric they pressed against. Yet, like a child, frightened and exhausted, she lay there. And then Henry didn't really think about it, he just shoved his arms in under her dirty back and thighs and he lifted her up and carried her to the bathtub. He protected her feet from the faucet water until it was just the right temperature and then he put the plug in the drain and he let the bathtub fill until just her knees poked out. She curled a bit, hugging the side of the tub as if it were a safe rock in dangerous waters.

He reached down into the warm water and touched his
wife's ankle. There was a flash of resistance to his gently lifting her foot to wash her, but then her leg relaxed and Henry
was able to gently soap her up to her knee and to then dip the
leg back into the water and rinse the soap. She still held on to
the side of the tub with one hand and she still kept her eyes
closed, but she was slowly coming to rest on her back. Henry
washed the other leg and then gently took the hand that was
in the water and began to wash her arm. As he neared her
shoulder, she turned her head away from him and stiffened
and squinted her eyes shut tighter.

"It's okay, Ruth," he found himself saying. "Just relax.
There." When he wanted to wash the hand that was clinging
to the tub, he decided to put her other hand on the other side,
so that she could hold on somewhere, somehow. He did so
and she let him, and then she pulled her whole body to the
new side of safety. Her body was still rigid, though she lay
flatter, less curled, in the tub. She let him wash her arm and
neck and then when he pushed her forward so that her back
was exposed, she whimpered a little bit. He cupped some
water first and lifted it over her back slowly, and then he
rubbed some soap in his hands and set the bar down and
moved his hands across her back, under the water, out, in a
slow, consistent rhythm, circles, hoping to warm her, relax,
talk to her. The smell of feces first overwhelmed the strong
soap but Henry never came close to gagging, hadn't even
noticed the smell since the first and only choke on entering
the bedroom. He thought, It is nice of Elizabeth to leave me
to this, and it is good of Paul to take John Henry. I don't want

anyone to see this, I don't want John Henry to ever, ever know. He thought, I don't know what will become of her or of me, and how can this day end? What will tomorrow be? Then he thought of his baby daughter's body, still at Dr. Greene's, and he assumed the man would come out to see them soon. Why had he done that with Ruth Anne? He could've kept her, maybe Ruth wanted to hold her one last time.

But then he was cupping water up over her back and shoulders and he focused on that and nothing else. Ruth started crying again, those high-pitched exhaustive wails coming from some well within her that Henry half feared and half hated because every cry was like a paper cut—pain so quick and intense it drew his breath away—and he just wrapped his arms around her shoulders, kneeling next to the tub. He pulled her close to him, thinking that he'd get in the tub with her if there were room, if it wouldn't frighten her. Instead, he held her and rocked with her. His wet shirtsleeves, pushed up to his elbows, clung to his upper arms. When he felt her lean back, let herself go in some direction that was vaguely *him*, he put his cheek to her head and whispered, "Sshhh, it's okay, Ruth. It's okay."

DR. GREENE CAME BY in the late afternoon. Henry had dressed Ruth in a clean nightgown and he had helped her to the couch, where Dr. Greene examined her as best he could, concluding that she needed rest and then they would see. "In due time," he said to Henry and Elizabeth in the kitchen, "we'll know what she's dealing with." Then he explained about taking Ruth Anne's body to Bob Martin at the mortuary and added that Bob would wait for instructions—but Dr. Greene couldn't keep the child there in his office, his home, all day and night and he hoped they would understand. He gave them some pills then, to help with the sleeping, he said, which was more important than anything else, and he left. He'd return in the morning.

Henry mixed some broth with the medicine and tried to spoon it into her mouth. She wouldn't take much, but there wasn't much to give. After ten minutes and one or two chokings on the liquid, Henry gave up, hoping she'd gotten the medicine. Elizabeth stood in the kitchen with her arms holding her own waist, looking out the window at the fields beyond.

Paul pulled into the drive at about six and left John Henry in the truck, as he had fallen asleep on the ride home. Elizabeth met her husband outside the house and took his arm and led him through the kitchen to the back porch. As they passed by the living room, Paul Sheehan saw his daughter propped up on the couch, still staring vacantly elsewhere with a towel laid over her shoulders as a makeshift bib and Elizabeth tugged him on: "I have to talk to you," she said. Henry could barely hear their voices out on the porch and then some silence before Paul's one husky sob. And this, most of all, told Henry the gravity of the situation, told him that Ruth wasn't likely to be okay. Her husband still hoped, and guessed, saying to himself, *Maybe*. But her father knew it with one look at her; he knew more.

They came inside off the porch and Henry came out of the living room, setting a bowl down in the sink. Elizabeth suggested taking John Henry to her house to sleep and Henry agreed. "I need a break, to tell you the truth," she explained to Henry. "I'll take the little one home and Paul will stay with you." She kissed both men on the cheek and left.

Alone in the kitchen, Henry feared Paul was angry, ready to explode at him. But Paul looked at Henry until the younger man met his eyes, and then Paul looked into the living room, at Ruth, and back. "I've seen my father and my brother do this," he said. "And I'm not going to watch my daughter, too." His voice was slow and sad but sure, like it was something he would take care of, something he could take care of.

Henry nodded and looked down at his feet.

"This is more than losing that little girl, Henry. Don't you think it isn't. And tell Dr. Greene this." They stood there in some more silence, until Paul added, "Do you want some company tonight? Someone's got to be awake with her. She's liable to run off and hurt herself."

Henry didn't agree that Ruth was liable to run off—he didn't think she was capable of it. Maybe it had been what she was trying to do the previous night but she wouldn't go again. He also could not think what it would be like to spend the whole night awake with his father-in-law, but he knew Paul wanted to be there, he knew he couldn't say no, and he knew he would like some kind of company. "Yes. I'd appreciate that. Thanks."

They devised a system. One would rest wherever was comfortable—in bed, at the kitchen table, outside. The other would sit with Ruth. They would trade off every two hours, and Paul would start. He went into the living room, selected a book of Longfellow poetry off the shelf, and began to read aloud, as he used to, Henry knew, when Ruth was little. "Listen my children and you shall hear," he began.

Henry listened for a while, sitting in the kitchen, and then began to wonder about his job. What would he tell them come Tuesday? Tell them Ruth was very sick and he couldn't travel anymore? He tried to imagine saying, *She's gone off* (like milk, which never turned back, or like a rudder, which returned sometimes with hard prayer?). Henry rubbed his foot along the edge of a warped floorboard. He looked up, at the back of his father-in-law's gray-specked brown head and the deeply weathered skin on the back of his neck.

As Paul read something he knew by heart, he willed Ruth's wellness, her return, with every bit of faith he'd ever known. He felt responsible for his daughter's state—he had thought about not having children because of his father's sickness and because of Matt's dark spells that finished with his leap into the Mississippi. It was a family curse, he believed, and although Paul knew that he, personally, had been lucky, he had never been given reason to believe that Ruth would be. Now that Ruth was sick, however, he knew he was wrong and he wished he'd heeded his father's death and his brother's moods. Ruth was a moody girl, but he had never really feared sickness for her. She seemed too strong, too strong-willed, to be overcome by it. He glanced at Henry and Ruth's wedding picture at his elbow. She was wearing her mother's cream lace dress and the length of it was blowing behind her in the wind. Her veil was off, but she was still holding her bouquet of white flowers and Henry had his arm around her waist, you could just see his hand creeping around at her side. He was wearing his black suit and vest with a straight tie. He was not looking at the camera; he was looking adoringly at Ruth. It was a nice photograph and despite everything—the farm, the baby, every way that Henry had disappointed and angered him—the photograph brought a smile to Paul's face.

Still, he blamed himself. For giving birth to Ruth in the first place; for letting her marry someone who would leave her alone so much of the time; maybe even for keeping her from college, which she seemed to want so desperately. Now she had lost this baby and it could be the death of her. Looking at her on the couch right there before him, seeing that vacant stare, Paul could've been looking at his father in his last days.

In the kitchen Henry rose and retrieved a piece of stationery, then returned to compose his resignation letter. Later, when it was his turn with Ruth, and the medicine had seeped in, she appeared to be asleep, at long last, and he leaned her over onto the couch and covered her with blankets. Then he put another blanket down on the floor beneath her, and lay there quietly, looking up, seeing flight patterns on the ceiling.

SEVEN

Down in the subway express, trying not to cry,
terrified of a smash up. All these people—listless, tired,
already dead. The pale-faced boy, poking his mother, who
read *The Mirror* . . . I wanted to say, "Which one of you
killed my boy!" I spoke to a nice Swede next to me:
"Where do I get off for 39 Broadway?"

—*Anne Morrow Lindbergh, January 6, 1933*

*W*HAT SHE FELT was only a sense of suffocating, like
lead had overtaken her body and was slowly locking it into
place. She knew what was wrong—she knew she was terrified they had taken her baby, because they had taken Colonel
and Mrs. Lindbergh's. If it could happen to them, of course it
could happen to her family, and what would she do then?
These flickers of recognition would come when she suddenly
listened for Anne and heard nothing, when her mind's eye
went to the cradle and, without seeing into it, she saw nothing. Once or twice, she remembered lifting Anne to her shoul-

der in the middle of the night, she hadn't known why, she had just done it. It was a bright moon and she could see Henry's form carving a mountain ridge with the covers pulled up over his shoulder. She had Anne against her shoulder, her little forehead just touching the skin of Ruth's neck.

The other recognitions—of not hearing Anne, of knowing that she wouldn't be in the cradle if Ruth looked—seemed like the beginning of an explosion and then the moment would be over and Ruth was again thinking of the Lindberghs, thinking she needed to protect her own. But then the explosion was past, far away, at the wrong end of a telescope, and no one had taken her baby, she was Ruth, she wasn't Mrs. Lindbergh, and she never would be.

The two days at home were one kaleidoscope, continually turning, of these feelings: suffocation; sadness and furor and fear; a tidal wave of panic; the calm of a tidal wave averted; and great self-loathing.

What she actually saw and remembered included simply the wall and its gentle cream-colored paper with yellow flowers which she and Henry had so carefully chosen; also, the feel of Henry's arms on her back and the cold side of the bathtub. She remembered hearing her father cry, too.

～

THE MANY DAYS AFTER, in the hospital, were blank. She slept in long, dreamless fermatas.

～

Later on, she sat in bed and watched the other patients and the nurses swishing back and forth with bright silver trays.

She wondered how much starch it took to get their hats to fold like that. There was a man across the big room who was tied to his bed. Every now and then he would thrash about and curse and spit and a nurse would come to him and speak with him and he would stop. There was a woman about four beds down who was always crying out from a nightmare. An old man who laughed the diabolical laugh of insane people in books. And maybe five other people just like Ruth, who simply stared about all day.

There was a large window with twenty-four panes just a few beds down from Ruth's. It looked out onto a grassy yard and in the afternoon, sunlight fell directly into the window and made the room warm and yellow. She liked to go there and look at the grass below, which was a pale ebullient green when she arrived and gradually deepened and mellowed during her stay. When she left, there were bright yellow and orange maple and sycamore leaves all around—sycamore leaves so big she imagined they'd float kittens across a pond.

She came out of the great sleep knowing about Anne, knowing calmly. She missed John Henry, who was too young to visit. Henry visited as much as he could, about three times a week. He'd found a job working in the garage in town, fixing car and tractor engines. He also helped his father-in-law with the farm. When he could go to Ruth, he did. The hospital bills were expensive and Dr. Greene had said to plan on a six-month or longer stay. It was important that Ruth get all her strength back.

When Henry came to visit for the first and second and third times that she was awake and sitting up—for he visited many times during the three weeks of sleep—Ruth cried, with quiet tears streaming down her face. They didn't talk about what had happened or what was happening. They talked about Henry's work and the farm and about John Henry. The child missed his mother, Henry said, but he seemed to accept that she had a bad case of the flu—and not a weak heart like his younger sister. Ruth knew that she mostly had been afraid she would die, and so once he started coming to visit, he saw that she would live, and he was all right.

The doctor in Iowa City had told Henry that there weren't many alternatives if Ruth didn't improve with rest. "You can keep her in a hospital for the rest of her life. A home of sorts. You know, she's not violent, I don't think she ever will be. But this could happen again at any time, with just a little stress, and she could stay there. I think you should know this."

When Henry visited and Ruth was sleeping—she still slept quite a lot—he would pick up her hand and kiss it and whisper, "Stay here with me, Ruth. Don't go away. Stay."

By the time summer was in retreat, she had begun to recover. After the fearful silence came a real, gentle calm, and finally warmth and a new patience. They started taking walks outside, and John Henry came. She chatted to him about reading with Grandma and about farming with Grandpa and Daddy. "Daddy took me up in the Swallow," he gushed.

"Where did you go?" she asked, calmly, feeling only terribly sad that she'd missed it—how could Henry do this without her? Well, she knew the answer to this, and it was all right.

Henry, who had looked a little panicked when John Henry first spoke, not having anticipated the moment or thought about what he'd tell Ruth on this matter, said, "Just to Iowa

City one day. Your parents were at your aunt's, and I needed some fuel. I didn't see the hurt."

"Oh, it's fine," Ruth said. "Did you like it?" she asked her son.

"I threw up," he replied.

And Ruth and Henry laughed, and John Henry, too.

She asked Henry how the Iowa City fieldwork was going and the farm, too, and what were their usual days like? "I want to picture it," she said. Henry told her, from dawn to dusk, as they walked slowly, hand in hand, with John Henry running around trees and chasing after squirrels, and Ruth was reminded of the time before they were married, the walks after supper and Henry telling flying stories—how long ago it seemed! Howsoever improbably, there was a similar optimism now, a similar horizon of possibility and hope.

Sometimes they had picnics—in July, they celebrated John Henry's third birthday this way. Ruth relaxed against a tree or in the grass, nibbling on cold fried chicken or sandwiches or pie, while the boy played with his father, and one day in September, with a blanket over her shoulders as her husband and son ran around, she startled herself with the desire to give John Henry a new playmate. She prayed that she could have another, don't let that be taken from her, too. She didn't dare say anything to Henry or anyone else. She needed time yet— time to rid herself of feeling desperate to replace Anne, to have another Anne. Time to get back, to know who she was now.

Her father came to visit sometimes, too, and he brought the chessboard with him. Ruth smiled and let him spread the board out on her lap, pull a chair up next to the bed.

She mentioned that they could play at a real table down the hall, adding, "I should be getting up and about anyway."

But he refused: "You rest."

Ruth knew he had to be thinking that she would eventually take her own life like his father and brother had. But she wasn't capable of this. She didn't believe she had either the strength or the courage for it, for her grandfather's suicide had, in a very strange way, always made her respect him, perhaps because it was an event out of the time of her own life and in some way mythical; her uncle's act, on the other hand, she despised, because she saw firsthand the sadness it brought her father. "Listen," she said once, because she thought he needed to hear it, "I'm not sick like your daddy or Matt was sick."

He shrugged, mumbled that he was glad to hear it. He pretended to simply keep on with the game, but then just before moving his rook someplace, he looked right into her eyes for a moment, looking as if see if he could believe what she was saying, looking and hoping.

After that talk, on pleasant days that weren't too hot, they played chess at the bench in the back garden.

Finally, just after harvest, she went home. Although her mother came every morning and stayed all day the first two weeks, Ruth gradually returned to a normal schedule. She felt and seemed different—flatter somehow—but it seemed she had recovered. Neither Ruth nor Henry, however, was exactly sure what this meant.

Henry was very fearful. He couldn't help but think that there was something specific that had set her off, and that it had to do with being in the house, alone, raising John Henry and Ruth Anne. And so he dreamed up plans, changes for them. He thought about moving them all to Chicago, then he'd be able to be home five nights a week at least, if not more. He could get the Chicago–Omaha route back, which meant he'd see Ruth every other day, or he could take the Chicago–Cleveland route, which meant he'd be home virtually every night. Flying among three different Great Lakes meant for crazy weather patterns. But it was a gamble that was perhaps worthwhile. Oswald had pitched the idea to Henry a few days after Ruth got home: "You're one of the best we got," he said over the phone to Iowa City. "Haven't found a true replacement yet."

"I appreciate that," Henry said. "And I can't stand the thought of leaving the company for good—I hope it won't come to that. But we do need more time to get settled—Ruth's a bit weak yet." Oswald, like John Henry, believed it was some renewal of the Spanish flu they had all known someone die from in 1918.

"The fall is an awful nice time to move up here," Oswald said.

Henry wasn't so much concerned with the promise he'd made to his father-in-law anymore; Ruth's health and the family's happiness were surely more important, and if Chicago, or Timbuktu, for that matter, would make her happy, they would go there and Paul would be all right with it, Henry felt sure. But for the moment, she was remarkably stable right there in Cedar Bluff. She had barely been home for a month, and he would leave her be.

CHRISTMAS CAME, then the New Year, and shortly thereafter, Ruth found she was pregnant again. At first Henry was unhappy because he had been nearly ready to propose a move to her—she seemed strong and rational enough to consider it. And then he was fearful because of Ruth's unhappiness during her previous two pregnancies. But the look on her face when she reported the news—pure, serene pleasure—persuaded him to put aside his qualms. Everyone else expressed concern at the news—her parents, Dr. Greene, the women in church. To all of them, Henry simply said, "She wants this baby and she deserves some happiness. She'll be fine and she wouldn't like you worrying so much." As for his own disappointment— Oswald and the company couldn't wait forever for an answer, he'd have to turn them down definitively, at least for now—he told himself he could bide his time well enough.

He wondered about taking her flying again. She hadn't asked to go, nor had she mentioned flying at any point while in the hospital. Before Anne's birth, he had refused to teach her to fly the Jenny alone because it was too dangerous and because he felt that she would have flown away eventually, not just around, as she'd said. What if she'd known how to fly the Jenny that night with Ruth Anne? He would have lost both of them, wife and baby daughter. And inasmuch as he knew he had tethered Ruth to him, to her family, to this place, by refusing to teach her to fly alone, he knew it was the right thing, lifesaving, to have done.

She'd said nothing about wanting to fly since her sickness, and Henry didn't want to upset her by suggesting it, but the further she got into the pregnancy, the more difficult it would become. If she wanted to fly, the time was now. So, over breakfast one sunny Saturday, he asked, "Would you like to go up in the Swallow today?"

"Oh," she said, surprised. "No. Not with the baby. And I've got too much to do today."

"Tomorrow, then?"

"Henry, no, I said," Ruth replied, her eyebrows furrowing.

He studied her closely as she stirred her coffee. She didn't say anything further, nor did she frown with unhappiness. "Let me know when you want to go up," he said. "Just say the word."

Ruth looked at him with clear, serious, and rather blank eyes, said nothing.

Henry, surprised, let it go at that.

RUTH TAUGHT JOHN HENRY to play chess that summer. Just as it had taken her father's mind off waiting to plant, the chess took her mind off waiting for labor. Her belly felt stretched and her belly button was inverted so that it poked out like the tied-off end of a balloon. She was far bigger than she'd been with the previous two. John Henry was five and eager to play a grown-up game. They didn't have their own playing board—just the hand-carved pieces that Ruth's father bought, somehow, for her tenth birthday, which were lined up on a shelf in the living room—so they went together to the lumber-yard to get a piece of two-foot-square plywood that was sanded at the edges and corners so as not to give splinters. Then they dug out the can of light blue paint Henry had used to paint his name on his plane. Ruth found a ruler and they drew with a pencil a grid of one-inch-square blocks on the board. They painted the board very carefully in the front yard, John Henry crouched low over his work and Ruth kneeling on all fours—using one hand to paint and the other to balance the odd weight of her belly. Anyone who could see her would have thought how strange she looked, crouched like that as if she were shooting marbles.

John Henry's natural watchfulness and competitiveness made him a very good chess player. Ruth taught him by twice stating aloud her every move—once before and once after. By the end of the summer, she didn't need to do this anymore. He could play.

⟶◦

IN EARLY SEPTEMBER 1933, labor came on like a slow cold front, visible from a great distance, and they made it to Iowa City with plenty of time to spare. Margaret was born as healthy as a straight, leafy sapling, and six days later—Dr. Greene wanted Ruth to stay two extra days, just to be sure of her strength—Henry brought them home to Cedar Bluff and to John Henry. Strangely, Ruth felt as if this one were a bigger homecoming from the hospital than the last. She felt relieved to be home again and the new little girl slept in Anne's old blanket as Ruth lowered her into the bassinet Henry had set up in their bedroom. It had seemed right to keep Anne's things, and seeing new little Margaret wrapped in something that had held Anne made Ruth glad.

She looked around the room with her old eyes, and she recognized memories of the time before the sickness, but it felt like walking through a museum with objective, safe detachment. Nothing threatened to overwhelm her, not even happiness. She sat down on the bed and pulled the bassinet toward her, reaching in and rubbing the teeny baby's back gently. When she looked up, she saw Henry and John Henry watching her and she gestured for John Henry to come to her, tiptoeing so as not to wake the baby. "Meet your sister," she said.

"Always sisters!" he said cheerfully, in a full voice despite his recent and careful tiptoe. Margaret awoke and began squawking in earnest. She was lovely and sweet and quiet and watchful and Ruth was more grateful for her than she'd been for the others, not that she loved them any less. This baby lay in one position for hours on end, sleeping, then waking and simply watching the world go by as if she were a census taker. Ruth had dreams for her, she would be able to fly if she wanted to; she could do anything. Amelia Earhart and Mrs. Lindbergh and Jackie Cochran and so many others had made it easier for her.

John Henry doted on Margaret as if he were the mother himself. He wanted to change her diapers; he wanted to put her to bed when she moved on to bottled milk. And he would read to her—stories from his schoolbooks, history lessons, anything. Henry also doted on his baby daughter, taking her downstairs to the kitchen sometimes early in the morning when she was awake and her mother needed more sleep. He would sit by the stove with her and sing the lullabies he had sung to himself every night for years after he stopped being able to remember exactly what his mother's face looked like, although he could remember her voice. Margaret watched him sing with her shining gray eyes on him and her mouth sometimes formed into a perfect O as if she were sucking on an imaginary straw.

All in all, she was not as much of a shock to Ruth's system as either John or Anne had been, and this was perhaps because Ruth herself was changed, not wholly, of course, but something, some tension wire, had been clipped. Watching her everywhere around him, with him and without him, intimate and not, it seemed to Henry like something in Ruth had been numbed, or decimated. She was calmer, this was true, and he was thankful for it, but he didn't know whether to believe it or not, or what its full ramifications were.

"Take it easy on yourself, Ruth," Dr. Greene had said the morning before she checked out after her sickness. "Keep in touch with me, do you understand? Come in and talk if you need it."

"Oh, I will, Dr. Greene," Ruth assured him.

"Well, if you ever need anything, if you ever start to feel bad again—be sure to come to me right away." He squeezed her hand.

Ruth thought of the man across from her in the mental ward who had been turned into a child after they cut into his head. It was a new surgery, the nurse had said.

"I'll be fine," Ruth said firmly, and Dr. Greene said good-bye.

November 23, 1933

Mrs. Charles Lindbergh
England

Dear Mrs. Lindbergh,

Although we're barely to Thanksgiving, the cold's already familiar this year. It set in early, mid-September, and some of my pumpkins froze on their stalks before Halloween. You always grow more pumpkins than you want to anyway, they're like weeds, so it was all right that a few perished. Anyway, it does seem like a year when cold *would* set in so early. It does not seem like a year when God is sitting on the porch, letting the warm, sweet twins, August and September, trundle around endlessly in the grass, chasing fireflies. No, He seems more interested in His more severe daughter, Winter, and all her accompanying thrift and chill, and she's come for a good long stay this time. From the window over my kitchen sink, I can look out over the field where we rotate corn with soybeans. I look at the stalks hunkered down onto the ground, and the field looks so tired I want to go out and sing to it. I want to think of a song to sing that will make us all feel better about the cold and this wretched world. We're due for snow tonight.

Henry's airstrip is just in the middle of the north field and he says the ground has been rough as rocks for nearly a month now. We didn't have much rain this fall, which is too bad because it's tough when everything freezes dry. My father prays most nights for a wet spring.

I'll tell you a beautiful sight I have, no matter what season: a nearly perfect row of maple trees, bounding the top of the farm. They were a fiery red-orange a month ago, but now most of those leaves have fallen on the ground and been blown around. From now until March, this line of trees will stand as dark as pencil drawings up against the early winter gray sky.

Henry manages to get up and fly quite a bit, even though he's not flying the mail anymore; instead he's a mechanic at the Iowa City field. He quit his route several months ago after being away too much. You can't blame a man for wanting to see his wife and children every night, I suppose, and after four years of me and John Henry staying home while Henry piloted for Mr. Boeing, he said it was time to find some aviation work closer to home. You see, when he flew the mail, he had to stay in Chicago through the week and then come home to Cedar Bluff on the weekends. Now, Iowa City is only about twelve miles west of us. There is a good road nearby, and in our Ford, he can get there in less than a half hour. His work there means they'll let him put his Swallow in a hangar from time to time. And the runway there, of course, has a beacon and some lights. After seven years of tying the plane up in the open field, rain or snow, heat or frost, our Jenny is much worse for the wear and hasn't moved in a few years. Now that Henry's got his Swallow and his job in Iowa City, I think he's wise to use the hangar space.

So you see, things are working out for us small-town, country aviation types. Henry's had quite a few people come down to the field for lessons. I think that in thirty years or more we'll see equal numbers of people with pilot's licenses as driver's licenses. When you see planes like our little Swallow, you see how easy it can be. We don't have anything so fancy as your Sirius, Mrs. Lindbergh, but then again we don't need one. Henry hardly flies out of Iowa much, let alone across oceans, like you do. So the Swallow does him just fine. Henry says that if we ever wanted to fly to California in the Swallow, we certainly could. I don't fly these days so I don't know myself, but Henry seems to like it.

I'm sure you don't know that I sent a condolence letter right after Charles Jr.'s disappearance, a year and a half ago, in the spring. You must've gotten so many letters, from important people, the Guggenheims, President Roosevelt, the Morgans, the Rockefellers, and the Astors, plus all the other people you must know from your father's life as a diplomat. I know you've been all over the world, Anne. Before you met Charles, even. I have often been envious of you. Very envious. And so I'm sure you received so many letters wishing you comfort in the sadness of your loss, that you could never have known my letter was among them.

I had a chance to go to a good women's college, St. Catherine's in Minnesota, but my father would not let me go, even as yours encouraged you so much. How I wish that my father raised me as yours raised his daughters! My father believes that a woman does not need education because she should stay on the farm, raising the family and helping her husband her whole life. College does not help with these things, he says. He is a good man, my father. Simple and direct and full of love he doesn't always know quite what to do with. I guess that's men for you. But also, he is stubborn as a mule in tall grass next to a clear, cool pond. The things I could have done or been if I had a college education like you, Mrs. Lindbergh. I could be a better writer and I could write things that influence people, as you and Mrs. Amelia Earhart Putnam have done. Maybe I could've been as good on a radio as you and maybe I could've convinced some man, my husband even, that I was indispensable in the rear cockpit.

You know, I had a baby who was nearly exactly the same age as Charles Jr., her name was Ruth Anne and maybe you remember the letter where I told you that her middle name came from you, even though Henry didn't know it. She was taken from me right after Charles was taken from you. At first I thought this was a terrible, terrible

coincidence—that we were both victims of the same
tragedy of fate. But then I realized my baby was taken
because I had been ungrateful at the beginning of my
pregnancy and because I was angry with you for having
Charles Jr. You see, I have always envied you immensely
because you have remained your husband's navigator
while I could only fly for one short year and a half before
John Henry's arrival kept me home. I saw that I was bur-
dened with children and family responsibilities and you
were not. And then I thought, maybe one can never have
everything and so maybe Mrs. Lindbergh's flying all the
time would mean that she would never have children.

I consoled myself with this; yes, I wished that you never
would have children. I wished there was one part of your
life that I didn't envy so much my eyes burned when I
looked at photographs of you and Charles, next to the
Sirius in Greenland or Cuba or London. I love my children, you see, I love my children with everything that I
am, because they are all that I am. I might have chosen to
do more flying, more navigating, but I was not able to do
both, as you are. You have continued to be able to fly—
and my gross envy caused me to think that maybe you
weren't given a choice, either—maybe it was your destiny
to fly and not have children as it was my destiny to have
children and not fly. I trusted in the law of things by which
I was a woman meant to have children; you were a woman
meant to fly. This was well before Charles and Ruth Anne
were born—this was after you and Charles were married
and mapping all those transatlantic and transpacific routes
around the world. You can see how it was easy to be convinced that you were destined to fly, not to have a family.
I believed, at the time, that no woman could do both. This
made my terrible, aching desire to fly hurt less.

When you gave birth to Charles Jr., I was proven wrong. I was angry and jealous and confused. I hated you, even while I admired you most of anyone in the world.

I was always a good woman, not perfect or pious or any one of many *better* things I could have been. But I was always, at the very least, kind and benevolent. But you, the things you experienced, the gifts you received such as only God in heaven could give—my envy of these things changed my onetime goodness. Drained it entirely out of me.

I became pregnant and gave birth to Ruth Anne. Even then I still loved you as much as I hated you and I gave her your name for her middle name. And I was happy and at ease with my baby even though the pregnancy was very difficult. I felt blessed. I had a beautiful baby girl and a sweet little boy. I thought the pregnancy had been a trial and my lovely Ruth Anne was a reward for passing.

Jealousy is a natural emotion, Mrs. Lindbergh, and although it may upset you to hear me say I envied you so much, you should also know that I always corrected these emotions. But when your baby disappeared, I couldn't halt or stop or control the way I felt anymore. I felt so terrible because I believed that I had wished for the horrible fate your baby suffered—no, not the fate he suffered, but the fate you suffered as his mother. I was getting what I darkly imagined at one point—a measure of fairness, which declared to you, as it had to me, that we could have one but not the other. Children or flying, not both. You got the strife that it somehow seemed I had hoped for. And I knew, almost immediately, that I would have to repair my thoughts, even though I never said them to any-one, even though I would hardly let myself have ill will towards you and your family except in the very darkest of dark Iowa nights in my own dark heart. And almost immediately, my repair was made. Ruth Anne was taken from me.

It was April, although brisk even for April—two nights earlier, my daffodils froze and keeled over, stiff as blades. Sometimes I think, we don't realize how dark our hearts can be, how much goodness can run out of us, until a mirror is lifted, until our darkest wishes are granted and we can see them in real life in all their wretchedness and shame.

We have been blessed with a brand-new baby just two months ago. Margaret Elizabeth. She carries the grace and beauty and peace of her older sister, who, I have no doubt, is navigating baby Charles around the heavens in some gleaming silver plane like the one Howard Hughes has been flying.

It comforts me a bit to think that you have not suffered alone, that I have suffered with you. For I have suffered a similar tragedy, even though you bear no blame for Charles Jr.'s death and I bear every blame for Ruth Anne's. I know what it is to hear a cry in the middle of the night and you think, half awake, "Oh, little Charles is hungry." And you then go in to the nursery and it is only when you open the door that you remember it is Jon, not Charles, that Charles is gone. I know what it is like to stand there and close your eyes and ears and to try and conjure up the sound of little Charles's cry, to imagine his face. And you realize you cannot.

I try to put Ruth Anne square and forever in my memory. I try to be sure that she is there. That I know *how* she was different from John and Margaret. But she's faded already. I see Margaret's little pale face and big gray blinking eyes and she reminds me of Ruth Anne, but I couldn't tell them apart. I have already nearly forgotten Ruth Anne but for the ache, which is, I know, of guilt and selfish longing, that seems a new organ in my side. When their absence is more than three times as long as their lives, how can we say we do not forget them?

The doctors and Henry tried to tell me that Ruth Anne had a hole in her heart. She was born with it. It was amazing she lived as long as she did, Dr. Greene said. But I don't believe him. I put the hole in her heart with my envy and my ungratefulness. I know this. And the only consolation I have for this little angel who used to sleep with her lips puckered, as if waiting for my nipple or a finger or another set of puckered angel lips to meet hers—the blisters she used to get from sucking so hard!!—the only consolation I have is knowing that she is with Charles Jr.

I do feel that I have paid my debts and this gives me strength. I will never be so greedy or envious again. I will never again wish more for myself than that I be a good and loving mother. It is quite a lot to bring children into this world and to love them and raise them to think well of the world, to love each other. It is not so much for me to give up fiddling around with maps and compasses and sextants in order to love my children, the children I have been blessed with.

I will not write again, Mrs. Lindbergh. I admire you still and I will always admire you and think of you, not least because our babies are together in heaven. There are many things about our lives that have brought us close together. And if I could go back and change my foolish, envious, young heart three years ago, oh, I would. I would do that before any other single thing—I would turn down any chance at being the first person to fly around the world nonstop if I could simply go back and change what I wished for you once upon a time. I would rather have our babies back than be Amelia Earhart, Colonel Lindbergh, and the Wright Brothers combined. Man in flight is a wondrous, lovely thing. But nothing, nothing, can compare to the wonder in a newborn's eyes or the eagerness in a one-year-old's reaching grasp. Nothing, no science, no discovery, can match these things. It is my great shame that I ever wanted anything more than these children, these beauties.

Forever in your regret,
Ruth Gutterson
Cedar Bluff, Iowa

Margaret was halfway through her first year when Oswald called Henry one more time, said there was one last job he'd offer him and then he'd stop trying. It was his old route again; the young kid who'd replaced him—the same young kid, awfully enough, who'd asked Ruth for directions to St. Louis even though she'd never been there—had crashed just outside Omaha in a bad storm, and died. "I know you'd like something to keep you closer to one field—but it's all I've got."

Later that night, as he stood with Ruth in the kitchen, folding bed linens, both of them enjoying the relaxed silence of sleeping children and tired adults left to themselves at last, he mentioned the phone call. "What do you think about moving to Chicago?" he said. "Oswald offered me a job a year back, and I had to turn it down, and now he's offered me my old route, which I'd only accept if we lived in Chicago. As soon as something comes up where I can be home every night— like Cleveland—I'll take it. But with this, you'll see me four or five nights."

Ruth considered this, working still, not looking at him. "And if we stay here?"

"Well, I think I won't take the job if we stay here. I don't want to be gone so much as I used to be. And he's said it's the last job he'll offer me."

Ruth folded a towel and brought it into her chest, hugging it there. "I'm fine, Henry," she said. "I'm truly fine. Fly for UAT if that's what you want to do—I think I could endure your absences. But I'll not move to Chicago."

Henry sighed and looked into his hands. "Why not? Once upon a time, it's all you wanted, to leave Cedar Bluff. I've half wondered if any of—" He stopped short of blaming Ruth Anne's death on their living on a farm outside a small town— it was both cruel and inaccurate. "I've just wondered what might have gone differently for us if we'd moved to the city right away and we weren't apart so much."

"If you're asking me to explain what happened and why," Ruth said, her face darkening, clouding with every second, as she set the towel atop a stack of towels and started to pick them up, "or what's changed—I can't say I know. I just know I want to stay here, next to my parents. This is home to me and it's a good place for the children to grow up. It's what feels right."

Henry sighed, feeling weak and overwhelmed. "I don't want to go back to how it was," he said.

"Then find a job that will let you come home to Cedar Bluff every night, because I'm staying right here. Daddy's going to give us the big house in a few years when Margaret's grown bigger." She took the stack of towels then and left the room, leaving Henry alone with one of the dogs asleep near the stove. He'd offered her a real plan, a real offer, sensible, even, and they could do it if they wanted. It seemed like the natural time, the natural advancement in their lives, and a little exciting besides. There was sense in her reaction, if it didn't contrast so clearly with what she'd wanted before her sickness. It was the difference, so stark, that bewildered him. Ruth's new quiet calmed Henry to a certain degree, but he missed her spark, her insatiable energy and enthusiasm, her bravery. It was these things that he had first fallen in love with that day at the end of the drive; these things that he had imagined would sustain them through his own less brave and honorable moments. Some nights, now, since the sickness, he watched her sleep. Other times he watched her move about the house, putting the children to sleep, finishing up the dishes. In watching, he searched for any sign that she hadn't lost her old self, that she was merely storing it away for a time when she could bear to feel it again.

In bed that night, Ruth spoke into the moonlit darkness: "I don't know why it is I've changed my mind about this, about feeling like I can't leave Cedar Bluff. But it is the way I feel, and I'm sorry if it angers or disappoints you," Ruth said, and tears began to slip down her face.

In that day's mail, to boot, she had received back the final letter she'd written to Mrs. Lindbergh, the first since the hospital, since Margaret, and the last, she had vowed, overall. But the letter came back to her "return to sender" and it was difficult, impossible, to tell whether it'd even been opened. Not across the top, anyway, as with a letter opener. And now, much as Ruth wanted to write again, apologize, she knew there could be no more. It was dangerous, this letter writing. She could make a diary with such letters, yes; but she'd write to no real person, from now on, if she must write at all. What, after all, if the Lindberghs came after her? They could contact the police if she tried to write again. She had to stop, and she could stop. Yet the *weight* of it all, the imagined humiliation, the sadness and longing she already felt for the friends she would have to abandon. She wept harder.

Seeing the reflection of her tears in the moonlight, Henry rolled toward her, gathered her in his arms, pulled her as close as he could, kissed her head, her ear, her neck. "No, Ruth. No," he said. "That's not it."

She cried softly, cried out what she had, and then slept, for which he was grateful. He lay awake, listening to an owl hoot from high up in the oak tree over the garage. Could they stay in Cedar Bluff forever, and would she fly again? Would he?

HENRY STARTED THINKING about crop dusting and about teaching flying lessons not too long after he turned down the job with Oswald. One of the guys in Iowa City reported that they'd had some inquiries about flying lessons, after the local newspaper ran a little story on Henry and the Air Mail. As for the crop dusting, he'd heard that some of the mail pilots did it on the side, and there was a man in central Illinois, over near Springfield, who had a big business going now with work across the whole region. It was actually Paul who'd heard about him from another farmer with family down there—and he told Henry about it, who called immediately.

"The money's good, real good, especially after the first season, when farmers see their yields go up—double, even," the man said over the telephone when Henry called to see if he could ask him how he got started. "And I'm not charging farmers so much—it's just that it's easy and fast, so I can do five or six farms in a single day."

The man was kind—more so once he determined that Henry was far enough away never to compete with him— and he invited Henry down to fly with him for a day. "You have an old Curtiss Jenny?" the man said. "That's what I fly. And I know where you can get one for a hundred dollars or so—less, maybe—and she'll do you just fine." Henry told him it was a Swallow he hoped to use and the man, somewhat surprised, said that would be fine, too. Henry eagerly accepted. He told Ruth he was going to an old pilot friend who was sick and that he would be back the following morning—he wanted to be sure the money was good and the plan was viable before telling her and, by proxy, the rest of the family.

The crop duster was named Martin McDonough and he had come to Illinois from Ireland only fifteen years before. "But I fell in love with flying right away," McDonough said. "Of course you know they've got a nice airfield here at Springfield, and I used to come over and get free lessons in exchange for delivering coal for their stoves and occasionally looking at their linen wings—my family knows textiles, you see. So I learned and then I read about some fellow in Texas

spraying his wheat for grasshoppers with an airplane!"
McDonough had a long, chortling laugh that emanated from
his belly and shook his voluminous beard—Henry wondered
how he could fly, in fact, with such a beard. "I could hardly
imagine it," he added, still laughing. "But I looked into it, and
now here I am, 'Martin McDonough, Farmers' Friend,
Insects' Enemy.'"

They were standing in the Springfield airfield office and he
gestured to an empty table, where they both took a seat. He
took a folded-up newspaper out of his shirt pocket and
showed Henry an advertisement with McDonough's plane
and the slogan written across it.

"That's nice," Henry said. "Did it work?"

"It's the *results* that work," McDonough exclaimed, leaning forward. "I've got a *waiting* list, my friend." He continued talking, explaining to Henry what sort of farms did well
with crop dusting, how frequently dusting was needed, how
to sell this idea to the farmer. "They're beginning to hear
about this. So hopefully people won't think you're as crazy as
they thought I was at first. And even if they do think you're
crazy—it just takes one season of results for them to stop
laughing. These are hard times," McDonough said. "No
farmer can scoff at what our work can do for them."

Next he took out a piece of paper on which he had drawn
a very careful diagram of his plane: there were two long barrels attached to the belly of McDonough's Jenny and wire
pulls that ran from the barrels into the cockpit such that he
just had to pull on one side or both and the pesticides would
spill out over the crops as he flew over. "You'll see it for yourself in just a few minutes, but I thought I'd lay out the plans

for you here—you can take this with you, too, if you want. I'm sure it's adaptable to the Swallow."

"That's very generous of you," Henry replied, putting the plans into his own pocket. They walked out to McDonough's Jenny, and they climbed in, took off, and dusted three farms over about two hours. Just as amazing to Henry as the actual dusting mechanism was the closeness to the ground at which McDonough flew. He couldn't have been more than twenty feet up. And the low, precarious turns he'd have to make at the end of the field! Sometimes a tree was there, or a utility line—this wasn't *easy* flying and Henry didn't like the feel of some of McDonough's moves—McDonough missed some of the Jenny's cues of protest and Henry found himself white-knuckled in the second seat. He also didn't like the smell of the stuff that was coming out of the belly of the plane. McDonough had a fancy mask; Henry had only his handker-chief tied over his mouth and nose. Despite all this, it was nice to be in a Jenny again—since Ruth Anne's death, the new Swallow gave him as good a reason as any to leave the Jenny where he'd pushed her to one June day several years before—in the shadow of the barn.

When they were done, McDonough flew them back to the Springfield airfield. They drove to a restaurant in town and McDonough tried to estimate how much money he had spent when he started. He also gave Henry the name of a farm products dealer whom he could call to get good information about which insect killer to use and where to get good bar-rels—scribbling all of this on the back of the plans he'd given Henry. They ate beef stew and toast and had coffee, and crumbs peppered the Irishman's thick, coarse beard. "Not everyone has the stomach for this work, you know," McDonough said. "It's dangerous, a bit," and Henry thought, Not everyone flies as badly as you do.

"But you're still game?" McDonough asked.

"I've had some experience," Henry replied.

"Oh?"

"I flew the mail for a while."

"Indeed," McDonough responded. "I'll say you have experience." He shook his head, amazed—and annoyed?—Henry couldn't tell. McDonough got back to eating, and was quiet.

Henry tried, but couldn't think of another single question to ask. Eventually, McDonough started talking about the airfield and its possible growth and Henry listened, nodding. At last, they paid the bill and McDonough reached out, shook Henry's hand firmly, and wished him luck. "There are more and more of us all the time," McDonough said. "I'm glad to help in any way I can. And you stay safe. I'll try to do the same."

Henry thanked him and estimated that he'd have just enough time to fly home and surprise Ruth with the good news. The skies had been clear on the way over and there was sun until well after seven in the middle part of May. He felt hopeful and virtuous—he believed he had found a way to continue flying without moving to Chicago. He couldn't wait to tell Ruth. He would be at home every day; and he would be flying every day; she could perhaps fly with him as much as she wanted. He felt, at last, that they might be all right after all, safe, and maybe Paul, too, would be pleased. Henry wouldn't be farming, but he'd be helping farmers.

He wondered what Philippe would think of the crop dusting—probably he'd find it both absurd and wonderful. Flying adapted to help something else in daily, mundane life. But then he'd find the barrels on the belly of a plane, ruining her beauty and symmetry, awful. With all the trouble and sadness of the last few years, Henry had looked back to easier times and France quite frequently; flying with McDonough, too, made him think of Philippe and how nice it was to have a partner in the plane. As he flew home to Cedar Bluff that evening, he thought of all the flights they took together when they no longer pretended to be having lessons—down over Marseilles and Monaco, flying low and seeing people look up, interested or worried, not quite used to civilian aviators buzzing overhead. A few times they landed in a bumpy field north of Nice where Philippe had some family and they spent whole afternoons and evenings walking through vineyards and eating magnificent meals with wines and meats and cheeses that Henry was slowly learning to appreciate.

Henry always missed having a partner in the cockpit—he missed Ruth, too. He had never had any letters from Philippe after leaving, and perhaps this was to be expected, since Henry knew that his friend was angry with him for leaving. Why hadn't Henry stayed? Because France and Philippe did not offer any of the things that Henry wanted from life—a wife and family, and not, preferably, on a war-torn continent. His happiness in France, with Philippe, was the happiness of youth and adventure, not permanency, and there was no logic to staying, although Philippe had done his best to convince him otherwise. "You like it here, I know," Philippe had said one day to Henry in the stables. "And you could have a bright future here. But you must decide that you want it—that it's for you. Listen to your feelings." He pointed to Henry's heart. "Don't go back to America unless you feel like you must. In there." Then Philippe took a long drag on his cigarette, looking away. When he turned back, he said very quickly, "You must also feel that you are sure you want to leave me."

Henry heard every word of this, and didn't respond because he knew he would never be sure that it was Philippe he was leaving—and yet he would go anyway, and this insistent departure held the truth and clarity that Henry couldn't speak. He left France to find a wife and start a family in America, and now he'd done that and he loved her without reserve or doubt; but still he missed Philippe, even after all these years, and especially after all these years—the difficult ones particularly. He missed the ease, the fun, their youth.

Until the day with McDonough, he had never thought of contacting Philippe, but the crop dusting idea got a partnership into Henry's head and he considered this for a while, about how he might present it to Ruth, to Philippe himself, and he wondered how in the world he would be able to seriously ask Philippe to move from France to Iowa for crop dusting. He would write a letter to Philippe, he decided as he flew home. He composed the letter in his head. But then he landed, came back to his senses as he was chocking the plane, and laughed himself to tears. He didn't need a partner, anyway, he told himself—and if he did, then surely Ruth would be willing in a few years, when the children were older. She had been enthusiastic about the idea when Henry told her. He explained it all to her over a game of chess and after she asked a few questions, saw how easy and sensible it was, he watched relief and happiness sweep over her. "I think it's a wonderful idea," she said. "It's perfect."

July 1934

Dear _____,

Henry proposed moving to Chicago, but I refused. I've learned, haven't I?, that Cedar Bluff is where I'm meant to stay, that I should be grateful for it. And so I am. We're making a life here. A good life. And now, Henry's had the brilliant idea of using his plane for farming—to spread fertilizer and insecticides. And if I had said I'd go to Chicago—he never would've come up with this. We have it all now. Right here in Cedar Bluff.

Mary Hitchens *does* know how to enjoy herself. She had some of us over for lunch this afternoon and I can't remember the last time I laughed so much. We played a few card games, first gin rummy, which I like well enough to play with Henry, late at night when it's quiet, but I don't enjoy quite so well at a party. After lunch, Mary had us playing charades with song and book titles and film stars and we could hardly breathe for laughing so much, especially when proper Alice Jaczys mimed a baseball player for "Take Me Out to the Ballgame." She hiked up her skirts and squatted down like she was swinging something and Alice, oh, she's ever so serious, and she looked serious doing this, too, her dark eyebrows pushed together, so concentrated, so believable. Mary was the first one to laugh and then the rest of us couldn't resist, couldn't contain it. No one guessed "Take Me Out to the Ballgame"— Jacqueline suggested "Casey at the Bat" but we all agreed Alice had the best acting abilities of any of us.

I admire Mary because she seems so at ease with herself, so reasonable and happy. Never moody. Her smile is so genuine, so patient and generous, and she always knows just when to call on me for a chat or a walk. She miscarried a child, her second, and now she won't have any more, and then, yes, as anybody would be, she was distraught and spent many weeks in her house, going out only when she knew she wouldn't see anyone. But then, eventually, she was better, and as her friend, I knew she was all right. I wish our children could play better together, but her Thomas is three years older than John, and you know how boys are—they have no time for the too much younger, the too much smaller ones. And since Thomas is their only one, Margaret'll have no peer there.

It would be best if Henry and Tom Senior were friendlier, but Tom is an (over)careful, judgmental man and he believes Henry is haughty and takes advantage of both my father and myself. Of course, that means we're letting ourselves be taken advantage of, which is neither correct nor a terribly respectful opinion for Tom to have. But Mary's so even, Tom's opinion doesn't weigh much on her and she tells me it shouldn't bother me, either. "You're the most honest woman in this whole town," she tells me, although I can't see she's particularly dishonest. "You should keep being who you are, both of you, and you shouldn't bother yourself with Tom's opinion, which is mostly about Henry being an outsider, if you want to know the truth."

To tell *you* the truth, I think this was all said to make me feel good. She's like that, Mary is. She strokes people, makes them feel calm and good and secure.

You'll like that after "Take Me Out to the Ballgame," Anna was given Amelia Earhart to charade and after dancing around with her arms spread, as if an airplane, she pointed to me, and Mary cried out, "Pilot!" and Elizabeth said, "Aviatrix," and Alice said, "Mrs. Lindbergh."

Margaret's just eight months old, and what a miracle she is. She's so perfect I can hardly try to write about her, as I'll not do her justice.

The early years of Margaret's life were the early and hectic years of Henry's crop-dusting business, and time seemed to evaporate around them. He continued to ask Ruth if she wanted a ride; he asked her every few months for several years; he even suggested that she get her private pilot's license. "I'm the head instructor," he finally reminded her, pleaded with her, one night in the summer of 1940 as they sat on the back steps watching their children in the yard. He wanted her to fly again. He wanted it *desperately*, he realized, as he sat there on the step, feeling anxious and a little angry that she hadn't been up in a plane with him in eight or nine years. Margaret was not quite seven and John, just eleven. They were running around catching fireflies in the lingering dusk of a June evening. Margaret, with more tentative and gentle hands, caught the glowing dots of insects more easily than her older brother did. But then he slowed down, too, and quickly accumulated a colony of five fireflies in his hand cage. Crickets and cicadas clicked and chortled and Margaret squealed a little every time she caught a firefly: "Oh! I got two now!" She came over to her mother and father and opened her hands to show them, but she was too slow and both bugs escaped, glad for freedom. "That's okay," Margaret pronounced gamely. "There's millions out here." She ran off.

"Have you been thinking about my suggestion?" Henry said to Ruth when Margaret was gone.

"That I get my private license?"

"Yes."

"Not this whole time, I haven't been thinking about it, no," Ruth said.

"So?"

"Oh, I don't want to do that, Henry," she said. "I'm not interested." She looked away from him, at one of their cats, who was stalking something in slow, measured steps along the house. In the dark, Ruth could barely make out a grasshopper leaping forward; the cat pounced, but missed.

"Why not?" Henry said. "You used to love to fly, and—well, you haven't flown at all in, what, eight years."

"It's closer to ten years. I just haven't wanted to," Ruth said. "And I still don't want to. That's all."

Henry did not entirely believe what his wife was saying. She seemed remote, even though the rationale for her not wanting to fly was obvious: the night with Anne in the Jenny. He knew that Ruth was angry, frustrated, with him for pushing the point, and he was angry in return. He wanted her to change her mind. He wanted her up there with him. It would ease his guilt. "But you love to fly, Ruth," he murmured. It was all he could think to say. "You loved it so much I can't believe you're able to change your mind about it. It was everything to you."

If he understood her, Ruth thought, he would understand that loving flying was just the problem, it was what had gotten her in all the trouble and sickness in the first place. She believed it was better if she simply did not fly again. Not in the near future, anyway. She half believed that someday she would wake up and trust rather than fear the burning desire to be back up in the air, with ground spreading out below her and clouds coming down to meet her and her stomach and head doing cartwheels of giddiness and gravity. In her most vivid dreams, she was still flying. She flew alone over an ocean and the blue rippled beneath her with occasional whitecaps and there was no land on the horizon, but she was not afraid. She flew with Henry and they had a plane with pontoons on it and they landed on a lake, a perfect mirror, which they skidded across as if on ice skates. They made love in flight, in the Jenny, the wind rushing around them and the roar curiously absent, so that they could hear each other's pleasure. She flew in her dreams, and when she awoke, there was a profound calm. Sometimes, she closed her eyes and willed herself back to the dream, and she could get there.

Henry watched carefully, looking for some betrayal of her words in her face, some hint that he was right, that she was pretending, somehow; he looked for some way in. But no. Her mouth cemented in place, her eyes sparkless and tired. And he felt his anger become tinged with sadness. He missed her. He missed that part of their marriage. Watching her hair blow under the helmet; her smelling like flight; and the way she talked after flying, the silky, confident calm that came into her voice.

"Just listen to me, Henry," she said on the steps that summer night in 1940. "Listen to my words. I'm not getting in an airplane. Not now and maybe not ever."

Henry listened, felt provoked by her tone, and spoke before he thought what to say: "Don't be such a coward, Ruth."

In the echoing silence that followed, it occurred to him, at last, that maybe he'd been wrong about refusing to teach her to fly the Jenny by herself—maybe he'd not saved her after all.

EIGHT

Fly slow and stay close to the ground.

—Advice given to the World War I American
flying ace Edward Rickenbacker
by his mother

D<small>R.</small> G<small>REENE CHECKED</small> in on Ruth as he could, which meant that when he saw one of the children for a chesty cough or a sore wrist or for shots, he would find a way to ask Ruth, privately, how *she* was doing. Once, in the winter of the year when Henry had called her a coward, Ruth told him she hadn't been feeling very well, although it was nothing physical, not her stomach, not her head, not her monthly that was bothering her. It was sleeping, she couldn't get to sleep, no matter how tired she was. It had happened, this sleeplessness, she explained, maybe three times in the last month or so.

"What do you do?" Dr. Greene asked.

"Oh, you know. I drink milk. I read. And if it's really bad, I cook things," she replied. "Bread, cakes, a roast once."

The truth, which she didn't share, was that these spells were spent standing in the kitchen, staring at the clock, and watching seventeen, eighteen, fifty-seven minutes sweep by. Just standing there, not moving, but feeling like she could burst into something, into nothing, at any minute. During the latest spell, only a few nights before seeing Dr. Greene, she had gone outside and run around the house a couple of times in hopes of chasing away her fear, the pressure, maybe *trying* to explode. It was winter, there was snow, and she was in her bare feet. It seemed desperate and silly even at the time but the snow felt wonderful and clean and shocking and better, better than standing before the clock.

And then the dog started barking, and Margaret peeked out her window; seeing a woman running around in a white nightgown, she thought it was a ghost, so she screamed.

Ruth looked up, caught her fearful daughter's eye, waved, which was perhaps the wrong thing to do, and came inside to calm and comfort her. She felt terrible but also thought it was funny. "It was Mommy, sweetheart, Mommy was out there looking for something," Ruth said as she tugged the distressed, half-asleep child on her lap. "There was a little kitten out alone in the snow and I thought I'd bring it inside to warm up."

"But where is it?" Margaret said, looking around. "Where's the kitten?" She was crying harder now. "Let me see it."

"Oh, darling, I didn't find it—she must've gone back to a cozy place with her mommy."

Little by little, the child relaxed, trusted her mother, and fell back asleep. Henry got up and asked what had happened.

"Bad dream," Ruth replied.

He stroked little Margaret's head and went back to bed. Ruth stayed with her, rocking slowly, kind of sleeping, until dawn.

It was all fine until the breakfast table in the morning, when Margaret announced, like it was the day's news, "Mommy was out running in the snow last night, looking for a kitten, and I saw her and thought she was a ghost and I screamed."

"That was your dream, Margaret?" Henry asked.

"That was no dream," Margaret said, as dramatically as a six-year-old can.

Henry looked over at Ruth as if poisoned. "What's going on?" he asked later, while they were doing dishes and the children were dressing for school.

She looked him straight in the eye, this was the only option, and said, "It was nothing, really. I just . . . well. It was nothing. Don't worry."

Henry kept looking, kept asking for better reassurance.

"I knew what I was doing," Ruth said slowly. "It was nothing. I couldn't sleep was all. I thought the snow would feel good."

She turned into Henry's nervous stare and he looked away from her, saying nothing.

"Henry Gutterson," she said, grabbing hold of his arms with her dishwater-wet hands and making him look her in the eye. "Imagine that you can't sleep all night long and that there's been four or five perfect inches of snow falling all the time—you've been watching it, how beautiful it is—don't you think you might, sleep-deprived, be tempted to run out into it, just for a moment? Just to be there for a moment instead of in front of the kitchen stove, thinking about not sleeping, listening to the tick-tock of the clock?" She raised her face and kissed him then. "I'm fine, Henry. *Fine.* I didn't mean to give Margaret a scare. It was silly of me. But how could I know she'd wake up and look out her window at three A.M.?"

"And if she hadn't?" Henry said. "Would you still be out there now? Frozen dead?"

Ruth burst out laughing, convincingly, and she felt Henry give way, too, and a smile crept into his face. "It was damn cold out there!" she said. "Do you think I'm a lunatic?"

Henry shook his head, smiling, letting her kiss him again, but not joining in her big, full laugh.

When she spoke obliquely to Dr. Greene about it, with no details of that particular night, he tried to press her further, ask her what, if anything specific, preceded the bouts of insomnia, and how she felt the next day and if she slept the following night, but he could tell she was done. Just that she was having trouble sleeping. "How often has this happened?"

"Oh, only two or three times."

But he didn't believe her. He watched her small, dense, expressive face, one strand of her brown hair conspiring to hide her secrets by falling forward out of its braid. Her bright eyes, shutting him out.

Dr. Greene sighed and ran one hand through his constantly mussed hair—if he pushed her too much, she might never talk to him. He wrote down the name of a mild sleeping agent that she could get from Nurse Conlin at his cabinet in town. "I hope you know that you can always come to me, Ruth," he said, looking up at her from his notepad. "If there's ever any-thing you need, anything at all. It's better to get to things early, you know, to talk about them when you can make people understand." He didn't want to sound like he was threatening her, and yet he wanted her to hear that she could find herself back in a hospital if she didn't take care of herself. Dr. Greene knew Paul and Elizabeth Sheehan and he liked them. They were the sort of people who got through tough times by denying their existence. This may have worked for them; but it clearly did not work for their daughter. She mustn't ignore this. He closed his bag, slipped his coat and hat on, and gave instructions for Margaret's cough, which had brought him to the house.

Ruth told him that she'd take good care of everyone, herself included. "I'll just have Henry give me a good whack on the head if this potion doesn't work," she joked, and Dr. Greene looked at her askance, smiled just at the creases of his mouth. "Ruth," he said, "Just be *careful*. Mind yourself."

She smiled—what a ridiculous thing for a doctor to say. "All right," she promised. "I will."

And then she could tell he, too, wanted something else from her, some better reassurance. Her husband, now her doctor. Why did she have to make them feel better when she was the one who'd been sick? "What I think, Dr. Greene, is that life is life," she said as she walked to his car with him. "And after a while, after some good things and bad, there comes a balance. But you know—you can't ever really feel the balance, right in the moment. How can you? It's not a feeling, balance. Not an emotion. I think if you feel the good and the bad, all the way, without being afraid, then in the end, somehow, there is balance. " She opened the door for him.

He looked at her for a moment, then up at the house.

"Okay, Ruth," he said, seeming to decide against some broader comment. He kissed her on the cheek, which shocked her. Then he got in and drove away.

For the most part, she lived by what she said to Dr. Greene that day—she learned not to look at her life in terms of a perfect happiness or even a perfect middle ground. Life was life—a mixed bag. Everyone always wanted to be flying; the whole world wanted that feeling of floating west on a clear morning with the sun at your back, all the time. It's just that no one, really, got to have it.

Along with this understanding came a settling into fits of sadness that, yes, did return, albeit not like before. She didn't fight them—easy into them, easy out of them, she found— and this gave her a kind of courage. It happened like this: she would find herself curling up on the floor after the children left for school. Curling up on the floor of the kitchen and watching the sunbeam coming in over her head, watching the heat ripple out of the stove to her right, seeing the dirt that gathered where the floor met the wall. She'd stay for ten minutes, a half hour at most, until she knew she had to get up because if she didn't get up, she was sick again. And it worked, she'd get up, stretch like she'd just taken a much-needed nap, and go out to the garden, where she'd kneel and tie up tomatoes or plant more beans. If she found herself again in tears out there, well, then the wind would blow off the back field and dry her face. If she was in the house somewhere, then she let the water fall into the soup she was making or into the laundry, dirty or clean. The tears disappeared in the boiling stock, burble of soapy water, or warm cotton. This was fine. Fine. She could stop, it just felt good to let go a lit-

tle, and the next day, she might as easily be laughing, humming a song Margaret had brought home from school.

Always, there was Henry and the children to focus on, to
come back to. A beacon in the night fog, far away sometimes,
beckoning her home.

~———o

THE HUNDRED-ACRE PARCEL they now owned (since John
Henry and Margaret each received twenty acres for the first
birthdays) was bigger than she could measure on the horizon
with her arms outstretched. In 1941, they swapped houses
with Elizabeth and Paul and the "big" house, the house Ruth
had grown up in, now hers again, fit in two cupped hands
when she looked down at it, south, from the opposite end and
high point of the farm, at the beginning of the airstrip. A large
boulder there marked Ruth Anne's grave. The land sloped
gently to the west, too, where the creek was, and clumps of
elm trees defined the eastern property line, where their land
met with the road, and across the road was the Cileks' farm.
Water traveled well over this land. From time to time, her
father had to reinforce the drainage ditches so that the water
didn't take over and start running any course it liked. She felt
her life was like this sometimes, and the sadness, the urgency,
was endurable so long as she didn't let it get too far out of
bounds. Give it a course, keep it there.

She was still writing her letters, but she had ceased to send
any of them, not even one a month. Mrs. Lindbergh must've
been frightened with so many letters before—it was almost
cruel of Ruth to have written them. And besides, since Baby
Lindbergh's death, the woman wasn't likely opening any

mail. But Ruth was used to writing the letters. She liked writing *to* someone and it was a secret place she went to, that no one knew about, just Ruth. What used to be a sanctuary from loneliness, these letters, eventually became a sanctuary of privacy, too, and maybe that's what children and a husband at home do to you, they climb into every nook and cranny of your life until you have to search, to boot them away with a swift kick in the bottom, to have something, anything, to yourself. Writing the letters was the place she got to be alone. She kept them in a milk crate atop the previous, sent letters, as a diary. She kept going with the articles, too, which she clipped meticulously like treasures and glued down into scrapbooks for the children. They were such good stories, after all, and the children should know that history—because it was their father's history to some extent. She kept the article books next to her new desk in the fancy parlor of the "big" house; they filled up twice as fast as the photo albums.

October 1941

Dear _____,

Henry took me to Chicago about a year ago for a short vacation, just three days—I'll not move my family there, but I enjoy a weekend in the city—Mother looked after the children. We went to see a play and ate a few wonderful meals and generally slept late and walked along the lakeshore. One day, there was a fog so thick you could dish it up and serve it with pie. You couldn't see the water from the top edge of the beach, where we were, nor could you see the grassy fields, or the drive, beyond us. It was walking in a cloud, with the sound of the lake lapping quietly, as if asleep, somewhere in the cloud. Although it was cool, the moisture made our hands slick. Henry said the mail planes, even, must be grounded.

There came a man, then, in a three-piece suit and hat and umbrella, held in the crook of his arm. A real dandy, and any other day, we might never have noticed each other, but with the fog, and nobody else out walking, coming upon each other felt like being in a private home. So we looked each other square in the eye, you know, like you'd never do otherwise in Chicago. Of course I saw something familiar there, and he thought so, too, and so we looked at each other again. Dean Cilek, as a child, would never look anyone in the eye, so I didn't for the life of me know who this familiar stranger might be. It's so lucky, then, isn't it?, that he said first, "Ruth? Ruth Sheehan?" Yes, I told him, it's me, and I knew by his voice, his low and wide and semi-deaf speech. "Dean?" I said, and he nodded, his eyes cast to the ground like the old Dean.

"Dean Cilek," I said again, grabbing ahold of Henry's elbow in alarm. He'd been gone from Cedar Bluff for twenty years, and most of us had given him up for dead, if not in actuality, then in our lives, anyway. He was lip-reading, I could see, so I was careful to speak slowly as I introduced Henry Gutterson, my husband, and then I wrote it clearly on the pad he extended to me.

"Daniel Clark," he wrote back, gesturing to himself. He then insisted on taking us to the Drake for tea, where he told us, in talk and a few notes, about the hoboes he'd run away with for two years, who treated him more kindly than anyone would believe, until the time he landed at the St. Francis in San Francisco as a valet, "where they liked me because I was quiet," Dean, or Daniel, said. Now he was manager of the whole St. Francis and had been sent to Chicago on business. I couldn't believe how good he looked, how successful, and who would've guessed it? Henry couldn't share the surprise, so he just enjoyed the couches and the tea and the views at the Drake. Dean asked about his parents and mine, too, but insisted I not say anything about seeing him. "I trust you, Ruth," he wrote. "Please."

How I wished that afternoon would last, that Dean would come back to Cedar Bluff from time to time! The truth is, I did write to him a few times at the St. Francis. But over, say, the last six to eight months, all the letters have come back, unopened, with a note that no Daniel Clark or Dean Cilek is there. First I thought Dean was just refusing me, but slowly . . . I don't know. I think he was making it up, everything or nearly everything he told me. I don't even know sometimes if we really saw him at all. He came out of the fog and went back into it, vanished, and what was there to prove we ever met and had tea?

"Seems like kind of a cheerless man," Henry said to me later that night. "Yes," I agreed, although I felt angry for saying it, and why couldn't anyone help him? As much as Dean looked well, *however* he did so, well kept, well-to-do, there was the same old sadness there somewhere, the flicker in his eyes that never quite took.

The funny thing is, the awful thing, he was a happy little girl those first years of his life when his father insisted he wear dresses and braids and work in the kitchen. He was rough and tumble just like you'd imagine a boy in girls' clothing to be—but he was a kid, as happy as any other, if more isolated in his own, muted, awful world. It's when he was made to change, when the betrayal was made known and suddenly it was boys' clothes and fieldwork, and people in town looking at him so strange, not being patient with his ugly words, that everything went awry for Dean. I don't think he'd rather be a girl, not ever, it's just that at an age so much younger than the rest of us, an age when he couldn't possibly withstand it, he learned that we are what others ask of us, what they want us to be, not what we *are*.

John Henry was twelve and a half when Pearl Harbor occurred. Although everyone assumed the conflict would be over long before John reached draft age, his father decided nevertheless to start his son in a thorough course in engine mechanics and in flight. All his life, the boy had been getting occasional flying lessons in the old Swallow, but Henry wanted his son to have a true head start on the Army Air Corps if they ever got hold of him. He began by installing a stick and rudder pedals in the second seat. Then, starting in March, when there wasn't usually ice on the wings, Henry woke John on Saturday dawns and they drove to Iowa City, stopping for coffee and rolls along the way and arriving at the hangar soon enough to be the first ones up. Bob Davis, the field's fuel man, did not think there was much an old mail pilot and crop duster could teach a boy about flying a P-51 or P-47. "Rolling in a Swallow over Cedar Rapids isn't too much like a Corsair or Mustang rolling out from the fire of one of them Zeros or Me 109s," Davis said to Tracy Gruendel, who manned the radio.

"Some might say that if you can roll a Swallow, you can roll anything," Gruendel countered. And then they both watched with their hands shading their eyes from the piercing early morning sun as the Guttersons accelerated to their left, or west, and lifted off over the marshland adjacent to the field, then over Highway 1, and on toward Des Moines.

Henry pronounced John Henry ready to solo after about three months of Saturdays and Ruth made his favorite meal—meat loaf and mashed potatoes and beets and carrots and pecan rolls—to celebrate. For dessert, there was a tall cake with an airplane carefully drawn in green and blue and red and yellow frosting. It had taken most of the day to get it all ready, and Margaret helped in peeling potatoes, sifting flour, and greasing cake pans. Henry did not give his son anything to wear or carry for good luck, mainly because he couldn't choose between his first flight helmet, an old Air Mail Service jacket, his pilot's license, compass, favorite gloves, or Philippe's white scarf. Ruth caught him ferreting about one day, asked what he was doing, and laughed a little at her husband's sentimentality.

Driving to the airfield, Margaret chattered, asking John Henry where he was going to fly that day. Did he think he'd make it to Chicago or San Francisco? No, John Henry told her. He wouldn't even fly to Cedar Bluff and back. "But that's, that's nowhere at all. That's hardly going anywhere."

"He'll go thirty miles or so, in total," Ruth said, smoothing her daughter's light hair against her head. "That's quite a trip for his first time alone." John Henry was quiet, watching the land pass aside his window. He didn't want such a big deal made of it because, for starters, he was barely thirteen and eighteen seemed quite far off. But even if the war lasted so long and he was called up, he wouldn't fly for his life after that, as his father had. He just didn't love it as much. He loved science—biological science, physiology, the human body. He would be a doctor, not a pilot. As for his first solo flight, he was anxious to be done with it, to have that pride, and to please his father, but he hoped his father would not make too much of it.

"I'd go to San Francisco if you let me get up in that plane," Margaret said, even though she never expressed much interest in flying.

Henry smiled and Ruth laughed. "Me, too, Margaret," Ruth said. "Me, too."

Paul and Elizabeth came, too, and they all sat on a bench outside the hangar from which they would see John Henry take off, circle down southeast over Lone Tree and Hills and Kalona, and then circle west and land to the east again. "Easy as pie," John Henry said confidently as he ambled off to the plane, his father next to him with an arm slung across the boy's shoulders.

There was a small sentimental good-luck speech, and then John climbed into the Swallow, Henry heaved the propeller, then pulled out the chocks and stepped away. John gathered himself together, taxied out onto the runway and down to the end from which he would depart to the east. He stayed there for a moment, and the rising drone told everyone that he was slowly easing the throttle back while keeping his foot on the brake. The plane began to move down the runway, picking up speed, until finally, with plenty of runway left to go, he pulled the nose up, and the Swallow lifted into the air.

Henry didn't take his eyes off the plane as it turned slightly south to head southeast over Lone Tree, as planned. Within a couple of minutes, the plane was out of sight. He jogged back to the group, where everyone was standing with their hands cupped over their eyes, scanning to the west and north, where he'd be coming back into view.

"He's doing beautifully," Ruth murmured to her husband. "He must have got it from me."

Henry turned his gaze from the sky for a moment to look at her and see a little grin. "I'm sure that's true," he said. "Except that I'm the one who's been out here with him at the crack of dawn every Saturday since April."

"His nose for navigation, I meant," she said, elbowing him. "You can't teach all of that."

"We'll see how his navigation is yet," Henry quipped, "when he makes it back here."

Eleven minutes later, according to Ruth's watch, John Henry's plane was seen again and he banked a beautiful turn to line up for his landing. He brought the Swallow down as gently as he'd taken her up, taxied back to them, and parked the plane exactly where he'd left it. Congratulations were given all around. John was pleased, but also relieved it was behind him, and anxious that the war finish before his seventeenth birthday, which it would, easily. For Henry, it was a milestone, the initiation of a new generation; another pilot was born; and Henry had a copilot, at long last. As for Ruth, she clung to pride in her son, for envy was too close at hand.

⟳

ONE YEAR LATER, Henry received a letter at the Iowa City airfield, and neither the handwriting nor the postmark, Miami, was familiar. He turned the letter over carefully and slid his pocketknife through the top.

"My old friend," the letter began. "I would like to see the great Mississippi River, as you once promised me. Will you make good on your promise? Or would you and your family like to come to Florida for a holiday? Myself and my wife Yvette would love to have you." There was more, saying briefly how Philippe had gotten out of France—just as this new war, "Surely more awful than the last, I fear, although who would've thought it possible," consumed his country—and to New York, where he met this wife, and then to Miami; and about his new Piper Cub, bright yellow, "like an egg yolk, and a little bit hideous." Henry stood in the field office, holding the letter for a moment, warmed by it, thrilled. He'd been glad when John Henry soloed because it promised someone new he could share flight with; but the idea of seeing Philippe again, of flying with him again—Henry couldn't remember the last time news struck him so happily. He took the letter home to Ruth and together they agreed to invite Philippe and Yvette to Cedar Bluff, as soon as they wanted to come.

"I welcome the opportunity to make good on my promise," Henry wrote back. "Come to Cedar Bluff anytime you like. I'm afraid we cannot come to Florida right now." He hoped his friend would come—how nice for Ruth to meet him after all these years—and he was curious about this Yvette, too, and a little surprised; Henry always imagined him alone. A few months later, there was a telegram saying they planned to come in a few weeks, was it all right? Henry cabled back, yes, please come.

They were a few hours early, around two in the afternoon on a June Wednesday, when George on the radio in the field manager's office called Henry over to listen to Philippe saying he was coming in from the southwest in about ten minutes. There was no way to have Philippe land at the farm— not on this, his first trip to Iowa and the land unfamiliar and his new, fancy Cub that might not like the bumps and clods and angle of the cornfield runway so much. With a few minutes to go, Henry put away his papers, neatened the tuck of his shirt, and pulled a comb through his hair. Ruth was due to drive in any minute now with the Packard, since Henry had flown the Swallow over in the morning and wanted to leave it with Jim, the mechanic, to have the rudder cable tweaked. Something wasn't right with it.

He stepped out of the office and put his hand up to shade his eyes, and there was the yellow plane, barely in sight, coming up from the southeast slowly, calmly. Henry watched, and after what seemed like a few seconds, the Cub was kissing the runway and gliding toward him. Henry waved his arm three times over his head as Philippe and Yvette approached. And then they were there, the prop was jerking to a stop, and the brakes were locked, and Henry stepped forward to the plane. The abrupt absence of sound when a propeller stops, he was thinking, is always remarkably quiet and lovely.

"Hello, *mon ami*," Philippe said as he opened the small door and unbuckled his seat belt.

Henry put his hand out and Philippe shook it and stepped down to the tarmac, where he threw his arms around Henry and slapped him on the back. Henry was glad it was so easy, like twenty days instead of twenty years had passed since they last saw one another, picking up right where they left off except Philippe didn't seem angry with him or disappointed with him, not from that greeting and first hug, anyway. Both stepped back after a moment and took in the other. Then Philippe turned and extended a hand to Yvette, who was all in white—her makeup, and her very blonde hair swept back in a clip—everything perfect as a movie star. That's some plane, Henry was thinking, if a woman can fly the couple-hundred-mile hop from Memphis, where they'd spent last night, and step out looking as fresh as Yvette looked. She wore sunglasses and offered Henry a cheek to kiss. "*Bonjour*, Henry," she said. "It's so nice to meet you."

Two little dogs, having roused themselves from an in-flight nap, arose from the back of the plane and started barking at the window to be let out. Henry looked very surprised and then laughed. Philippe laughed, too, and reached to pick up one dog up in each arm. "*Celui ci*," he said, shaking the dog under his right arm, "is Wilbur. And *celui là*"—he jostled the dog under his left arm—"is Orville."

"Oh, put them down," Yvette said. "They've got to go to the bathroom, I'm sure."

So Philippe did and they barked a little bit but otherwise just hopped along behind their master as he checked the plane, their tails erect and flicking in the wind like nervous wind socks.

Philippe looked well, with an accumulation of lines and wrinkles around his kind dark eyes and still-straight, stern mouth. If the skin was looser around his chin and his chest was not as robust, then the very tip and cleft of his chin and the square of his shoulders remained definite and proud. These things would always make him handsome, Henry thought.

Ruth stood off a hundred yards, in the shadow of the gas

pump, taking a few minutes to look, unnoticed, at this man about whom she had heard so much; and his wife, who was perfectly lovely, perhaps too lovely for this visit, in beautiful white perfectly pressed linen, dressed for some French chateau, Ruth thought, not their farmhouse. She imagined immediately how Yvette smelled: powdery and expensive.

Philippe was as handsome and self-possessed as she had imagined and their plane was beautiful, which she'd also expected, since Henry showed her a picture of it in a magazine. What she wasn't, perhaps, prepared for was the exuberance of Philippe's greeting and hug, the rush of it, the slight desperation, and Henry's surprise and nervousness and relief and happiness, all at once, which was so palpable, embarrassing, that Ruth averted her eyes, despite her invisible remove at the gas pumps. She was glad she wasn't where Yvette was, just behind Philippe, her glance seemingly averted, too. It was as if the two men had entered their own world, ignorant of all else. Philippe gestured at the feed-corn-colored plane and said something, then grinned broadly and laughed as Henry shook his head.

There were also two little white dogs with giant brown spots on them flitting about Philippe's heels and Ruth worried what their own dog plus the wild cats would do to them. Henry gestured toward the office and Philippe stepped back, reached into the plane, and retrieved two small leather suitcases. Then he put one arm across Henry's shoulder and the other around Yvette, whose dress was gathering the breeze. She was young, Ruth could see. Five years younger than herself, maybe, which would make her fifteen years younger than Philippe, and Ruth wished she'd worn her yellow dress with the narrower waist, which made her skin warmer and her eyes darker. But then she told herself this was silly, there was no contest, and she'd never been competitive like this before—honestly, never. Why now?

At last they neared Ruth and she stepped out of the shadow to say hello. Philippe set the suitcases down so that he could properly kiss her on both cheeks and then held her at arm's length to examine her, like her mother did with the children after she hadn't seen them in a while or when Margaret was wearing a new dress. Then he pronounced her "beautiful" and "perfect" and "nothing less than what I'd expect."

Ruth was embarrassed with this exaggerated performance, especially with lovely Yvette all in white right there, waiting to say hello. Up close, too, Philippe was everything smooth and sophisticated and confident that she'd imagined he would be. She hoped Philippe would find her to be a suitable wife for his friend, and that their home, Cedar Bluff, Henry's life, would garner similar approval. Philippe was important to Henry, after all; he was an older brother of sorts. Ruth extended her hand to Yvette, who took it limply and said it was nice to meet her, and was there something she could drink? The young woman looked a little pale and Ruth knew they could stop somewhere for something if she was really so thirsty, but decided to press on home; whether this was a cruel instinct or not, it was the one she followed.

"Yes," Ruth said, "there's gallons of lemonade and tea at home." Then she reached down and petted the dogs; she let them smell and lick her hands—maybe they would take notice of the dog back home.

It was a nice day, not too hot, and a nasty spell of humidity had lifted just that morning. It had been a good summer so far and the first tomatoes were in. They would eat them with potatoes and chicken for dinner. Driving home, Philippe praised the airfield's smooth and straight runway and commented on how beautiful Iowa was, the lushness and the space and the purity. "Of course, I felt a relief from the war tension in France by going to Miami, but that place is—so completely different from my home. Here, in the country-side—this feels more like home to me."

"And where are your children?" Yvette asked. "There are two?"

"Yes, they're home," Ruth said. "John is helping his grand-father with a sick cow and Margaret is with her grand-mother."

"Your parents live very close by?"

"We live in the house I grew up in—my parents live at the top of the farm that my father still works, in a newer, smaller house."

Yvette looked at Philippe and laughed. Ruth was taken aback at her rudeness. "We'd never last next door to my par-ents," she explained. "Philippe hates them."

Ruth looked at Henry. "Oh," Henry said, taking a cue. "It's wonderful having Paul and Elizabeth so close. The children love the farm and their grandparents. And they let me have my own landing strip—usually I take off and land right there."

"Do you think they'd let me land on Park Avenue, my love?" Philippe cooed to Yvette.

"God, no." The woman looked out the window as if sud-denly bored.

At home, Henry walked Philippe around the farm and Ruth stayed back with Yvette, pouring her some lemonade and trying to talk about the flight, about anything. But Yvette would only say that she hated flying, that she much preferred a proper cabin on a train. "Flying is faster, I suppose, but it's so violent, you know. Up and down and side to side and loud! But," she sighed, "Philippe does adore it and it is quite nice to travel by your own schedule."

"Were you born in Miami?" Ruth asked.

"Oh, no, no," Yvette answered. "We came from Paris just as I was born, in the beginning of the first war. To New York, where Philippe and I met. He likes to say I am American," she said with a laugh, "but I am not. French is my first language, and I don't *feel* American."

"Oh," Ruth said, shaking her head and smiling a tight smile. "Men *are* terrible like that, aren't they?" It still wasn't clear to Ruth why they lived in Miami, but it seemed impolite to press her guest. She tried to think of something else to say or ask but failed, and then their glasses were empty and Yvette excused herself to her room. Ruth felt relieved, and guilty. She started dinner, and Yvette slept or rested for the remainder of the afternoon while Henry stayed outside with Philippe.

⟨◦⟩

MARGARET AND JOHN loved Philippe and Yvette and their dogs. The cats, even, let them alone. Philippe brought everyone presents, which he handed out at the end of the first night's dinner, ignorant of the fact that Yvette was still eating carefully, precisely, with excruciating slowness and detachment, even though he was seated next to her. "Yvette, *mon dieu*," Philippe said, when he realized she was still eating. He gave some hurried communication in French, a scolding, it looked like, for her sullenness and desultory eating. If he was talking to her as if she were a child, she certainly seemed to be asking for it, although Ruth knew she was also behaving like a child to get attention from her husband, who seemed to have totally forgotten her. After their brief exchange, Yvette let John Henry take her plate away, and presents came forth.

Ruth unwrapped a beautiful cut-crystal bottle of French perfume: *eau de toilette,* Philippe carefully pronounced for her. Margaret was given a small intricate lace handkerchief, which she promptly dabbed her nose with and then pretended a sneeze—always the performer. John got a fine, soft shaving brush with an ivory handle. He looked a bit confused and embarrassed because at thirteen, he was nowhere near shaving, plus he had his father's soft skin, which meant a mustache and beard would wait still longer. Still, he recovered enough to thank both Philippe and Yvette, although a slight blush tinged his cheeks when he spoke to Yvette. Finally, Henry tore open his tissue-paper package to find a white silk scarf, much like the first one Philippe had given him. Except this one had his initials stitched at one end in fine, glossy cream-colored thread. Below it there was a date in 1919. It was the date of his first flight—also the day he met Philippe.

"You didn't need to get any of us presents, you know," he told Philippe, "But we all appreciate them."

"Oh yes, thank you," Margaret piped up. "I shall keep my handkerchief and use it when I am a young, beautiful woman."

"But you already are," Yvette said—Margaret seemed to be the sole thing that charmed her so far—and little Margaret stood up shyly from her chair and went to kiss her on the cheek.

Later, the adults sat on the porch to drink one glass of some brandy that Philippe had brought with them. It was a perfect Iowa evening, with the sun setting lazily over the tall lush green cornfields that went black and mysterious as dusk slipped into night. Henry pointed to the Jenny peeking out from the side of the barn about four hundred yards off to their right. Her high wing and struts and light blue-gray body were a regular part of the Guttersons' landscape, particularly since she hadn't moved in over a decade, but she certainly looked odd to someone not used to seeing a plane nestled into a farm-yard. And so Philippe laughed a bit at first. "She is like a shrine at the center of all this corn," he said. "It is like the corn grows up around her, to do her honor. Your landing strip is like a royal promenade."

"That would be nice," Ruth said. "It would be nice if she brought us that kind of luck."

"Oh, I think she does," Henry said. "Flying has brought us nothing but goodness." He slipped his arm around Ruth, squeezed just barely, hoping she forgave the insincerity of the statement, and she did; she didn't like the statement itself, yet she agreed with his saying it. To hint otherwise might bring Philippe too much into their lives. This man, regardless of his charm and intrigue and devotion to Henry, should not be privy to their secrets, nor should his wife.

The subsequent days followed the same pattern as the first. Yvette spent much of each one in her room—she arose late and took a two-hour rest every afternoon. Philippe said she fatigued very easily, especially in the humidity and all the matter in the air. When Yvette was awake and around, she was often reading or sitting quietly, listening, or gazing, or simply lost in her own thoughts. Ruth vowed not to notice the woman's behavior too much—Yvette was not used to farm life and she didn't find it charming, why should she? She came from cities. Besides that, Yvette seemed shy and a little sad to Ruth, who knew that if she herself were in the position of visiting them in Miami for the first time, with Henry and Philippe so fond of each other that they forgot the women entirely—Ruth, too, would want to stay in her bedroom all day.

"We were a very good team," Philippe said to Ruth the third morning over coffee, while Henry went off to get more fertilizer and Yvette was still in their room. "I haven't had any partner like him since."

Ruth listened carefully and said, "It's too bad Yvette doesn't like to fly."

Philippe nodded. "Yes, although she'd never be a partner to me like Henry was."

Ruth felt an urge to insert herself in this calculus somehow—to make sure Philippe knew what a good flying partner she, a woman, had been to Henry. But there was no way to do this gracefully, and it was a selfish instinct besides. "Henry's so pleased to have you here," she said instead. "We both are."

"I wonder how many farms are for sale up here, or just a house and a piece of land," Philippe said. "Do you know?"

"You and Henry could work together," Ruth said, playing

along. "You could run two planes. There's always more business to be done."

Philippe nodded and then flattered her. "And I can steal
you away from him and have two lovely wives all for myself,"
he said.

Ruth laughed heartily and shook her head, realizing right
then how much of a joke this was. Philippe wanted Henry,
not her; toward Ruth, he felt jealousy. It was a brilliant morning and soon to be too hot—for the first time all summer, her
feet had touched a warm floor when she left her bed at dawn.
Although a breeze persisted, it was clear that some sweltering July weather was imminent. Silence hung between them,
and Ruth gave up trying to fill it. She rose to clean the cof-
feepot.

Henry returned from the store shortly thereafter and asked
Philippe about the Latécoère mail service—did he ever join?
And if not, what had he been doing, with whom had he been
flying? "You should be an instructor," Henry said. "You
taught me rather well."

But Philippe shook his head and said simply, "Since you, I
have no other copilots, my friend." Henry laughed because
he knew this was a lie, at least in part.

But Philippe insisted. "No, I am serious," he said. "I wished
never to replace you and so I didn't."

Ruth, who was wiping down the counters, heard the
urgency, the weird urgency in this comment, and she turned
her head slowly to look at her husband. What would Henry
say? How did he feel? Looking at his familiar face, the dark
hair now flecking with gray, his hazel-green eyes, and his
kind mouth, his trustworthy, honest mouth, his stilled hands,

she could not tell and she did not want to stay. She made a quiet excuse to leave them, and did so.

"As for the mail," Philippe said, "I decided I did not need the risk. I have enough money; I can fly whenever I want. Why start risking your life for a paycheck? If I want to cross the *Méditerranée*, I can do that. If I want to fly from Morocco to Cape Town, I can do that, too. I do not need some other man telling me to do these things, telling me to carry paper in my plane."

"Well," Henry said, looking after Ruth, wondering why she had left so abruptly, with the washcloth in the middle of the counter, "I've got to get up there and earn my dinner," he said. "Are you copiloting today, Monsieur DeBreault?"

"*Certainement,*" Philippe said, and then climbed upstairs to see what Yvette was doing.

Henry found Ruth outside, taking clothes off the line. "I'm going to take Philippe up with me today. Could you make us some sandwiches for lunch?"

"Sure," Ruth said, unpinning a sheet, folding it, and laying it on top of the others in the basket. She would not look at him, although he stood there, waiting for her to finish so that he could kiss her and thank her for hosting Philippe and Yvette, especially since Yvette was so odd.

"Ruth," he said gently, reaching out and touching her wrist as she worked, her eyes still set on an indefinite spot in front of her, away from him. "Are you all right? Did I do something?"

"I'm tired," Ruth said with a sigh, her glance slipping toward him and then away again. "It's been a long week."

"I know," Henry said, taking a sheet and clothespins from

her hands, setting them down, and taking her into his arms, which she barely permitted. "We'll be back to normal soon," he whispered into her hair, knowing this was true, knowing and hating that the visit was exhausting and perhaps confusing for her, but grateful nonetheless, for maybe all this camaraderie with Philippe, about flying, would stir her to go back to a plane.

June 1943

Dear _____,

Mary has told me that she thinks I'm better, that I used to always seem on the verge of falling off something, or of "dissolving into a puddle," as she puts it. "It's not that you aren't, or weren't, strong," she tells me. "It's that you were too strong, willful. It makes people nervous."

And you'd think such a speech would be warm, congratulatory, even though congratulations are ten years too late. But in any event, the speech was a kiss-off, to explain why I wouldn't be invited to a dinner party at Anna's the next week, and why Anna and Mary were taking their families on vacation together, to a lake in Minnesota, and not inviting Henry and me and the kids. "You're better— you're not like you used to be, but I guess you still make people, Anna at least, nervous."

"What about you, Mary?" I said straight to her.

"You shouldn't have told me about the nights you can't sleep," she said first. "Or if you tell me, you've got to tell someone else. It's too much for just me." Then she shook her head and suggested—"Maybe if Tom and Henry got on better."

Aren't women supposed to gather around each other, you'd think they would. But this is perhaps a situation along the lines of Charles Darwin's theories: every person for herself. And you mustn't tell anyone your problems, because they'll save themselves instead. Throw the poorer swimmer off. I think of Dean Cilek sometimes—did I do as much as a young girl could've to help him?

And if that weren't bad enough, we're being visited right now by Henry's oldest friend, Philippe, and his wife, Yvette. Although I'm thrilled for Henry to see this man, who's nearly a brother, I've had more then enough of Yvette. For god's sake, she's the most haughty, miserable, rude creature I've ever met, and I don't care what she looks like, it shouldn't matter. She makes me seem steady as a doctor. And if I didn't think I was half out of my wits in frustration with Yvette and for this situation with Mary and Anna, I'd swear Philippe was jealous of me, although I can't figure out how it would work. He doesn't seem queer, but still, there's such a tension that exists between myself and Philippe that I wonder if it isn't hatred sometimes, clinging to me like corn silk. I can't wait for them to leave.

After dusting the Fosters', the Annenbergs' and the Hansens' fields, Henry and Philippe started back to Iowa City. They flew along the river, Henry pointing out things over the side of the plane as they went—a huge Army Corps of Engineers dam and reservoir, then the Iowa River, which they followed down toward town, and finally the university football stadium, fieldhouse, and the old state capitol. With the airfield in sight below town, Henry started to bring the plane down, but Philippe held his stick (a second set of controls were there since teaching John Henry to fly) firmly in place. After wrestling with it for a few seconds to no avail, he looked behind him to see Philippe grinning broadly. "We've got to get fuel," he called back.

Philippe merely shook his head. "Let's keep going. West. California, my friend," he screamed into the wind.

"What?" Henry said, having missed a few words and not believing the ones he'd heard.

"California," Philippe shouted again. "*Vas y.*"

"No," Henry said, uncharmed by his friend's joke. Still, Philippe would not let go. So Henry wrenched the stick and took the plane into a dive. The Swallow was a good plane and Henry knew her like he knew his own face. When teaching John to fly, Henry had let him hold the stick for the most part, but when he felt John was pushing the plane in a direction she couldn't go, Henry had steered them to a better course. Now he was just barely comfortable with the dive he was risking and he hoped his friend would be startled into letting go of the stick. But when he tried to pull up, he saw that Philippe was holding her in the dive. Henry was furious; he could think of doing nothing apart from climbing into the back cockpit and throttling—no, killing—Philippe. What the hell was Philippe thinking? There was also the matter of the rudder, which Henry still didn't feel was quite right, even after its recent adjustment.

The Swallow was picking up speed and they needed to straighten up right then or she wouldn't be able to manage it. Three more seconds went by without Philippe giving up control, and then finally, just as Henry was cursing himself for calling Philippe's bluff by initiating the dive, for installing the second stick in the first place, for not carrying a parachute anymore, for being too low to jump anyway—for most everything—Philippe pulled her up. The shift in force made Henry's veteran stomach do a little flip and he closed his eyes and prayed that Philippe was quite finished with the games for one day, and that the rudder cable would hold. The small forest he saw beneath them tilted and curled as in a carnival mirror.

And then she stalled—the dive must've flooded the engine somehow. Now they were powerless and too far away from the runway to land there. Henry quickly looked about for a good place to land but saw only the treacherous spot of woods and beyond that a hog farm, a large fruit orchard, and a road running perpendicular to their course. He aimed for the road, planning the necessary ninety-degree turn. With a couple of hundred feet left between them and the ground, they arrived at the road and Henry pushed the pedals and the stick hard, with the wind, and they gently, barely, swung to face the south. Philippe had long since let go and Henry was able to push her as hard as he knew she would go, and the rudder held. And then they were hardly aloft and still banking and Henry pulled out, leveled the wings as much as he could with so little time and space. She wouldn't be exactly aligned with the road, but it was better to land a little crooked than to land on a wingtip. Finally, there was no air, no space, left and they were down, smacking the dirt road three times before settling, and the wheels went over into the ditch along the road and the wing dipped low, too, caught itself in the ditch, and they flipped diagonally, tail over nose, one wing ahead of the other, before finishing upside down.

There was silence and then Philippe laughing, like he had the time in the Alps. "We should have gone on to California," he said. "Now look what you've done."

This was old rugged pilots' humor, the sort of thing Philippe assumed he could enjoy with Henry—it was just like the old days, wasn't it? —but Henry was far from amused. He unstrapped himself and got out of the plane. He stood on the road and surveyed the damage. The propeller was broken and a wing was wrecked. The tailwing looked splintered, although Henry couldn't really tell because it was embedded in the soft ground of the ditch. The dust and spray barrels were crunched like wads of paper and the small amount of pesticide that remained was trickling out everywhere, over the wings and onto the ground. Philippe was still in his seat, laughing, but Henry was furious. They were several miles south of Iowa City and several miles north of Hills. Henry began walking up the road, with Philippe still strapped into the upside-down Swallow, laughing like a record needle stuck on one long, deep scratch.

Philippe knew he had made a grave error, but then he couldn't have done anything else. His affection for Henry was overwhelming, plain and simple, and Philippe couldn't have him, which he knew from the moment Henry introduced his wife to Philippe: And *this is Ruth*. His eyes for Ruth were the eyes of both a proud father and a passionate admirer, almost a Narcissus, Philippe had thought, unconsciously gazing too long at his own beautiful image. This single moment—this gaze that Henry had for Ruth but never for Philippe—and the days on the farm that had passed thereafter, which only served to underline that first moment—had made Philippe miserable and crazy and made him nearly drive the plane straight into the ground, killing them both. As he stayed there in the Swallow, gradually sliding out of the upside down plane and lying on his back, looking up at the wreckage as the odorous, dusty matter from the tanks seeped out and gathered in a sort of puddle ten feet away, Henry having long since disappeared without a word up the road, Philippe let his tears run down his temple, into his hair, until the sun went down and the dusk wind dried his face and he heard a big truck from the airport rumbling up the road. He wondered if he would not rather have been dead.

Henry stormed off to the nearest farm, furious with Philippe, and scared, scared at his first crack-up in about five years, scared at the intensity of Philippe's will. His insistence on having Henry all to himself for several hours each day, his speaking French sometimes so that Ruth couldn't understand, his overbearing flattery of her and the children, and this galling indifference toward his poor, beautiful wife, Yvette—these things had made Ruth uncomfortable and Henry resentful, even if he loved having his old friend around, loved having Philippe's attentions. But this nearly fatal stunt in the Swallow was too much. Philippe must leave. Despite the fun they had had, he could no longer pretend that their friendship could return to what it used to be. Why wasn't it enough for Philippe to come to Iowa, stay with Henry's family for over a week, and fly together again, for a little while? What was it that had made Philippe nearly willing to kill them both?

He would tell Ruth that the Swallow had blown a hose,

causing a small but lethal piece of metal to lock things up in there and engender the stall. The guys at the airfield who fixed the plane would know this was not the case, but it didn't much matter. They were not going to say anything to Ruth. The plane would take nearly six weeks to fix, which meant Henry would have to borrow a plane from the airfield and rig her up. The delay and canceled service, plus the customers' skepticism of Henry's flying abilities given his crash on a bright, clear, calm afternoon, would mean the loss of nearly a third of his business that season and he'd have to win them back over the winter as he encountered them at church, the market, the feed store.

Philippe and Yvette would clear out quickly, on the excuse that Yvette's sister was ill and they needed to fly to New York. There was a thank-you note for the visit—which mentioned nothing about the Swallow except, "I hope she's getting repaired to fine form, let me know if not," and then nothing. Philippe would not offer to pay for the repairs, which Henry thought was the least he could have done.

When Henry got to Ruth that afternoon after the crack-up, with some of the Swallow stacked up in the back of a truck and her sitting on a bench outside the hangar, watching the wind sock blow while one hand absently kneaded the other, wondering how bad it was, and worrying, he kissed her on the forehead, then pulled her up to him and kissed her square on the lips. He didn't usually do this in full view of the other mechanics and pilots, but he didn't care. He was sorry, so sorry, for so many things, and lucky, too; she was all he wanted, all he ever should have wanted, and if he never flew again, but had Ruth by his side, his life would be complete.

She kissed him back with relief and a little, shy passion, knowing that he'd dodged some menace, knowing *they'd* dodged some menace and now it was over; they were back. Then she made him hold still so that she could look at a cut over his eyebrow and then his purpling wrist, maybe broken again. She drove home, with Henry putting his head down in her lap, and relief flooded her like air to the nearly drowned.

NINE

We are all fighting it—fighting the transitory, the evanes-
cence, against death and the shortness of life and that futile
feeling—the "Qu'as-tu fais?" feeling.

—*Anne Morrow Lindbergh, September 25, 1933*

*I*T WAS THE FIFTH of October, a Wednesday, ten months
since her parents had gone. "Mrs. Donnelly? Margaret
Sheehan Donnelly?" a voice on the phone said when she
walked into the house and ran to the ringing phone at five
P.M. "This is Captain Ron Davis with the United States Coast
Guard."

She was almost relieved to hear it wasn't a telemarketer, as
most calls that began "Mrs. Donnelly?" at five P.M. on week-
days were. "Yes?" she said. "This is Margaret Donnelly."

"Mrs. Donnelly," he said, "I am calling you from Honolulu,
Hawaii. And I'm afraid I am the bearer of some distressing
news for you."

"Yes," she said, conscious of having anticipated any such

call for nearly a year now, conscious of feeling her breath quicken and her body relent.

"I understand that your parents, Henry and Ruth Gutterson, have been missing for a while?"

Margaret said this was correct.

"Well, there was a piece of tailwing washed up on Christmas Island, a good bit south of us here, a few weeks ago. The call numbers on the fuselage, I'm afraid," he said, "correspond to a charter plane touring all the islands, which your parents were on five months ago."

"Five months ago?" She actually managed a little laugh because it was so ludicrous; they'd been dead all of these last five months. There was relief, too. But no surprise about the news itself. "Why are you only calling me now?"

"They didn't leave correct information," the captain said. "They left false names and addresses, which we only know now, of course. They gave us the phone number to their home in Iowa, I believe, but no one was ever there to answer it. So we started to think that maybe they didn't have any family. Even so, we put out some feelers to hotels and such and people had seen them, but they had left the same name and information those places and they had paid cash. We had almost given up when, on a stroke of luck, someone at the charter service discovered the FAA flyer and put two and two together. We had the Cedar Bluff police send us a copy of their handwriting just yesterday, and now, yes, we're certain it was them."

Margaret felt her hands shaking, fury at the edges. "But that FAA notice went out to every private airport nationwide in December. They should've had it in April, before they got onto that plane." How many other places, she wondered, had her parents been where the flyer was sitting right there on someone's desk?

"Well, you'll have to talk to the charter service about that. But if they got a paper in December, it's not surprising that it had fallen beneath a few things by April."

Margaret squeezed her eyes shut, pinched the bridge of her nose, and leaned against the wall. "Have you found anything else?"

"Not so far. And the tailpiece doesn't give us much idea where they went down or when. The amount of water that moved through this area with some doozy storms this past month, let alone the last five months—they could've gone down two hundred miles from where that piece was found. And, well, I don't have to tell you that with five months' time passed, lots will have been, well, long gone by now."

"I don't expect to find their bodies," she said flatly. "I was just curious if there could be any more of the plane."

"Yes, there could be. But it seems unlikely. Like I said, it's a minor miracle we found anything."

Margaret thought for a moment, tried to figure out what questions she could ask this man and what she needed to ask the charter service. It was difficult to think clearly. "So, could you just run through for me what happened? When they chartered a plane, where they were going, things like that."

"Of course," the captain said. Margaret liked his efficiency and matter-of-factness. There was no unnecessary warmth or pity. He explained that there had been a charter pilot with them and they were supposed to be flying around the islands, but the last contact was well south. The guy in the tower at

Hawaii County Airport informed them that they were well off their course—at 13 degrees north and 160 degrees west—and they said they were encountering some fierce turbulence and were going to turn back. But then contact was lost. This was about two hours after takeoff. The date, exactly, was April 3.

"How does anyone get lost in this day and age?" Margaret asked, realizing this had been her initial fear, deemed ridiculous.

"We looked for them, trust me. Hawaii County called us and we alerted all fishing boats in the area—there weren't many, given the weather—plus sent two cutters and three search planes of our own," Captain Davis said. "But there was nothing. To be honest, Mrs. Donnelly, we're still trying to piece it together. Christmas Island, where the piece of the tail was found, is nearly seven hundred miles south of Hawaii and the last contact was somewhere in between. They could've been trying to get a landing strip and the weather was easier that way—the storm was pretty much moving north-northeast, and so to fly southwest was flying a little bit out of it. Still, that's a long way to go for a landing strip, even in the middle of the Pacific, and the pilot said they were turning back."

"Could they have simply run out of fuel?"

"It's possible, yes."

She sighed. There didn't seem to be much else to tell. It wouldn't do any good to cross-examine him. "Okay," she said. "You'll call me if you find or learn anything else?"

"Yes, absolutely, Mrs. Donnelly. And again, I'm so sorry to be calling you with this news."

"Any news at this point . . . " she said, trailing off. "It's not unwelcome. Thank you."

He offered his condolences once again and they hung up. She was at the kitchen phone, still in her raincoat and still with the mail under her arm. She set that down and let her hand fall to her side, where she knew Fern's cool muzzle was waiting. The sun had nearly set and the kitchen was dark. The only sound was cars swishing by, home, horns, and bus brakes squeaking. Fern started scratched her ear and there was that slight percussive sound of toenails scratching through fur against cartilage and skin, and then she started panting because she was expecting to go out.

Margaret ran Captain Davis's call through her head as if she were trying on the information for size. She didn't have to wonder how she felt—it was relief, plain and simple. Not happiness, not pleasure, but relief in having full-on pain, at last, in having certain pain, rather than wonder. Not even the frustration of the charter service's ineptitude could diminish the stillness she felt seeping all the way through her. And was she relieved that they'd been dead, most likely, for so long? It did mean they had only been running away from their children for five months, which was a lot different from ten. Perhaps they had been trying to come home in the spring, after all, as Margaret had hoped—maybe Hawaii was meant to be the end of it, the farthest reach of their wandering before turning back.

⌒

JUST THE MONTH before, John had told her he'd given up, that he felt certain they were dead, and that perhaps it was time to really close the farm up—not just put the valuable things in storage and leave couches and beds out with sheets draped over them, but to store everything, make the house empty. It was a Saturday when he told her, right after his glider lesson, and he and Susan stopped in Lincoln Park for lunch on their way downtown. Susan and Terry were in the backyard, looking at the new cherry tree they'd planted to replace the old, failing magnolia. Margaret was slicing cheese for sandwiches and John leaned against the counter next to her.

"Well," he said, looking away from her briefly, out the window, and then looking back just as Margaret glanced at him and noticed his eyes were brimming. "I think they've gone," he said.

She focused on the hunk of cheddar and her knife. "Do you know something I don't know?"

"No," he said, shaking his head. "Just this feeling. And the fact that we've heard nothing in five months. In the whole nine or ten months they've been gone, we've learned three things. Bank withdrawals in two places and one phone call, to Philippe, who wasn't alive to receive it. If they aren't dead, then they are dead to us. They mean to be dead to us. And so, maybe we should accept that they're gone."

This surprised her—both because it seemed extreme and because John had generally been more positive. "You can't really believe that," she said. "After the way this time has gone, and the confusing, inadvertent, silly little appearances they've made—you're going to tell me that you're sure they're dead?"

"I just feel it," John said simply. "I think it's the right thing to feel." He seemed relieved. His was a smile, or a face, of relief.

"Do you really believe this, without any evidence?"

"I am—it feels nice to do something. To decide something."

"To take control," Margaret suggested.

"I guess."

"Well," she replied, "I'm still expecting them to pop up on a talk show, or in the crowd at a *Monday Night Football* game. Maybe on *The Price Is Right*."

John laughed, because she was asking for it, and because he didn't know what else to say.

"Since when have you felt this way?" Margaret asked. "What made you decide?"

"I don't know whether it has to do with the glider lessons or whether I'm just fed up. But I started to feel it a little bit, this sense of, well, letting go, when I started flying, and it was why we gave you the flying lessons for your birthday, which—"

"I—" Margaret broke in, starting to explain herself.

"No, don't use them," John said. "It's fine. Really, it is. I'm sorry I pushed them on you."

"It was a nice thought," Margaret said, and meant it. "Anyway."

"I just worked it out in my head today, up there. How long they've been gone. What we do know about them. Whatever is the name of that rule about the simplest solution likely being the right one?"

"Occam's razor." Margaret nodded, ignoring the petulant voice in her head saying her brother had resolved their par-

ents' death in about the time it took to cook a roast or
rearrange the living room furniture. "I'm glad for you," she
said. "But I think it might take me a little longer."

In the hard squint of her eyes as she looked at the sandwich plate she was assembling, John saw how distressed he
had made her and he backed off, let her go. He felt foolish,
for what he'd been trying to do anyway. And what was that
again? He didn't even know. He just wanted her not to be
sad, he wanted to do something, and he did feel better, giving
up on them. If it was spiteful, he didn't care. And maybe he
needed her to agree with him. If she agreed that their parents
must be dead, that would be something, wouldn't it? They
could get on with their lives. But she wasn't buying it. Even
with the information the Lindbergh letters gave her, or maybe
because of it, Margaret had been like a small animal caught
in a trap this whole year, and still was no better. Maybe it was
easier for John because he remembered, if barely, Mother
being in the hospital, and it factored into his earliest knowl-
edge of her. He stood next to his sister and put his arm across
her shoulder as she worked. She was taller than his wife, her
shoulders stronger, straighter. Susan was so very narrow,
although Margaret was, in fact, thinner. He patted her arm
and she patted the small of his back in return.

It was a September day that was already nostalgic for summer, warm, but with a duller edge, and then the leaves.
Football was replacing baseball. Apples were coming in and
he was supposed to go to an orchard up near Wisconsin the
next day, with Susan and their grandchildren. He had wished
before that Margaret and Terry had borne children, they
would have been such good, loving, devoted parents, look

how devoted to their dog they were, for chrissakes, you'd think they *did* have a child. That September Saturday, he wished this could've been, more than ever. Children renew us; they renew life itself, it's true, and they'd be a help to Margaret just then.

Over lunch, they talked about John's gliding lessons. It was the first time Susan had watched, and although she was originally apprehensive, she left the field more excited than John.

"It could not have been more graceful," Susan said. "None of this accelerating or decelerating to hit the runway just right—"

"Well, that's not exactly true—" John broke in.

"Okay, so you lifted or depressed some flaps. What I mean is that there was no loud throttle gunning or pulling back. It was so much more peaceful than all that. What I can't believe," Susan went on, "is how far those things can go without falling out of the sky."

Terry joked, "I won my elementary school's paper airplane competition in the third grade. I got my plane to cross the entire gymnasium because I managed to wait until a big gust of wind came in through the doors that opened onto the playground. I thought it was cheating, really, except no one ever said anything about it."

"I thought it was so beautiful," Susan said, looking at John, reaching for half a ham sandwich, "that I'm considering joining John for a ride once he's certified."

"That's wonderful," Margaret said, half enthusiastically. Although she supported John's new enthusiasm and was glad for him, she found herself wishing that all elements of flying—at least the flying done in small private planes with someone she loved in the pilot's seat—would go out of her life. At first she thought the flying lessons for her fifty-fifth birthday were a cruel, insensitive, and crass present, and then she came to see it was just badly miscalculated. The four of them had met for dinner at their favorite steakhouse downtown and John and Susan gave her a card with Snoopy as the Red Baron on front. Inside, they had slipped a gift certificate for lessons at Palwaukee Airport in Wheeling. "Apparently they have a great flight school there," Susan told her. "I have a friend who just got her license and she said it was the best experience of her life."

"What a great present," Terry said. "Very thoughtful, guys."

Margaret was a terrible pretender when it came to gifts that confused or displeased her and this one did both. She was so bothered by the gift, and she didn't exactly know why at the time, but it was all she could do to put the certificate back in the envelope without bursting into tears. She'd turned down the opportunity to take lessons and solo when she was a teenager, deeply disappointing her mother and baffling her father, and John knew all this. Way back then, had she felt like she had won something by holding firm in her refusal? Sure. Did she think, now, four decades on, that this small victory had been worth her parents' large disappointment? No. There are things that parents want us to do that matter more to them than to us, and it never mattered as much to her to say no as it would've mattered to them if she'd taken at least one lesson. Soloed once. She hadn't really understood this at the time, and now—it was ancient history and she still had no interest in flying. Besides, they weren't even around to know, to be pleased by it. Still, why, however, a gift of lessons nearly brought her to tears was unclear—hormones, she told herself.

Margaret ate her steak in peace and listened to stories of the new grandbaby, Ruth, who was eight months old already, how was that possible? More about the Ireland trip John and Susan, alone, were taking—Terry still had relatives there, so he was trying to explain where they were from and how they got to England, and then to Canada, where Terry grew up.

John could tell, looking at the straight, flat lines around his sister's eyes, that the flying lessons bewildered her and he felt terrible, but he hadn't necessarily expected her to understand it, at first. He had hoped that, as she thought about it, she'd come to see the lessons as a chance to understand Mother a little bit more, somehow. She was so hung up on the fact that their parents' actions didn't make any sense, that she had missed something, and the Lindbergh letters sent her into a tailspin of confusion and sadness. John didn't see any more sense in it than she, but he didn't feel like he had missed something, either. Maybe he was more prepared for them to make no sense; maybe he was just asking less of them; or maybe he was fooling himself. In any event, he had anticipated that Margaret would need to think about the lessons, but he hadn't guessed they'd make her so sad.

They split two big hunks of chocolate cake. Susan had brought one candle, which she discreetly lit and Margaret discreetly extinguished, in one breath. They had made a pact, the four of them, since their fiftieth birthdays, to never put more than one candle on the cake.

As they waited for the valets to pull their cars around, John took her aside. "Look, I know the flying lessons might seem like a morbid gift," he said. "But I think it's sort of like climbing back on the horse that throws you off—or like facing your worst fear. Or think of doing something that Mother did, just to see what it feels like. I've been flying again lately—Susan does not even know. She thinks I've been playing a lot of tennis." He chuckled at this small infidelity. "But I feel peaceful up there. Like nowhere else. And maybe that's what it was like for her."

Margaret nodded, and their cars arrived.

Recalling all of this at the lunch table while John and Susan oohed and ahhhed about gliders, Margaret thought about what her mother would have been like, flying after all these years, getting up to the only place where, according to the letters anyway, she felt truly free and alive, a space of paradise, nearly indescribable, not just peaceful, as John suggested. Maybe they never came down, they just kept going, on and on, up there, leaving behind all the concerns that had kept her from flying the whole rest of her life, namely, her children and then her grandchildren.

While Susan was clearing dishes, John quietly suggested calling some storage places, to put everything in Cedar Bluff away. They'd talk about the house later. There must be legal issues. Margaret felt a little overwhelmed but he wasn't really asking her to respond. He stepped out the front door, kissed her, then Susan did, and they said they'd call later. The idea of renting some storage and removing the articles of her parents' life to a space for which she held the key both shamed her and satisfied her. When they came back, they would have to beg, she mused. They would have to apologize and make her understand, which could take months, years even. She would let them know what it was like, wondering, not being able to get on with your life.

And yet, regardless of not quite believing or understanding John's certainty, she knew he was probably right. It made good sense. If Officer Sargent had called her the next day to say they'd been found and they were dead and he was sorry, she wouldn't have been surprised. But even then, the wondering would continue—why and how and when, where? She guessed John felt the same, even if he didn't know it, because how could he really, truly, stop wondering? How could he just decide to stop?

~

YET ANOTHER MONTH passed; they did nothing about storage but call for prices and availability; and then came the evening of the Coast Guard call. When she hung up the phone, Margaret stayed in the kitchen, sitting down at the table and looking out at the garden and the evening light going from gray to real darkness punctuated by neighbors' squares of light all around, when she heard the front door close. Eventually—how much time had passed?—the hall light went on and the closet door opened. Terry took off his overcoat and hung it up. Then he came into the kitchen, flicking on the overhead light as he passed the switch. He saw her and was startled. "Jesus," he said. "You scared me. What are you doing?" He didn't look at her but went to the mail, picked it up, opened a few things.

"Eh?" he said when she didn't answer.

"Oh, just sitting here."

"Did you just get in?" he said, opening up a credit card bill. "Why are all the lights off?"

"It wasn't quite dark when I got home." She turned her head to look at the clock on the microwave. "A half hour ago."

"What have you been doing? You look like you just walked in." Terry finally set the mail down, got a glass from the cabinet, and went to the refrigerator for some apple juice. Like clockwork, every day, he did this.

"Thinking, I guess."

Terry poured his juice and then looked at her carefully and silently for a moment.

"What's going on?" He put his glass down and came to stand near to her. He kissed her on the cheek.

"They found a plane they think my parents were on. A King Air. Went down somewhere near Honolulu five months ago."

"Oh, honey," he said, taking hold of her arms, which were crossed in front of her. He tried to pull her up to him but she resisted for some reason and he relaxed, pulled a chair out next to her, and took her hand. "Five months? Who called?"

"The Coast Guard. They said a piece of the tailwing washed up on Christmas Island a few weeks ago. A charter service out there says my parents went up with one of their pilots back in April. They were just flying to Kauai, to the northwest, although Christmas Island is seven hundred miles southwest, which doesn't make much sense."

"No," Terry agreed. He tried to catch her gaze as she looked off into some invisible corner just to the right of him. Then he pulled her to him again, and she let herself go this time. She felt his shirt moisten under her eyes and she felt his collarbone, pronounced and strong in his lean, softening body, and she bounced gently against it with each ugly, embarrassing sob.

The Coast Guard called John, too, and he reached Margaret about twenty minutes after Terry got home. "Well, they went out with style," he said.

"You talk about this like it was a suicide," she said.

"Wasn't it? The risks they took—you're telling me they weren't something like suidical?"

She didn't answer him. She knew John was a big proponent of do-not-resuscitate orders and even euthanasia. Still, these were his own parents. She was crying again, and John said he wanted to drive down and see her, be there. She handed the phone to Terry, who agreed it was a good idea for John and Susan to come, if they could. Terry'd get some food.

They all sat in the TV room, sipping water or wine or scotch and making the phone calls they needed to make, John and Margaret alternating as much as they could. They got on the phone together to call their father's one remaining sibling, Uncle Jack, in a home in Madison. And when they were finished with the phone calls, they talked about having a service, a Mass and a luncheon, there was no rush, of course, but when was convenient and where would they have it? John said he'd make some calls in the morning to find a place for a luncheon. They'd have to go through the will, figure out the farm. "Not tonight," Margaret said simply as John rattled off the to-do list. "Not now."

"Of course not," he said.

They watched a basketball game while Terry called his own mother and sister to report the news. No one said much—neither Margaret nor John had any idea where to begin, not for themselves or for each other. John, too, was glad the wait was over and that there was a conclusion after all—a conclusion, even, that his parents seemed to have chosen in some way or another. And yet everything seemed so wrong, so off. However much it was a fitting ending, as he himself had said, it was an incredibly stupid one.

They both tried to imagine it, their parents in the last moments, the panic that even Father must've felt as the water approached. Did he take the wheel? Did he say: "I've banged up planes more times than I have fingers to count. I've rolled them end over end, side to side, you name it. I've landed with engine fires, broken wheels, with no visibility whatsoever— not even my own nose on my own face. I know what it feels like when the ground rushes up to meet you so fast it feels as if a hand is swatting you on the cheek at a hundred miles an hour. I know the relief and the laughter and the headache I get when I finish upside down, held in by my boot straps, looking at a fine crop of corn that pokes up nearly to my nose"?

Or did he not utter a word because he knew this forced landing would be his last? Margaret would've crawled to the very back of the large King Air cabin. She would not have been able to watch out the cockpit window. She would've strapped herself in at the emergency exit, where there was no window, no way of seeing what was coming. She could never watch her death approaching like a high-speed train.

And what were their regrets? Did they wish, at long last, that they hadn't taken such a foolish trip? Did they wish that they'd called their children, just once? And how horrible is it that Margaret and John couldn't help but hope that in their parents' final moments they experienced a rush of regret and sadness, of panic that they would never see their children's, or any of their grandchildren's, faces again?

John decided that his mother was wearing her red silk dress with the pearl buttons. She wore this dress to an awards ceremony when the Iowa Aviation Association gave Father a distinguished service award a few years back. John imagined Mother in this dress, strapped into her seat, with her arms folded across her chest. She would have had the far-off look in her eyes that he knew by heart, except maybe Mother was biting the corner of her lip in fear. Maybe she pulled down her shade and leaned her head forward against the seat in front of her. Maybe she put her head in Father's lap, if he was next to her; or maybe he was up front, trying to do something, and she was alone in the cabin, her head pressed against the upholstery of the seat and her hands clasped together, slipped between her knees, held tight there. "Henry," she would have called out in a near-whisper. "Henry, come back to me, here."

And then it was late, the game over. John and Susan drove back up to Wilmette and Margaret wondered what she'd do next, since sleep wasn't likely. "It will be easier now," John said to her as he left, hugging her briefly and kissing her cheek. She said yes, she knew that. He suggested that they look two weeks ahead for a funeral—that far out, their schedules could easily be loosened up a bit and they could have time to think about what they wanted to do. There was no particular rush.

The next day, John checked into the plane, the charter service, all of it. He found out the King Air was fairly new and in good repair. Manufactured and sold to the charter company in 1980, it had three thousand hours of flight time on it and was designed to fly for two to three times that long, which is to say that she probably had another ten years in her, if not more. There were ten seats—a single seat most forward in the cabin, near the door, then three rows with two seats each, and finally a couch for three, adjacent to the bathroom. A four-inch trim of a lacquered wood ran along the cabin wall and each tan leather seat had its own drink holder plus footrests. The cabin walls were taupeish. They stocked the pantry with Lifesavers, honey-roasted peanuts, pretzels, and Doritos in the red bag, ham and cheese sandwiches on rye, and roast beef on pumpernickel. There were chocolate chip cookies and brownies with walnuts on top. Eight-ounce cans of Coke, diet Coke, ginger ale, 7 UP, and orange Fanta. There were small bottles of Bacardi rum, Gordon's vodka, and Gilbey's gin. The ice machine was broken on the day his parents flew and thus the company had put a cooler of ice on the plane in case the passengers wanted a drink.

King Airs cruise at about 250 miles per hour, or half as fast as an average jet. His father had worn his old flight jacket, the heat of Hawaii and the stiffness of the leather notwithstanding. The charter manager remembered this. "He was wearing a vintage flight jacket and I asked where he got it and he said he'd been an Air Mail pilot," the charter manager said, speaking freely only after he discerned that John was not going to berate him for the FAA flyer mix-up, as Margaret had when she called. The man whistled through his teeth. "Ain't that something, an Air Mail pilot," he said.

He also told John that the pilot who went down with his parents was thirty-five years old and his name was John

Lowenstein. He had been a pilot for Allegheny Airlines for ten years and decided that he didn't want to travel quite as much. Then the airlines went under and he decided it was time to move on. He had loved Hawaii on his honeymoon. His wife, a schoolteacher, wanted to live in a warmer place than Boston and so they moved. "If you had to choose between Boston and Hawaii, how long would you have to think about it?" he said with a laugh. Anyway, Lowenstein found his way to Hawaii Charter about five years ago, the manager said, and just recently had become co-owner. Lowenstein had a good sense of humor, the manager said. "He was always cracking some joke or another. Real full of life." He left behind a three-year-old daughter and his wife. Did John want to contact them?

"Maybe someday," he said. "I'm not sure what I'd say to them just now." He took a Boston address. The pilot's wife had moved back to be near her family, the manager said. It was too hard for her to be in Hawaii.

Driving home from the hospital that evening, sitting through nasty traffic prompted by resurfacing on Lake Shore Drive, John tried to ascertain how he felt differently, now that his parents were dead, and he couldn't tell. He didn't feel much differently. There was no punch of sadness or grief or shock and he knew it wasn't coming. The stupidity of what they'd done, the selfishness, that was all still there, wasn't going away. He was glad they'd made a choice so monumental at the end of their lives. He was glad for this, he told himself. His parents were strong, assertive people and it was good they had lived their last year assertively, doing exactly what they wanted. It was good.

The freeway ended, turned west, became Sheridan, and John had a ways farther north to go still. At a stoplight, his vision went blurry, then he couldn't breathe but for the heaves he hardly recognized and he pulled over, pounded on the steering wheel, let the cars pass him, and made a lot of noise. It was dark enough, no one could really tell.

WITH MARGARET'S GRIEF for their death came a manic remembering, a determination to fit her memories into, around, the letters, to weave them together so as to allow them in her understanding of her mother. If Margaret could do this, she told herself, she could accept her parents' end, their decision to go. And so she remembered coming home from school when she was young, and her mother's eyes red and swollen with crying, and how she believed for some reason that Mother was allergic to dandelions, that they did this to her eyes, and maybe Mother told her this, or maybe it was John, she didn't know. But once when Mother got up from a Sunday nap, and Margaret and her father were making, with little success, a cake for Mother's Day, Margaret said, "Mother, I thought you were sleeping but your eyes are red like you've been picking dandelions." Dad had laughed and patted her back and said, "We all need a good cry sometimes, Margaret."

She had been nine maybe, or ten. She wasn't making the cake by herself but she did understand immediately that the dandelion story had been a lie. Her mother left the kitchen and did not come back until Father went upstairs at suppertime, brought her down with his arms wrapped around her, practically holding her up, and her eyes and her face looked worse. He sat down with her and Margaret served the dinner—meatballs they'd made with slightly more success than the cake. Mother didn't really eat, a few bites, no more, but by the time cake was served, she was smiling and seemed to be coming back from whatever place it was she'd gone. She ate two pieces of cake. Later, when John and Margaret were doing the dishes, she gathered them both into a big hug and said she loved them very much, that she was sorry if she misbehaved sometimes.

Instances like this were very few and far between, especially as Margaret got older, but recalling it with their death, for the first time in years, was like finding a book that'd been pushed back behind the others on a shelf.

Margaret knew it wasn't anyone's fault, what had happened in the last year, in the last eighty years, and their family was wonderful, she was a wonderful mother—nothing, really, could touch that. The letters seemed to threaten everything and nothing, and it would likely stay that way, because you can't change your memories when you're fifty-five years old, not at any age. Still, she couldn't help but feel that if she'd known about her mother's depression sooner, much sooner, well, it would at least have explained a lot. Her inscrutability. Her sometimes maddening distance.

But then, the good memories, too, of sitting on her lap in the car, with Dad driving, John in the back, and the radio on, and Mother humming along—she loved Bing Crosby so much. Or lying down at bedtime and Mother rubbing her back, no matter if she was six or sixteen. Margaret remembered her sadness and she remembered her laughter spilling all through the house like April sun, her tickling John and Margaret, chasing them around as a pretend monster. In high school, Mother ordered literally dozens of college catalogues, looking through every one, dog-earing pages she found important or interesting, and when Margaret teased her that she was trying to ship her only daughter off somewhere far away, Mother said, "Never hem in yourself in, Margaret. You must seek out exactly what you want and go after it. And not just now, but always."

Although it was normal parental encouragement, she kept it in her memory like a worry stone, and rubbed it throughout college, law school, even now. Then with she and Terry trying, too late, to have children, and their not being able to talk about their failure, not for years, Mother just listened, telling Margaret it would be fine, to think about adoption, to get some rest and be nice to herself. A new dress maybe. A vacation. Someplace with lots to do, not a beach, for distraction. And Margaret listened.

The other oddities, like hauling them to Amelia Earhart's house or the scrapbooks, or getting so mad and tetchy on the subject of her own flying, the crying jags—Margaret and John may have rolled their eyes at her if she weren't looking, but that was all. There wasn't anything to talk *about*. Not really, and if none of the rest of this had happened—if they'd never flown away, if Margaret had never found those letters—none of this scrutiny would have occurred to her. Because Mother was, on average, much more even-tempered than not. She never lost her temper or was afraid, not even when Father crashed the plane on a fence or cow or even into the barn as he did several times—mostly she laughed at him. She was a good person and a good mother; she loved her children and her husband. What else was there to know?

⁓

THE MEMORIAL SERVICE and luncheon took place on Monday, October 17. It was cold and damp and gray outside, the sort that goes straight through you, gives you a headache like a hangover. Funeral wreaths and bouquets of every color and size lined the walls of the church; a dozen more arrangements were left at the house. Hordes of people turned up and the church was packed. The story had become something of a news item, with a front-section article in the *Des Moines Register, Chicago Tribune,* and *Sun-Times,* plus, oddly enough, a front-page article in the middle of the *Wall Street Journal.* The flowers came from distant, unknown people in places such as Hawaii, England, New York, and California. John and Margaret recognized all their parents' friends plus other locals as well as their own friends; the partner to whom Margaret was closest, also a friend of Terry's, Dan Dashiel, came from the office, and John's longtime secretary, Barb, came, too. Terry's sister came from Des Moines, but not his mother, which Margaret was glad of; her Alzheimer's was a handful. Easily half the church were strangers.

John and Margaret had decided to let the priest choose the regular readings, then they each contributed something, nonscriptural, as extras. Margaret read from the Amelia Earhart biography, annotated by Mother, that they found in the attic, and a snippet from Anne Morrow Lindbergh's early journals, in which she talked about flying with her husband. If it seemed morbid at first, they quickly agreed on it. Mrs.

Lindbergh was, after all, some kind of friend or idol to Ruth, a constant companion, and no one else but Margaret and John would know the real meaning of including her in the service; no one else would be asked to understand it, not even Terry and Susan, because how would Ruth's children talk about the letters, with their spouses, with each other—how do you talk about your mother's diaries? You don't.

For his reading, John managed to dig up Dad's old Air Mail Service manual, the flight instructions from Chicago to Omaha, which was his route for nearly ten years. John also read a few lines from old mail stories taken from a history book on the service. Margaret had barely set foot in St. Joan of Arc since her own wedding. Now, as then, Terry was the steel rod keeping her upright, his hand always at the right place in her back, supporting her through the service and the luncheon, always seeming to say, *Not much more*.

Two women came up to Margaret after the Mass as she disentangled herself from a tactless reporter from Cedar Rapids. The women were Mary Hitchens and Anna Klemman, whom Margaret previously remembered only dimly as Mother's best friends, or at least the ones she saw the most of, at book clubs and luncheons. But then, of course, since the letters, Margaret knew more about them—Mary, in particular, who once truly hurt Margaret's mother, and thus Margaret had nothing to say to her—wished, in fact, she would leave. Anna's health had greatly declined in recent years, such that she didn't recognize many people—neither Margaret nor John, for instance—and she talked to herself a great deal, loudly and usually into silence, reminding herself to take her pills, buy some paper towels, or "phone the children."

"I'm driving down to Florida tomorrow," Mary said to Margaret outside the church as everyone was milling about. "I guess it will take me about four or five days. I'm going to take my time, you know. I'm an old lady."

"I'm going to the car while you talk to the girl, Mary," Anna said, and Mary nearly stopped to remind her who Margaret was, but then didn't, and Margaret was glad.

Mary was Mother's age, give or take a few years—and she radiated vitality and health. The only thing that seemed to be fading in her was any talent she once might've had for getting to the point. She stood by Margaret for fifteen or twenty minutes as everyone passed by and said "Hello" and "I'm sorry" and "I'm so sorry" and "We'll see you at the restaurant." Margaret kept hoping, then praying Mary would leave. Maybe she'd think it was too long to leave Anna alone. Or maybe she'd see that Margaret had a lot to do—things to get together, even the church to go back into so that she could get the readings off the lectern, some of the flowers they had brought in. And she wanted to be sure the priest knew where he was going—they had, of course, invited him to the luncheon, although she had a difficult time even remembering his name. He was new to the parish; it wasn't entirely clear that he even remembered who her parents were. Margaret excused herself to do all these things, and when she returned, Mary was still there, at the back of the church, still there even though fifteen minutes had passed and everyone was gone.

"Your mother would have liked the readings you chose," Mary said when Margaret finally turned her attention to her. "She adored Anne Morrow Lindbergh. Used to talk about her lots."

Margaret stood stock-still. Did Mary know?

"Oh, she really loved Mrs. Lindbergh." Mary laughed a sweet, if cackling laugh. She told Margaret a couple of what she said were Mother's favorite stories about the woman— operating a radio from way above Central America, flying an amphibious plane up around Iceland, and how she and Charles always outfitted their plane for sleeping in it, "Like truckdrivers, right?" Mary laughed. At the end, she added, "I think your mother wanted to be Mrs. Lindbergh. You know, flying all the time."

"Yes, I know," Margaret said, her chest growing tight. She looked out through the glass doors—Terry was sitting there in the car. "But of course, your mother"—Mary was chattering on more insistently now, gripping Margaret's forearm for emphasis—"your mother was never really the same after baby Ruth Anne died. Something in her just went away," Mary said.

Margaret felt slightly as if someone had hit her on the back of the head, and all she could say was, "Right, I know, Mary. You're right."

Mary nodded and still held on to Margaret's arm in a half excitement that reminded Margaret of a child with a big secret to share, and she couldn't believe what this woman had just said, like it was gossip. Margaret, finally, shook her arm quite hard and jostled Mary free—nearly knocking her over in the process. "I've got to get to the lunch, Mary," Margaret said to the old woman's surprised and slightly hurt face. "I've really got to go."

Mary's shock washed away then as her balance was regained—she'd grabbed a pew—and she began babbling

again, something about not being able to come to the restaurant and she was sorry and maybe they could exchange
Christmas cards? But Margaret was gone, to the car, driving,
long before she was actually gone. She waved without looking back, and went through the doors into the chill.

In the car, she cried softly and Terry gave her his handker-
chief, held her hand. She didn't explain.

At the restaurant, a steakhouse that was never open for
lunch except that the owners were good friends of her parents, there was a large ham and a beef roast, sliced for sandwiches, some scalloped potatoes and applesauce, vegetables
and dip, biscuits and zucchini bread. Margaret kept hearing
Mary's voice: "She was never the same." She kept feeling the
insistent squeeze on her arm.

Mother's walking friend Jeanie Cooper, whom Margaret
didn't know very well since she'd just come to town in her
retirement a few years back, was very nice and helpful and
also teary. "I loved your mother so much," she said. "She was
a wonderful, smart, funny woman. Oh, how I'll miss her!"
As for everyone else, it seemed that they all, like Margaret,
had done their grieving in odd ways over the past ten months,
and the news of their death and their memorial service there-
fore served as more of a catharsis. There were very few tears.

She found herself mostly concerned that everything was
going well—that the iced-tea pitcher was full, the coffeemaker was working, the cookie tray had been replenished,
and there were knives in the different mustards set alongside
the ham and roast beef and cheese and party rolls. A couple
of times she looked around the room, at the men who had
watched her grow up and watched her parents and one

another grow old. Would they all say things like Mary Hitchens? Could they all confess disarming observations of her parents, things that meant Margaret could never know her parents as well as she wanted to, as well as she used to think she did?

There were so many things out there—so many things besides Anne Morrow Lindbergh and Ruth Anne and depression and flying that she didn't even know the beginnings of, she didn't even know their shape. The dawning of this sense—the sense of phantom shapes and influences in her parents' characters—was where she had begun this, the year in which they would die. And the bold pronouncement of this sense, in Mary Hitchens—because even reading the letters, Margaret had no idea *why* Mary had said to Ruth what she did so many years ago—this was what marked the end. It all seemed washed in murky grayness.

⌐⌐⌐

AFTER THE LUNCHEON, Margaret, Terry, John, Susan, children, and grandchildren changed into jeans and walking shoes and bundled up and went out to the north field, just as the sun was settling over nearly frozen gray ground. A marker had been placed there the day before, next to Ruth Anne's boulder. It *was* cold—colder than the morning. A bitter, confident wind had kicked up and was coursing across the unobstructed landscape. It took twenty minutes to get there, and Margaret led the way as much as John. At last, there was the boulder, and the marker, just a simple rectangle, like a big brick —or a chock for airplane wheels, one of the grandkids pointed out—which had only their names written on it. All that marked the spot were the tire ruts that went around the boulder, and the decades-old rosebush, wound around the decaying fence post, vital enough, against most odds. It was pretty from here, a commanding point, a look out, the top of the runway.

What to say? John's children seemed to be waiting. Talking among themselves a little, explaining to their small ones, not about the boulder but about the runway, where they were and what was happening. But their ears were half cocked to John and to Margaret. Finally, he found a voice: "I'd like to suggest that we all think of some stories today. Just mull over them all, your memories of this place, of them, and pick one. Tell someone. Tell your children. Write it down and store it away. At Thanksgiving, Christmas, holidays to come, we'll read them. I loved my parents," he said, his voice finally cracking, "and I'll miss them."

Margaret nodded, not being able to lift her gaze from the ground, not wanting to make contact with anyone. Finally, she looked up at John, met his teary eyes, nodded again. She dropped her rose at the marker, kissed it, and then the boulder.

Back at the farmhouse, some used the bathroom and Margaret walked around, making sure the windows were all locked tight. On a closet shelf, oddly enough, John had found a box of pictures taken over the side of the old Jenny while flying. The edge of her cowling was barely visible—a slanting black obscurity at the edge of the frame, and far below, a quilt of land with perfect straight stitches of color distinguishing corn from wheat, sod from soybeans, lawn from sidewalk, water from brown firmament. Some were of a body of water, a reservoir, the river, or even Lake Michigan, with water spreading just to the edges of the frame, known to be water only because of its uniformity.

Together, the pictures created a life, and he imagined putting them all together to make a giant treasure map, that would reveal a source, a resting place. His mother and father had taken the pictures, perhaps to show people where they had been, what it looked like, because who would believe it, back then? Today, they looked like surveyor's photos, like something anyone might see looking out the window of a USAir flight across the Midwest, but not then; then, it was a miracle, God's view. The pictures had long since yellowed, all creams and taupes and near-greens slightly warmer, yellowed the way gasoline exhaust yellows the metal it rushes over; the way age yellows skin and teeth and bones.

❧

As THEY DROVE HOME, the sun set in the middle of Illinois and Margaret felt hollowed out, eviscerated; she didn't know what to feel anymore, and when would it all end? She learned so much more about her mother this last year, straight up to Mary Hitchens's comment, but nothing was *clear* to her, she just didn't understand. Terry tugged her hands out of her mouth, to keep her from chewing her nails, and she was glad she didn't smoke, and she thought, Maybe we've done a good thing. Maybe it's better not to have children. No one will ever have to feel this way, to go through this, about me.

She picked up the pile of mail that they'd brought back from the farm. Dozens of condolence cards were addresssed to the Gutterson family. Margaret paused with one letter sealed in a heavy cream formal envelope; it was addressed to

"Margaret and John Henry Gutterson" and the engraved return address on the back flap read Darien, Connecticut. She couldn't think of anyone she knew in Darien, and slid her penknife across the top, pulling the letter out. A *Wall Street Journal* clipping was folded inside.

October 12, 1988

Dear Margaret and John Henry,

I read this article in the *Wall Street Journal* today with great dismay. As you may or may not know, your mother wrote to me, over many years, and she was a very kind, loving, passionate, and brave person. And devoted, too. As a mother; as a wife; as a pilot. I never knew your father, but I can tell you how brave he was, to have flown the mail back when he did. Charles always said they were the craziest bunch of men, Air Mail pilots.

I wish I'd properly let your mother know how much I thought of her over the years. I didn't, not in time anyway, and I regret that. What I knew of her was so terribly honest and heartfelt—she was always feeling, feeling, feeling, and I suppose this made her a little impulsive, and made her think of such adventures as this last trip—which, if it was selfish (undoubtedly, it was), it was also true. She was true, your mother. All on the surface. I never did meet her in the flesh.

I wish you the best in this difficult time and I shall cut a rose today and put it on my desk in tribute to your parents.

Sincerely,
Anne Morrow Lindbergh

TEN

Flying again. The things I had forgotten. Things going under that
still suspended wheel. How slow the cars, the pattern of houses
doubled with their shadows, box like houses. How still the water!
A boat cutting the water like shears—the heavy satin, rippling
back, falling away on either side, frozen waterfalls, woven cloth
fields . . . and over the earth, a clear, calm light, quiet. One could
sit still and look at life—that was it. The glaze on life again, that
glaze that art puts on life. Is that the fascination of flying?

—*Anne Morrow Lindbergh, March 30, 1933*

THE WATER BELOW was dark and threatening and
Ruth decided she preferred to fly over land, Iowa of course or
someplace like Texas, where there was so much flat and space
and you felt as if you were coasting across a giant shelf above
the rest of the contoured world. She thought of taking off in
Southern California in January and the first time over Cedar
Rapids in the fall, five months before, when all she could do
was laugh and marvel at all the new houses and roads, so

many, and how big the highways were. As the ground fell away beneath her and her stomach lagged behind her body and her sunglassed eyes squinted at the fierce sun, she felt the whole world, her mind and her heart and her soul, expand and rise; her grounded horizon of cities and fields and desert slipped into a blue and white glow of possibility and presence, and everything became so big, so lovely, like an awesome golden platter rimmed in silver with lapis lazuli and pearls. The engine was loud and the little plane bumped along through a few air pockets on the way up. She looked down, out the side window, and she said to herself, "Here, here I am, at last."

It was incredible over the Pacific now, this expanse of water, the power of its mere image, endless and daunting. Ruth's back was bothering her, she shifted in her seat, trying to stretch or ease it, and her knees! So much walking. And she was nearly through her arthritis prescription. What if she'd never seen the ocean, or never seen it like this, anyway? And how many people had never seen Iowa, didn't know what it felt like there? Dozens of people on the trip hadn't even known where Iowa was situated. Next to Pennsylvania? they'd ask. Or no, wait, next to Washington, the state? Ruth found it appalling. Wouldn't it be nice, right then, she thought, to be in the Jenny and not this King Air, to feel the ocean air on her face?

At first the trip and its anonymity were glorious and thrilling and from it sprang youth and a grace to repair their regrets, to see the things they should've seen twenty, forty, sixty years before, to just go, to fly away. She had even written Mrs. Lindbergh, mailed it, the first time in how many years? Oh, she'd made it, they were there, in the world, after all.

November 15, 1987

Anne Morrow Lindbergh
c/o Charles A. Scribner and Sons Publishers
Fifth Avenue
New York City

Dear Mrs. Lindbergh,

It has been nearly fifty-four years since my last letter to you. It was 1933, the year following the one in which each of us lost infant children. I am sorry that I did not write to you when Colonel Lindbergh died in 1974, but I thought much about you.

He was a great, great man and you don't need me to tell you that. But he was a person who lived by his own convictions and never by what others wanted or expected of him. If only we could all live so truly!

It seems to me that lives grow and change in infinite ways and at different rates—and it is still funny to me that my husband Henry and your Charles started at about the same place—in the northern Midwest, flying for the Air Mail Service. Since the last letter you had of me over fifty years past, Henry and I have not moved from our farm in Iowa, nor have we become important people in any sense. What we have done is raise two fine children—one a doctor and the other a lawyer—and we have stood by and watched as the single-engine biplane spawned the Tri-Motor, then the DC-3, and now all the jets. I wonder how many Curtiss Jennies—remember the original mail plane?—could fit inside this new monster, the 747!

My daughter tells me women still do not have exactly the same choices as men in this world—we never will because we are such different species, men and women—but so many things have changed since our youth. I wouldn't trade anything that I have had for something that I haven't, however. Of course this is not to say that I haven't had my unhappiness, my disappointments. This is only to say that I don't believe life has been unfair to me. Fairness, of course, is never something God bothers to explain to us, does He? But still, I am at peace. I have lived a full life.

I do wonder what you would say to me if you were to respond to one of my letters, just once. Probably you have never gotten a single one of them. Or maybe you've gotten a few, and, having decided that I was completely crazy, you have disregarded all the others. I cannot say that I blame you. I am very sorry if I ever disturbed you. That was never my intention.

After all these years, I got back up in a plane last October. Henry helped find me an instructor who thought the both of us to be legends after he stumbled upon some old pictures in a deep, dark archive at the University of Iowa library. Pictures of Henry and me flying the mail together back before 1928 and John's birth; pictures of us with John after he soloed; pictures of Henry in front of twenty different planes over forty-odd years. This instructor was a real nut for history and he wanted to hear all about our lives, everything.

"You'd think we were the Lindberghs!" I said to him once when he was asking so many questions. "You might as well be," he said. Next, he agreed to take me up in his 172, see if I couldn't solo at long last. And I did. I won't tell you what it felt like because you know. You know the ecstasy, the physical and spiritual sensation of lifting from the earth and entering that space that scientists quantify and only pilots swim in. The feeling of being pulled up above the audience as if on a wire, a great wire that will let you go where you want, a wire that you trust as you trusted your mother's hand on your shoulder or your knee as she read to you or showed you how to cook an egg. The world takes on a different property—namely of being separate from you, a feeling of pure detachment, a feeling of power, as you say, "the glaze on life."

Henry and I are about to do a bit of traveling just now—perhaps I'll send you a postcard!—and when we're finished, I suppose we'll finally settle into the rest of our lives. I have a feeling that everything has happened to us that's going to happen, and my feelings like this are usually spot-on. We're 80 and 87 years old, after all. I suppose it's about time to face the curtain's fall. Henry will probably live until he's a hundred and ten. He has that feel about him. He seems vaguely middle-aged to me even though he's been napping in the afternoons many years longer than I. As for me, I don't expect I'll see 85.

You've been a good friend to me, Mrs. Lindbergh, whether you know it or not, whether you care or not. Still, you would have liked me, I think. We would have been great friends because at one time we had a lot in common; and always, I believe as much as I believe in flight itself, have we been similar women. It is too bad that you have never known me as I have known you; you have certainly had the chance. And perhaps, after all, you have read every one of my letters and perhaps they have seemed as close as diary entries, as your books sometimes seem to me, and perhaps you have never known how to respond, that it was not by choice but by inability. But, you must know, I love and admire you no matter.

Your friend,
Ruth Gutterson
Cedar Bluff, Iowa

It was the postcards that Philippe and Yvette sent in the early sixties—after fifteen years of nothing from them, they suddenly began sending postcards again—and these cards started the trickle of a plan, an extended wandering, in Ruth's mind. Pictures of the Statue of Liberty, the Smoky Mountains, Mount Rushmore, the Grand Canyon, and Big Sur; of Gatlinburg, Atlanta, the Alamo, Boston Common, and Washington, D.C., came to their mailbox once every week or so, for almost a year. "We're seeing the United States," Philippe wrote. "Seeing the whole thing, slowly. You must do this sometime." In another card: "This is simply the experience of a lifetime. We might next fly to South America. I have not done enough of this. And why not? I have no reason. What's yours?" And finally, on the last postcard, from San Diego: "Won't you two join us? I know your children are grown; your parents can take care of themselves. You have nothing to lose. Come meet us in Mexico City! I'll be the ambassador and you can be the Lindberghs!"

Both Ruth and Henry read these cards with some amount of fascination and envy. They wouldn't meet Philippe and Yvette, no, the four of them would be impossible; the Iowa visit in 1943 told them that, Henry said, and Ruth agreed, but they would go themselves, sometime. They did go to Hawaii in 1965, flying in a 707. Ruth slept soundly in a seat that reclined and for the first time she and Henry looked out over the land together and discussed what they saw in normal tones. No shouting, no pounding, or pointing, or clearing of goggles—and no shuddering or shaking. They left the plane without a headache or any vague sense of vibration in their bones—Henry was amazed. For Ruth, the 707 did not really count as getting up in a plane again—passenger airliner travel was as close to her old flying and navigating experiences in the Jenny as eating cherry-flavored candy was to eating a cherry. And she had cut a wide swath around the Jenny, until she more or less forgot it was there, even though for decades the plane sat behind the barn, without wheels or struts, belly to the earth from which she once lifted, and she rotted. Her dull, khaki, doped-linen body retained every storied stain of oil, dirt, and blood, from god knows how many engine gaffes, cut hands, and other flying creatures that perished in contact with her. Eventually, a small maple sapling started right up through the Jenny's body and millipedes and slugs appreciated the soft, cool wetness in that space.

None of Margaret's or John's friends were particularly afraid of dark, dank, spacious barns, but the Jenny was another matter. Games were played there, in which one was dared to climb in the old plane at night and stay, alone, for a count to one hundred. Other times, they all huddled inside together and John told ghost stories about the men before his father who had flown her and were now dead and probably their spirits lived in the Jenny. But Ruth had so strenuously averted her attentions that she missed all of this, until John asked if they could build a haunted house in the Jenny for Halloween, charge five cents for entrance. A haunted Jenny, he said. It would be a big success.

But Ruth turned ashen and sent him out of the kitchen. Under no circumstances would there be any "haunted Jenny," she said later. It was too dangerous.

In Hawaii, they spent ten days walking all over the volcanoes, beaches, and forests—the sort of landscape Ruth had barely been able to imagine as real even with pictures in books and on television, it was so fantastical and lush and otherworldly. When they got home, they talked of Paris and London—Henry wanted to take her there, to Europe, he said, and renew a promise from before their engagement. They planned to go in 1967. The spring before, Ruth bought an elegant hat and a new dress in anticipation of the fancy dinners they would have. Then her father died a couple of days before the trip.

Henry had taken lunch out to the eighty-year-old, who was working on the tractor a couple of hundred yards into the north field. They had five years since contracted with a younger farmer to do most of the work but when the equipment broke, Paul liked to try and fix it. When Henry came home from morning lessons at the airfield, Ruth said her father had been out there for hours and wouldn't Henry take him an egg salad sandwich and some lemonade, see if he couldn't fix the thing? Ten minutes later, Henry came upon Paul, laid out on the cool shady side of the tractor, his face fixed in a peaceful, contented stare, as if he were watching the clouds or an airliner go by, a wrench still in one grease-coated hand and his legs slightly apart. A bruise had developed on the side of his head—from hitting the side of the tractor on the way down, and he had passed.

There was no way to carry him to the house by himself,

and so Henry took his shirt off and covered the man's front; then he wiped his hands clean and gently pressed Paul's eyelids closed. He walked back to Elizabeth, catching the John Deere man, at last, on his way into the field, telling him to go on back to the store for the afternoon. To call the undertaker when he got back to town and come back the next day, if he could.

Elizabeth asked to be taken there, saying nothing else until she arrived at her husband in a slowly lengthening noon shadow. She sat on the ground and took his head in her lap and commenced swaying forward and backward, barely whispering something like a lullaby as if coaxing a colicky baby to sleep. Henry felt invasive as he watched this and yet he wasn't sure what to do, either. Elizabeth said to him, "Go, Henry. Leave us. Get Ruth." And then she went back to her husband of sixty-odd years. In the last steps that took Henry out of earshot, he could make out a single heave of grief, and then another, and then he couldn't hear anymore.

Ruth ran from the house all the way through the fields as if there were something yet to do, and Henry knew she wanted to get to the man before he was any further gone.

For a little while, he was afraid that the death might spark her sickness, but it didn't. Instead, she found a purpose in being strong for her mother. She supported her as they walked out of the field that night, at dusk, when Joe Gustafson and John Frieberg and Charlie Cilek came down and helped Henry carry Paul to the undertaker's car. Elizabeth insisted on staying in her own bed in her own house and so Ruth stayed, too, making tea and coffee and toast as requested, pacing the house the whole night, wondering how her mother's life would change, wondering if her father had gone to a better place, and hoping such a place existed.

Elizabeth stayed in the house alone, then, for two and a half years, carrying on much as she had the previous seventy-two years. One day she awoke without her right side and moved to Hillsdale just beyond Cedar Bluff to the west, where they had pinochle leagues and a pond near the cafeteria. Ruth visited there with someone else—Henry or the children, when they were home, or Mary Hitchens—four or five days a week. They pushed Elizabeth on the path around the pond and they showed her photographs or a news article that might interest her. Ruth always asked for a recipe or two even though she never really needed them. Elizabeth would spend twenty minutes talking about how to pit a cherry her perfect, secret way, how to know when there was the right amount of sugar in a pie, when to thicken with tapioca and when not to. Her face would light up with focus and enthusiasm when giving such counsel. Her hands would lift—even her right hand would rise a half centimeter from the leather armrest on the wheelchair.

Ruth could never really tell if Elizabeth was happy or unhappy at Hillsdale because the woman was simply resigned to it, as she seemed to have been to the rest of her life. And yet during her four years there, Ruth became closer to her mother than she had ever been. Without her father, Ruth had no opportunity to criticize her mother's silent obedience; she had no opportunity to hope for her mother's support against him, and as such, no opportunity to be disappointed. She tried to arrive in time for Elizabeth's bath a few days a week. Ruth, with only a little lifting help from a strong woman named Roberta, could bathe Elizabeth slowly, and well. As such, she came to know the worn edges, ends, and folds of her mother's body almost as well as she had known her own children's. The curious reversal in this was not lost on either mother or daughter and Ruth found herself hoping that Margaret or John Henry would be as devoted to her. Yet at the same time, she resolved that she would never live out her days at a place like Hillsdale. Not ever.

One day in the last spring of Elizabeth's life, when the crocuses were up and open to the sky and bluebells were sprouting and the grass was green as the Irish flag, she was unusually talkative and reflective. They circled the pond four times because it was such a nice afternoon and Ruth had plenty of time and she could tell her mother liked the breeze on her face. The smell of mud and rain and seed and newness swam around them. Elizabeth closed her eyes and talked about the running races she and her sisters used to have to the end of the fence line and back, about seeing President Roosevelt on the train in 1908, about meeting Paul for the first time and how she was charmed by his slight Irish brogue. She dozed in the wheelchair for a while with her head lolling to the side. When she opened her eyes one and a half laps later, she said, "The hardest thing and the best thing anyone has ever done is be a good mother, Ruth."

Ruth nodded and did not say anything; what could she say in response to this anyway?

And Elizabeth let several minutes go by before she said, "I know you know this. But I wanted to say it even so." She reached one trembling hand up to the handles at the back of her chair and she fumbled for her daughter's hand, found it, patted it.

Her death came in the fall of that year, 1972, on a cloudless October day full of chill and color. Ruth felt both abandoned and free, guilty and relieved. She went to Hillsdale for some months afterward, once a week, to visit Elizabeth's roommate, whose children lived far away.

Over that next decade or so, there were days when Ruth would be washing breakfast dishes and she would look out the kitchen window over the yard and driveway, to the barn and the fields beyond it. She could not believe that four decades had passed since Ruth Anne's death, that she was well past sixty, on the way to seventy and beyond, because she felt the same bewilderment at how to spend the rest of her life as she had felt at twenty-five. She was surprised, sometimes, that she had lived so long already, married, and raised two children who made her proud and brought warmth and ease to her. But there was still the question of what to do. There had been the trip to London and Paris that was canceled by her father's death, still waiting to be rescheduled. And they would go, someday, across America, too, like Yvette and Philippe, and wouldn't it be fun to just pick up and go, without a plan, to just go?

Ruth was not unhappy. She had an ever-increasing amount of time to read and play chess and go for long walks and visit her children and grandchildren, which gave her a surprising amount of pleasure. Just after Elizabeth's death, Margaret hit a tough time when she and Terry found they were infertile, and Ruth was glad to go to Chicago for a weekend, to welcome Margaret home, to answer her phone calls, at least, every day. For so long, Margaret had been a career woman—they were a career couple and it seemed to make her happy. She told her mother she didn't feel ready for children, and while Ruth certainly had understood that feeling when Margaret was in law school, there were alarm bells going off in her head by the time they were both thirty, and Margaret, at least, was still "not ready." Terry got two puppies, golden retrievers, and named them Rawlings and Wilson—his parents had been in sporting goods—and he taught them to fetch tennis balls and Frisbees. Ruth saw this as clear a sign as any that the man wanted children, but she kept her mouth closed.

And then, finally, Margaret just woke up one day and decided she wanted children. It was just like her, to decide so impetuously, so intuitively. She had rarely been a child or a woman who did things because she was *supposed* or *expected* to, but rather operated on pure desire and will. She wasn't selfish, however; on the contrary, she was possessed of self-knowledge and confidence that meant she was never afraid to give of herself. Anyway, to Ruth there seemed little ambivalence or indecision in her daughter's life and she envied this.

But when they tried to get pregnant and failed, Margaret was crushed, not least because she wasn't accustomed to failure. Terry was nearly sterile, and so, Ruth had to believe, secretly, was Margaret, at age thirty-seven. The marriage would be fine—that was clear. They loved each other and got along as well as childhood playmates. But Margaret was so sad, guilt-ridden, and angry, too. Ruth told her time and again how full her life would be without children; how valuable her career was, how rare and impressive, the only female partner in one of Chicago's best firms; and if they could think about adoption, there was that.

One day, out of nowhere, Margaret said she hoped Ruth had never taken personally any of her own decisions about career and home and family, that she was never explicitly choosing *against* what Ruth's life had been, and "I just, well . . ." she said, in a rare moment of speechlessness. "I don't want you to think I don't admire you and your life and your choices, because mine have been so different, and now that I won't have children, more different still."

Ruth was both touched and a little amused. "I've never had the choices you've had, for one, Margaret," she said. "But no, I've never thought that." And although this wasn't true, not wholly, anyway, because of course Margaret was choosing against being an Iowa farm wife and mother—as a successful big-city lawyer, could her choices have been more opposite, more opposed?—Ruth didn't feel personally offended by it.

There were still the letters, still written and never sent; it was a habit as ingrained as making jam in August. Every now and then she would read of someone, one of the old-timers, Jacqueline Cochran, one of the '99ers, and she would clip the piece, write something. It gave her the same sense of calm as Henry breathing next to her, behind her, in the early hours of the morning when she awoke and looked out the window at the day's arrival.

If she still felt like she was waiting for something, wondering what was around the corner, it was a feeling that she had become quite accustomed to. She knew there was something else there, to come. But she was no longer in such a hurry to get there.

Henry, too, felt at ease as they approached their golden wedding anniversary. The spark in Ruth that he once feared would never reappear had restored itself in time, as water diverted to another body. Her spark came through in her decisive and energetic mothering and now grandmothering and in the running of hers and Henry's life; in the obsession with aviation fact and history; and in her absolute refusal to go near a plane, not a small private one anyway (she happily climbed aboard an airline). He realized gradually that her will to fly and her subsequent will to stay grounded were one in the same. And although Henry mostly believed that if Ruth got into the cockpit of a small plane with him, she would know a joy she had denied herself for thirty, then forty years, he eventually trusted that she knew what she was doing, that she was wise not to fly. He thought of the ghost story about the woman who wore a perfect scarlet ribbon around her beautiful neck at all times and the husband who finally could not resist removing it to see *all* of his wife's neck. As it came away, her head fell off. If Ruth wanted to keep her scarlet ribbon in place, so be it.

When, at last, she then tore the ribbon off herself, first with her lessons and then soloing, he had long since given them both up to age; and he had long since stopped wondering how it worked in Ruth, how she had kept herself from flying for so long, and if she was happy enough. Watching her, that day, climb into the 172, strap herself in, and signal for the instructor to prop the plane for her, he knew she hadn't given it up, not ever. And then, when she came back down, there it was in the corners of her mouth, the pitch of her eyebrows, the lift in both places. Here was Ruth, after so long. Back to Ruth, all of her. Again.

They had been talking about the trip for twenty years, and shouldn't he have known that with the flying lessons would come Ruth's insistence, at last, when they were too old, with a great-grandchild on the way? Henry had been ambivalent. He couldn't imagine putting his children and friends through the worry of not knowing where they'd gotten to. But Ruth had been adamant. "Why does anyone have to know where we are? Let's just pretend, for a day, for a week, that no one in the whole world needs us. That it's just us, you and I. The children will figure out that we're just fine and then they'll understand. I don't want to hear them tell us we can't do this—we might agree with them. And we won't be gone long, just until spring. How many of our friends go south for the winter?"

Because the counter to this argument was so obvious, so broad—the idea was simply cruel and ridiculous—Henry had not been able to issue it successfully. "I don't think it's a good idea, Ruth," he ventured, as she spread the tour books out before him—California, Nevada, Colorado, Arizona, New Mexico, so many. "Not to tell them, that is. It seems mean to me."

She was looking at him, her eyes shining, and she reached across the table to take his hand, which he wouldn't give her. He looked out the window, it was raining, and he thought of the moment nearly five decades before when, among lightning bug flashes and their young children's screeches of glee and amazement, he had called her a coward. That single moment had, in some sense, been the coal for her present, crude diamond of a plan, and he knew it. Or, at least, the penance for those, the harshest words he'd ever spoken, was his complicity now. Besides, if he objected to this trip, if he tried to change her plans, if he tried to tell the children, she would fly away without him. And he loved her too much, needed her too much, after all these years.

IN THE BEGINNING, Henry humored her a bit. And then he was heartbroken over Philippe, who had called just days before the trip to say he was sick and wasn't sure he'd live to their reunion in May. Henry first thought of going to Miami immediately, but then resolved, No, I'll make it a few weeks, and this is Ruth's trip; we'll go where she wants first. She's waited long enough. But then, from Santa Barbara at Christmas, when Henry called to check in, say they'd be there in a few weeks, the housekeeper answered, said she was sorry, but Mr. DeBreault had died. Would Henry insist on going there? Going home? Henry replaced the phone, slowly, sat quiet for a few moments, and then got ready for dinner. He didn't sleep that night, Ruth knew this, but she didn't ask about it.

They stayed an extra day there, Ruth sitting at the pool with a book and Henry staying in the room, where he wrote a secret postcard to Margaret and John, sent it to Margaret's home address in Chicago. "We're fine," he wrote. "Don't worry. I'm sorry. See you soon, before the frost breaks." It was raining when he mailed it and he had jogged to the box outside their hotel in Santa Barbara, released the postcard—a picture of horse at a river at sunset, quite pretty, he thought— heard it hit the bottom of the box, turned, and slipped back to the hotel, trusting his old friend the postal service. How was he supposed to know that the felt-tip ink would run, there had been enough rain on the card before it went into the box, it was indecipherable? While he was gone, Ruth was drinking coffee at breakfast, scrawling a letter to Mrs.

Lindbergh on the back of a brochure from Hearst Castle. From Santa Barbara, they would head to Arizona and then to Texas, and finally they hoped to get over to Hawaii once again. From there, home, in time for spring flowers.

March 31, 1988

Dear _____,

I have begun to worry that the children will be horribly angry with us for never giving them any warning of our little trip. Have we been so terribly selfish? I think we have. We are in Hawaii now, and after a few more days here will likely return. Placing a telephone call or sending a card at this point seems a little ridiculous, as we'll be home so soon. Although I had such an awful dream last night, Margaret in a car accident, that I nearly picked up the phone at 2 a.m. just to be sure she's all right.

I read a story in the paper last week about Ruth Law Oliver, an old pilot I used to follow, since she flew at state fairs and such across the Midwest. She actually was the first person to fly mail to the Philippines—and she was a wonderful daredevil. I saw her do the loop-the-loop in 1921, and you'd never seen a thing like it. The same rules didn't seem to apply to her, in her airplane, as they do to the rest of us. Anyway, she was wonderful and I've told my granddaughters all about her. But I've always been puzzled why she quit flying so suddenly, at the top of her game, in 1922. And this story I've just read in a magazine says her husband got fed up with her flying one day and sent an announcement to the local paper saying she'd retired. She saw the news just as everybody else did, over morning coffee, and she lived by her husband's design.

She must have loved him very much, or she was a fool. Both ways, I'm sad she stopped flying. Do you think she snuck up there again one day, like me?

If ever there was proof that flight is a disease, and airplanes the vessels, and there is no cure, I'm it. My whole life has been shaped by it; my whole being transformed; and yet it's never been quite right for me to fly. Never destined or ordained. This much I know. And I hope my children can forgive me without understanding.

Still over the Pacific, and where were they now? It had been nearly twenty minutes since they last saw land, or could it have been longer? Ruth looked at her watch, one-thirty; had they left at ten-thirty or eleven-thirty? Oh, she really couldn't remember. But where were they now? She looked out her window; the horizon looked dark but she knew nothing about flying in these parts of the world. Or what it would be like to go down in water, whether you would hit harder or not as hard, whether the plane would splinter faster or slower or not at all. She tried out the physics in her head. How much friction, how the surfaces would react against each other, would they die on impact or when the sharks got to them or would they drown or freeze. She supposed it would be better to go down in the South Pacific than in the North Atlantic.

They would be heading back soon, when they'd had enough of Hawaii; they were both eager to stop packing and unpacking, and in the King Air, Ruth felt the urge to be back, so strongly. She longed to be standing at the kitchen sink and looking out the window and knowing how the whole day would unfold. She longed for the Iowa air, for the grocery shopping she could do with her eyes closed, for the finches and sparrows and the mourning doves and the new family of starlings that had taken up residence under the eaves on the south side of the house. A *murmuration* of starlings, she knew. She longed to see farmland, the Mississippi in all its coursing murkiness, and the superhighway I-80, splayed east to west from Davenport to Council Bluffs with eighteen-wheelers flowing along like blood in a vein. And she wanted to be near her children again, to pick up the phone when they called, to step into a room and remember it as their bedroom, smell both of their vague scents. She wanted to tell them she was sorry for whatever worry she caused and she wanted to tell them what she and Henry had seen. She missed Margaret's vexed huff, John's all-knowing nod, both children's perfect kisses on her cheek, no matter how old anyone was. After eighty years of Iowa and motherhood, she hadn't expected to want to go back so much—to long for it as she had longed much of her life for the rest of the world, anything besides Cedar Bluff. But there it was.

She went forward to see Henry, in the head pilot's seat, messing with some instrument he didn't understand. The charter pilot, John, was in the bathroom and Ruth watched the autopilot as Henry reached for some manual or another. His once-dark-brown hair was now a sturdy, defiant silver and his eyes squinched in a hundred tiny folds at the edges from too many years in the wind and sun and cold. His green eyes were the same or even clearer, nearly translucent, as they were the day they met, and Ruth loved him beyond herself. Loved him as she loved her own hand, which is to say he was vital, nearly the most vital part of her, he was the key to every-thing she did, everything she touched.

What was wrong with the fuel tanks, Henry wondered, because there was a red light telling him they were danger-ously low, which seemed impossible, too stupid. He didn't know this plane or its instruments. Lowenstein was certainly taking his time in the toilet and Henry was starting to get a little bit nervous. Somewhere behind him, a half hour, maybe, there had been lovely volcanoes and cliffs and beaches but too much wind, a fierce storm kicking up. Where was the near-est place to land? All of a sudden, he felt unusually panicky and told himself that Lowenstein would be back any second. There would be reserve tanks, or a bad fuel gauge, and they would be, in fact, fine. After all his years of flying Popsicle sticks wrapped in tissue—for him to get nervous in this safe, sophisticated King Air seemed ridiculous. He peered out at the horizon, a darkening, foreboding midnight blue before him, and sighed.

In the bathroom, Lowenstein swallowed his four aspirin hard, hoping his headache—god, did he feel awful—would dissipate. What do you call a pilot suffering a paralyzing migraine? he joked to himself with a wan smile. Johnnie Crash! He splashed his face and stepped back into the cabin. As he turned to the cockpit, he watched old Mr. Gutterson lean across the cockpit and kiss his wife in the middle of her forehead, right at her ever-whitening hairline. They rested against each other like that for a moment and Lowenstein continued to watch. Mrs. Gutterson must've come forward while he was in the bathroom. It was sweet, the two of them, eighty-something-year-olds, up there.

"Let's go home," Ruth said into the pressurized silence of the cabin.

"Yes," Henry said. "All right." He was ready, too, even after a burst of energy these last few weeks, which were really more his than Ruth's. Since the mailing of the postcard and getting past Philippe's sudden death a little, he had begun to enjoy himself, eventually taking over some planning. Baja California and a little bit of Mexico had been his idea, just the thing for January, and the Grand Canyon, Tucson, Flagstaff, Scottsdale—he understood why so many old folks retired there. Hawaii had taken his breath away, yet again; he couldn't believe Iowa was on the same planet. But most of all, he enjoyed giving Ruth, at last, something she wanted, what she deserved, and this was more satisfying to them both, more thoroughly warming and calming and life-giving, than he ever could have dreamed. They had put over ten thousand miles on the car in five months' time; she was finally getting her trip.

But now he, too, was ready to be an old man back in Iowa. Now, at last, someplace offshore of Hawaii, heading to Maui with questionable skies before them and a pilot who'd decided to spend fifteen minutes in the john, Henry looked forward to kissing the cornfields again, to the predictability of spring, summer, fall, and winter on the farm, to the home of all his memories, of his children and grandchildren and great-grandchildren.

Lowenstein watched this tender scene for twenty seconds before something wrong hit him, something happened, and he went down to the floor of the cabin.

As they both turned back to see where the noise came from, it was Ruth who had the sharp, panicky intake of air and said,

"Oh my god, what's wrong with him?" Henry, despite his earlier panic, recognized their death when he saw it.

It wasn't very long before the engines went hush and there it came, in a silver blue-black, sweltering mass. Ruth looked forward, then at Henry, then forward again, thinking it would have been nice if they could've opened a window. She turned back to Henry. She lifted her dress and slip just slightly so that she could sit on his lap, facing him. She wrapped her arms around him and held on. He buried his face in her chest, he sighed once, and they were silent.

ACKNOWLEDGMENTS

THIS BOOK PROFITED from many keen readers and editors, among them my siblings and their "pluses"—Meghan Hughes and Kimball Mayer, Jim Hughes and Holly Stewart—and my mom, Sheila Hughes. Karen Anderson, Holiday Reinhorn, Alexis Claiborn, Erin Murphy, Jen Renzi, and my godmother, Suzy Perozzi, were also great readers and supporters. Thanks to the copy machines at unnamed financial institutions, and to my brother and Taryn for access therein.

My husband, Tim Groves, has provided not only honest opinions but also endless good humor, fan mail, and back rubs. Thank you.

As books have their shepherds, my agent, Paula Balzer, has given invaluable enthusiasm and faith to this project, and friendship to me. I am also grateful to Jill Bialosky and Deirdre O'Dwyer at Norton for their thoughtful, welcoming reception of *Dear Mrs. Lindbergh*.

As a secondary dedication of sorts, I need to mention my grandfather, George Priester, who flew an Argo Standard from Chicago to a cornfield in Industry, Illinois, to court my grandmother, Veta Bedwell Priester, in the early 1930s. Though their story bears no other similarity to Ruth's and Henry's, my grandfather's long life in, and passion for, aviation have bequeathed a love of flying to several generations of his family. As he nears his ninety-fifth year, he still goes "to the airport" every day—to an office near the main runway of Pal-Waukee Airport in Wheeling, Illinois, which he founded.

Finally, the only regret I have as *Dear Mrs. Lindbergh* goes to press is that my father cannot put this book on a shelf in his office. He showed me the necessity of clean sentences, the vitality of detail, and the grace in subtlety. He was also the book's sharpest editor, and is responsible for some factual accuracies that very few others could ascertain. To him I owe much.

NOTES

page 7: Lindbergh, Anne Morrow. *Locked Rooms and Open Doors: Diaries and Letters of Anne Morrow Lindbergh 1933–1935.* New York and London: Harcourt, Brace, and Jovanovich, 1974.

page 11: Glines, Carroll V., Colonel, United States Air Force, *The Saga of the Air Mail.* Princeton, N.J.: D. Van Nostrand Co., 1968.

page 44: Lopez, Donald. *Smithsonian Guides: Aviation.* New York: Macmillan, 1995.

page 76: Bilstein, Roger E. *Flight in America: From the Wrights to the Astronauts.* London and Baltimore: The John Hopkins University Press, 1994.

page 99: Lindbergh, *Locked Rooms and Open Doors.*

page 129: Bilstein, *Flight in America.*

page 151: Lopez, *Smithsonian Guides: Aviation.*

page 177: Lindbergh, *Locked Rooms and Open Doors.*

page 212: Lopez, *Smithsonian Guides: Aviation.*

page 246: Lindbergh, *Locked Rooms and Open Doors.*

page 277: Lindbergh, *Locked Rooms and Open Doors.*

BIBLIOGRAPHY

Berg, A. Scott. *Lindbergh*. New York: Berkley Books, 1999.

Bilstein, Roger E. *Flight in America: From the Wrights to the Astronauts*. London and Baltimore: Johns Hopkins University Press, 1994.

David, Paul T. *The Economics of Air Mail Transport*. Washington, D.C.: The Brookings Institution, 1934.

Earhart, Amelia. *The Fun of It*. New York: Putnam, 1932.

Glines, Carroll V., Colonel, United States Air Force. *The Saga of the Air Mail*. Princeton, N.J.: D. Van Nostrand Co., Inc., 1968.

Lindbergh, Anne Morrow. *Locked Rooms and Open Doors: Diaries and Letters of Anne Morrow Lindbergh 1933–1935*. New York and London: Harcourt, Brace, and Jovanovich, 1974.

Lopez, Donald. *Smithsonian Guides: Aviation*. New York: Macmillan, 1995.

Rado, Sandor. "The Problem of Melancholia," in *The Meaning of Despair: Psychoanalytic Contributions to the Understanding of Depression*. Willard, Gaylin, M.D., ed. New York: Science House, Inc., 1968.

Rendall, Ivan. *The Adventure of Flight: Reaching for the Skies*. London: BBC Books, 1988.

www.airmailpioneers.org

DEAR MRS.
LINDBERGH

Kathleen Hughes

The story of Henry and Ruth has two origins. The first is a news story in late 1997 about an elderly couple who went missing while driving home to Iowa from Thanksgiving at their child's home in Chicago. I was living in Iowa City at the time, finishing graduate school. I never did find out what happened to the couple, but I began to wonder what they might have done for themselves if they had planned some kind of adventure or mystery trip. Furthermore, I wondered, what past events would motivate two octogenarians to disappear for a little while? I am sure I missed the small capsule report that described the couple's discovery in good condition; I did try and go back and find it on microfilm several months after the fact, but to no avail.

At the same time that I was thinking about this couple, I was reading several reams of letters that my paternal grandfather wrote to his first cousin on a daily basis in the late sixties and early seventies, around the time they both lost their spouses. My grandmother died in June 1972, four months after I was born, and so I never knew her yet grew up very aware of her absence in my grandfather's and father's lives.

Grandfather and "cousin Mary Catherine" grew up as near-siblings, the only children of sisters who lived on the same block of Seminary Street in Greencastle, Indiana. Mary Catherine eventually settled in Easton, Pennsylvania, while Grandfather stayed in Indiana. Grandfather's letters were both surprising and familiar; the letter that described his delight in a new soap, Irish Spring (he loved all things Irish), and its healthy lather jibed with his giving his grandchildren boxes of the soap to take home and the ever-present smell that it exuded in his two bathrooms. I also knew he loved raw onions but felt awe at the three-line-long letter that described only his lunch of "onions with butter on crackers, and a glass of milk" one day in the week after Grandmother's death.

And so I was considering how much one cannot know about grandparents, what gets lost between generations, even if a general sense of things—such as my child's generalized sense that Grandmother's death destroyed my grandfather—is carried along. I thought of the distance between children and parents, too. Though parents and children know one another in ways no one else can, parents and children also miss critical things about each other, too. Children, especially, never got to know their parents as children, or even young adults. Half a parent's life, often, is a mystery to children.

Now shift to my maternal grandparents. My maternal grandfather, Opa, began to fly in 1928, when he and his brothers ran an auto repair shop in Oak Park, Illinois. A man offered to give my grandfather flying lessons in exchange for looking over his airplane engine. When Opa fell in love with a girl who lived on a farm in distant southern Illinois, his flying lessons came in handy and he flew down and landed in her cornfield to court her. Gradually, my grandfather combined a career on the Chicago-Northwestern Railroad with a passion for flying, and he bought and developed Pal-Waukee Airport in suburban Chicago until it became one of the largest private airports in the world. When I was little, Opa used to take me flying in little Cessnas and Pipers and he'd ask casually, fifteen hundred feet up, "Did you lock the door?" He'd work the pedals and give me the illusion that I was actually taking off and landing the plane all by myself. Select elementary and middle-school holidays, I'd go into the office with him and "work" by answering the phones ("Priester Aviation, may I help you?"), sharpening pencils, making copies, and taking a long lunch in The Hangar restaurant, eating a BLT and a chocolate shake in dark leather banquettes beneath picture boards of Amelia Earhart and Charles Lindbergh, watching little jets and planes descend overhead and kiss, then hug, the runway.

My maternal grandmother, Oma, died when I was ten, and I watched Opa's world, like grandfather's, become defined by his loneliness, by his widowerhood, by all the objects and random slippers and canned fruit stored about that had been hers. As the years went by, I wondered about Oma in the same way I wondered about Grandmother: What had she been like beyond a ten-year-old's view of her? What had she been like when she was young? What were her passions? And what would life have been like for her if she had been more passionate about flying than her husband?

From these various autobiographical pieces, but with no part of any real person (apart from my sense of my grandmothers as very strong, independent women), rose Henry and Ruth. I started with the image in my mind of a young wife, saying good-bye to her husband in a cornfield as he climbed into a plane and flew away. I then combined the idea that this same couple would disappear without explanation for a "mystery adventure" sixty years later. Ruth and Henry, and their disappearance, were born.

I suppose that it seems obvious and logical that letter writing would find its way into the story—but they were not part of my original concept. I began them after researching Anne Morrow Lindbergh for a while—reading her diaries—and coming to feel that Ruth would find Mrs. Lindbergh a kindred spirit and an admirable woman. In Ruth's intense loneliness, I thought, she would find solace in writing to Anne Morrow Lindbergh.

DISCUSSION QUESTIONS

1. Do you find Henry and Ruth's trip understandable, or unfathomably selfish?

2. How would you explain Ruth's breakdown?

3. How do you think baby Ruth Anne dies?

4. Why do you think flying especially captures Ruth's imagination?

5. To what extent is Ruth a product of her time?

6. What are the barriers to Ruth's happiness?

7. What role does Philippe play in the book?

8. How would you describe Henry's affection toward Philippe? Does he feel the same way that Philippe feels about him?

9. What is the significance of Dean Cilek?

10. How would Ruth's letters have seemed different if Anne Morrow Lindbergh had never replied?

11. Do you think Margaret will eventually come to a clearer understanding of her mother? Does John have any advantage or disadvantage over Margaret in this respect?

12. How much has the world changed for women since the 1920s? How much has it stayed the same?

13. If you were to take a trip along the lines of Henry and Ruth's trip, where would you go?

14. Would you want to read a cache of your mother's most private letters?